RITUAL OF PASSION

Slowly, his eyes never leaving hers, the Irish king drew Shannon into the bright glaring light between the two fires. She twisted her wrist in an effort to escape his grip, but quickly realized that it would be no use. The king looked out over her head at the rest of the dancers, who now stood panting and glistening in the firelight. Most of them had found partners too, she realized, though a few of the women seemed to be frowning at her with something like disappointment on their faces. She ignored them and searched wildly for Lasairian—but he was nowhere to be seen.

There! There he was, at the back of the crowd, staring at her with a look of surprise and concern. She started to cry out to him, but her voice was lost in the shouting of the king.

"People of Abhainn Aille, you have found your partners for the rites beneath the moon! I will tell you this: Your king has found his partner, too. His task is to be the mate of the Goddess, to be her husband and protector. And she whom he chooses to be the Goddess for him shall be as his Queen for this night, this night of Beltane."

"Leave this one to find her own partner!" shouted an angry male voice. "Leave her to me!"

Shannon twisted around to see Lasairian pushing his way through the crowd, fists clenched, his face burning with outrage. He was defying his king for the sake of a woman he barely knew.

MISTRESS OF THE WATERS

JANEEN O'KERRY

LOVE SPELL BOOKS   NEW YORK CITY

For the real hero in my life.

LOVE SPELL®

May 1999

Published by

Dorchester Publishing Co., Inc.
276 Fifth Avenue
New York, NY 10001

ISBN 0-505-52309-4

The name "Love Spell" and its logo are trademarks of Dorchester Publishing Co., Inc.

Printed in the United States of America.

PRONUNCIATION GUIDE

Abhain Aille—*AH-ween AL-lee*

Beltane—*BEL-tin*

Clodagh—*CLO-dah*

Eire—*AIR-eh*

Lasairian—*Lah-SAIR-ee-an*

Samhain—*SOW-en*

Chapter One

On a fine evening in early spring, as the sun began to set in the cool clear sky, Shannon Rose Grey walked across the university campus on her way to the student center. As always, she passed the old stone fountain at the center of the quadrangle; but this time she found herself slowing to watch the fall of the water, and heard as though for the first time its quiet singing sound.

She paused beside it.

Taking a copper penny from her skirt pocket, Shannon tossed the coin into the gently rippling waters. "For luck," she whispered, and then continued on her way, the fountain still singing as she left.

Shannon heard their voices well before she entered the room. She knew they were talking about her.

"Why are we asking her to do this?"

"She's such an introvert! She never talks to anyone. She'll never help us."

"All she does is bury herself in her books. She doesn't care anything about people, only about reading."

"She doesn't even date!"

"Well, so what? What does dating have to do with the Renaissance Faire? Ian told me I should ask her here tonight, so I did. She could be a great help to us—and maybe it'll bring her out of her shell, at least a little."

"Shell? Armor plate is more like it! What do you suppose is wrong with her?"

"I've heard stories. Something about her family—something tragic—"

"Yeah, I thought I heard that too. Something that happened a few years ago—"

"Oh, stop it! None of us knows anything about it. She's just a shy girl who could use a few friends, that's all. She'll help us, and we'll help her."

Shannon paused in the hallway, just outside the door to the classroom. A strand of her fine blond hair fell over her face, but she ignored it. Why should she go in? Why should she put herself through this?

It was true she felt obligated to Abby, who had gone to some trouble to find her and then had pleaded with her to come to this meeting. But who was this Ian that Abby had just mentioned? Shannon did not know anyone by that name.

She closed her eyes. There would only be more curiosity about her shyness and reticence, more unvoiced questions. Why, really, had she come here?

Yet she had to admit that the young and lively voices, the voices of people her own age, had caught her interest. It had been quite some time—she could not remember the last instance—when she had simply joined a group of friends to have some fun.

She made one last effort to turn away and found that she could not. With a deep breath, Shannon stepped to the doorway, pausing with her hand on the worn wooden frame.

They all saw her at once. "Shannon!" called Abby, hurrying over. "You made it! I'm so glad you're here. Come on in! Do you know the rest of these guys?"

She smiled gently, allowing Abby to walk her into the large classroom. "I think I know Kathy—and Donna—we have classes together—but that's about all."

"Well, good, that's a start! Now, come over here and we'll tell you what we have in mind."

The five women and three men sat casually at the small writing desks in the classroom, while Abby leaned up against the instructor's desk at the front of the room. Shannon slid into one of the seats and sat very still, hands folded on top of the desk, hoping that her fair skin was not as red as she knew it must be.

There was the briefest moment of uncomfortable silence. "Well, then," Abby said, giving herself a small boost to perch on the edge of the desk, "let's get started. The Faire is only four weeks away, and I've invited Shannon Grey from the Gaelic Arts program to help us out. Shannon, this is Beth, Gayle, Cindy, Kathy, Donna, Phil, George, and Ian." Each nodded as they were introduced, and made a gesture of welcome.

She nodded back at the sea of friendly but unfamiliar faces, hearing not only their murmured greetings but their unasked questions as well.

She did her best to look through them, not at them. Yet one face came into focus apart from all the others. There, behind the rest, smiling at her, was a tall, broad-shouldered young man in a black T-shirt and black jeans, a man with dark curling hair and beautiful dark eyes.

He managed to hold her gaze for a long moment. It was not merely a polite expression of greeting that he wore, as the rest of them did, but a warm and welcoming smile, as though he knew her, or wanted very much to know her.

Shannon gazed back at him, frankly staring at his smooth skin and broad shoulders. She was held by the gleam in his large dark eyes ... could not look away from the slight touch of color, of excitement, at his cheekbones ... until Abby began to speak again and she quickly turned away, blinking, forcing her attention back to the matter at hand.

"So anyway," Abby continued briskly, "we are the official committee for the Renaissance Faire, the festival that the university holds each year on the first Saturday in May. And we've decided that it's going to be just a little bit different this year."

Yes. The Renaissance Faire. Shannon had seen it the last two years. It was a fun, if rather lightweight, campus street festival of pseudo-medieval singing and dancing and costumes and silly games, along with a plethora of paper-hat kings and cardboard-sword knights.

"How will it be different this year?" she asked, barely managing more than a whisper. Her face burned with the knowledge that all of these strangers—and Ian—were staring right at her, but she kept her eyes on Abby and waited for the response.

"We'd like it to be a little more authentic, at least in some ways," said one of the other women. "For one thing, we want to have an old-fashioned maypole dance."

"It's never been done at the Renaissance Faire before," said another.

"And we thought you'd know how to set it up, and how to do it, if anyone would!" finished a third.

Shannon stared at them all, stunned. "You thought I would know?" She shook her head slightly. "Why would you think I would know?"

"Well, you're one of only five people enrolled in the Gaelic Arts study program, and the only Irish Language major on the whole campus," said Abby, sliding down from the desk. "Who better to ask?"

"But—isn't the maypole some kind of European folk custom?"

Abby shrugged. "We asked one of the Medieval history profs, and she didn't know much about its origins. She said the maypole is really much older—that it had its roots in the old Celtic rituals. But we couldn't find anyone else who really seemed to know for sure. The prof said to find someone who knew a lot about the ancient history of Celtic countries, and Ian said you'd be the one to ask."

"Ian." She almost looked back at him again, but dared not. If he smiled at her that way again . . . if his dark eyes caught and held her again . . . even now she could feel his presence, so close in the room, just a few feet away, he was gazing at her even now, she did not need to turn around to know where he was looking, to know that he was looking at her.

Shannon drew a deep breath and looked squarely at Abby. "In Ireland, in the old days, there was something held in May called Beltane. It was a pagan ritual. But I don't know if it had anything to do with a maypole or not."

She sighed. "I'm sorry. I only know the more recent history, the last few hundred years; I never studied anything nearly as far back as the pre-Christian times. I don't think the modern celebrations have much of anything to do with real history. It's just been too long, and too many things have changed. Too many things are different now.''

The tension hung in the air. Shannon turned and her eyes flicked from face to eager face, all of them waiting for her answer. Her gaze rested, again, on the beautiful dark-haired man, on Ian.

''I'll see what I can find out,'' she heard herself say.

Instantly the tension vanished as they all spoke happily at once. ''Good! Great! Our next meeting—We'll see you then—Can't wait to get started!''

''So you'll come to the next meeting? And of course, you'll come to the Faire on May first,'' said Abby.

''Yes,'' Shannon answered, turning back to Abby. ''I'll come next week, and I'll be at the Faire. But I only want to do the research,'' she added quickly. ''I mean, I don't want to dress up or anything.'' She'd seen some of the costumes the participants wore—bedsheets and tinfoil, mostly. Really not her style.

''Great! I'm so glad you're going to be part of the com-mittee. Hey, maybe you can help us next year, too! We can never get enough good people to work on these things.''

Shannon smiled politely. ''I'm afraid I won't be here next year. I graduate at the end of this semester, and after that I'll be going to live in Ireland.''

They all began talking at once again. ''Ireland!—You're kidding!—How fantastic!''

''Do you have family in Ireland?'' Abby broke in.

''Not any more. But most of my family traces back to there. It's where I want to live.''

''So that's why you're learning to speak the language?''

''Yes. I'll be a teacher of Gaelic. Some people there are working very hard to preserve it, and it's still spoken in a few places.''

"Wow . . . you sure are lucky. Well, at least we've got you to help us for a while. How soon after graduation do you leave for Ireland?"

Shannon hesitated, and started to look behind her again, but stopped. "Just as soon as I can. After I graduate, just as soon as I can."

The meeting went on for a short while longer, as the Renaissance Faire committee took up the fascinating topics of street permits and vendors' licenses. Shannon tried to look as though she were listening politely, but her mind had taken a different turn. As before, she knew that the dark-haired stranger continued to stare at her, and she wanted nothing more than to turn around and face him.

Finally, the meeting ended. Everyone got up to leave. Shannon said goodbye to each of them and accepted their thanks yet again, and by the time she started for the door there was only one person left in the room.

"Shannon."

He stood alone near the center of the room, smiling at her again, his expression warm and gentle. He placed both hands on the back of a chair and stood there leaning on it, as though careful to keep a barrier of some type between them.

"Ian."

She kept her reply as formal as possible, her purse held close in front of her. Though he was several feet away, he had so enveloped her with his presence that it seemed she already knew what it would be like to stand face to face with him, close enough to feel his warmth.

It was as if he had already touched her, from far across the room.

"I'm so glad you came tonight," he said, standing very

still behind the chair. "I was afraid you would not when the time came and you were not here."

Shannon barely comprehended what he said, so captured was she by the sound of his voice. The strong Irish accent, the beautiful lilt of the words! As her heart began to beat faster, she dared to make a little test.

"I am sorry I was late. I stopped to throw a penny in the fountain," she said to him, in careful Gaelic.

He looked faintly surprised, quite interested, and highly amused. "And why did you do that?" he answered, also in Gaelic.

"To make a wish," she responded.

Immediately he spoke a few more rapid sentences, but she soon raised her hand for him to stop. "I'm sorry," she said, switching back to English. "I've studied for nearly five years, but you're too fast for me. You're—you're a native speaker!"

"I am," he said, also in English. "From a place you would call County Galway, in the nation of Ireland."

"Then—whatever are you doing at Bowling Green State University, in the state of Ohio?"

He moved out from behind the chair, one hand still resting on the back of it, and stopped. "I am here just as you are," he said. "To learn . . . to grow . . . to discover. I am searching, as you have been searching."

It was hardly a satisfactory answer, and an odd one. But before she could say anything, he took another step toward her. "You said you dropped a penny in the fountain. An American penny is made of copper, is it?"

"Copper, yes," she said after a moment, nodding her head.

"And why did you offer your penny to the water?"

She raised her eyebrow. "I don't know. For luck, I suppose, or to make a wish. Everyone does it.''

"Luck." He nodded, thoughtful. "And what did you wish for?"

She raised her chin, and looked straight into his dark and shining eyes. "To find out how it is you know me, when I've never met you, and why you gave my name to Abby, and why you think I of all people should be the one to explain May Day to the Renaissance Faire committee."

For the briefest moment he looked quite startled. Then just as quickly he laughed out loud, laughter that sounded like a song. "You have my apologies! I should have explained myself to you."

He took another step toward her. How tall he was, and how fine and strong his shoulders. His skin was fair and smooth and touched with color, his long arms graceful by his sides.

Shannon found herself blinking, trying to focus on him. He was so very different from any other man she'd ever seen. He was like some wild and magical thing from a far different place, and it seemed to her that if she did not keep him here by her will, he might just vanish back into whatever strange world he had come from.

"When I lived in Ireland, I was a student, and learned many things, yet I longed to know the worlds beyond my own . . . far beyond. It happened that I was offered a chance to come to this place, and never would I turn down such a chance. So, you see, dear Shannon, I am a student here too, just as you are, and that is how I came to know Abby. She told me of you and your study of Gaelic, and I told her that she must invite you to work with them at the Faire so that I might have the chance to meet you myself."

He seemed to her like a most beautiful strain of music, elegantly and classically played, while beside him all the other men were merely crude and raucous noisemakers.

Flustered, she searched for words. "You told them to ask me here? Just so you could meet me? Why—why didn't you just come up to me yourself?"

He looked at her, his eyes smiling but sad, and shook his head. "You would never have accepted such an offer. You value your privacy so, and I must respect that. I did not wish to frighten you away or have you think me discourteous.

"But now we are here, and we are speaking together, in English and in Gaelic, and I can compliment you on how lovely you look in your fine smooth dress of yellow and white. And I can say that I hope you will walk with me to Isabella's, where we could share coffee and sweet biscuits—I believe you call them 'cookies.' "

It was no use. She felt helpless, hypnotized by the beautiful words, and the sight of that face, and the unswerving attention he paid her. He had not teased her about being shy or tried to goad her into talking or smiling or laughing.

No, Ian had made her feel that she was beautiful and fascinating just the way she was, that he had no thought or care for anything else, and that his world would simply end if she refused him.

And she began to feel that hers might do the same if he walked through that door without her.

She took a breath to speak, but could only nod, slightly at first, and then a bit more firmly. "Isabella's," she repeated, and he smiled again, moving to the door to hold it open for her.

Carrying a steaming white mug of chocolate raspberry coffee, Shannon sat down at a glass-topped table and began carefully studying the interior of Isabella's Cafe. She would

16

not normally have been so interested in the decor of a coffee shop, but right now it was important to look around at something, anything.

It was all that kept her from simply sitting and staring at Ian.

Fortunately, Isabella's was quite a charming little place. The counter was stocked with cream-filled pastries, enormous chocolate chip cookies, and fresh-baked carrot-walnut muffins. On the flowered wallpaper behind the counter were blackboards listing a grand selection of coffees, chocolates, and teas. And along the walls were antique shelves and sideboards, all draped in ribbons and lace and bright silk cloth and covered with china figures and baskets of silk flowers.

She liked it very much, and wondered how Ian had come to know about it.

In a moment he was back, sliding into the white wrought-iron chair and easing his long legs carefully under the fragile table. "Now, here is a drink for a king if ever I've had one," he said happily, setting down a mug and a plate.

She glanced at the steaming cup, piled high with whipped cream. "Hot chocolate?" she asked, with a little smile. "I guess you do like chocolate," she added, looking at the plate. It was stacked with huge chocolate chip cookies and two slices of Black Forest cake.

"One of the great delights of the modern world," Ian said. He took one of the cookies, broke it in half, and offered it to her.

Eyeing him cautiously, she took the piece from his fingers. She could not help but notice his hands, the fingers long and slender and strong, the nails short and neat. "Thank you," she whispered. He only smiled at her in return, his gaze steady and calm, and at last she placed the

17

cookie on a pink napkin and reached for the white china pitcher of cream.

"Didn't they have chocolate in Ireland?" she said lightly, just to make conversation, just to take her mind off the way he had so smoothly and easily drawn her in. It was much easier to concentrate on stirring cream into chocolate raspberry coffee than to wonder how this strange man could make her feel as if he'd known her all his life. At this moment, she did not want to know how he could make her forget everything else in her world, as if he were the master of a world all his own and he had just invited her into it for a time.

"Well—they do indeed have chocolate in Ireland, but not like this."

She looked puzzled, and his eyes began to shine with merriment. "In Ireland there is no Isabella's Cafe, and since there is not, there is no Shannon Rose Grey to share the chocolate with. And it is simply not the same." He took a long drink of the hot chocolate.

When he set down the heavy white mug, there was a little touch of whipped cream above his lip. She stared at it, slowly setting her coffee spoon down on the glass table. There was nothing she wanted so much as to reach up to his face and brush the sweet cream onto her finger. Her hand began to move—then quickly, with a little shock, she stopped herself.

With a deep breath, Shannon raised the coffee cup and took a quick drink. "So," she began, casting about for something, anything, to say. "The committee wants to do an authentic maypole dance."

"They do," he answered. "And it sounds like great fun."

"I'm sure it will be," she said carefully, "but like I said

before, if there's a connection between May Day and Ireland, I don't know what it is.''

"You were on the mark at the meeting. You made the connection.''

Now she looked at him again. "What connection?''

His dark eyes changed, becoming mysterious and almost remote. "Beltane.''

Chapter Two

"Beltane." Shannon shook her head, setting down the mug. "You mean the old pagan ritual? It had something to do with spring, and building bonfires, but that's all I know about it. Are you saying that Beltane was the original May Day?"

He smiled faintly, but his face still held that expression of seriousness, of knowledge of great mysteries both past and present. "I am saying that Beltane is the key to what you search for. If you study it, you will find what you seek."

"For the May Day celebration," she said, looking closely at him.

"The May Day celebration, you will learn about that, too," he said, and his eyes once again took on their look of brightness and amusement. "So. You plan to move to

Ireland in the summer. Is there some special reason why you have chosen Ireland?''

She glanced up and smiled. ''I've heard about it all my life. My family came here from Ireland, a couple of generations ago.''

''Have you been there recently?''

She looked down at her coffee. ''Not for several years.''

''Yet you plan to work there.''

Shannon nodded, slowly, still gazing down. ''I love languages, and I found that I like to teach. Some people there are working very hard to make sure that the ancient Irish language lives on. I would like to be one of them.''

''A teacher! Ah, teachers are wonderful folk. But surely if you mean to teach Gaelic, you will need to know its heritage, its origins, to teach it properly, will you not? You'll have to study the ancient ways at some point. Gaelic has been spoken for far more than just a few hundred years, you do know.''

''Of course I know. It's old, very old. But I'm learning.''

''And you believe that the place to do your learning is Ireland.''

''I do.''

''You have family there, do you?''

''No, I'm afraid I don't. The last of them came here early in this century. But—''

''No connections?''

''Not yet. But I've sent my resume off to a number of schools and companies, and I've gotten a few responses already. I'm sure I'll find something.''

''Resumes. I see.'' He took another drink of the chocolate. ''Where will you live?''

''I'm working on that, too. It won't be difficult. There

are small flats for rent, and sometimes rooms in private homes. It doesn't matter too much at first—I just want to get there."

"It is important to live in a place where you feel you are needed." It was a statement, not a question.

"Yes," she said, looking up at him again. "And—"

"And what?"

"And challenged," she finished.

"Challenged?"

"Yes. Challenged, and needed."

"Are you not needed here?"

"I have no place here."

"Where is your place, Shannon Rose?"

She hesitated. "I am still looking for it. Someplace where no one will laugh at me if I say that my hobbies are collecting French paintings and watching the Russian ballet. Where I can do something useful, but—but still be myself, without apologizing for it."

"Ah. I understand. The modern world can be most—demanding. Impersonal."

"Yes, it can." She looked away from him, allowing her thoughts to come to the surface. "It can be gray, and dull, and grinding."

"And you long to be surrounded by beauty and magic, by quiet and by peace."

"I do . . . yes, I will admit that I do."

"So you don't know exactly what you are looking for—you only know that it's time to go and find it."

Shannon stared at him. She was sure that her amazement must be showing on her face, but for once she did not care if someone knew what she was thinking.

He did understand how she felt. He hadn't pressed her for answers. It was as though he'd already known the things that she would say, and simply wanted to hear her say them.

"I sometimes think that all of life is a search for magic," Ian continued, "and I believe that magic is what you search for. I know I have long searched for it myself, looking for it most often in music, and in beautiful words, and in the faces of women."

"And what did you find?"

He looked down for a time, and then turned his dark gaze on her once more. "I found . . . that oftentimes there is nothing so magical as the search itself. And that nothing you desire will be found if you are running away from something, instead of running toward it. Are you running away, Shannon?"

He smiled at her. In a moment, his eyes were almost laughing. Instantly she was once more on her guard. Was he merely teasing her, just trying to get some sort of reaction out of her? She should have expected that it would happen sooner or later. But even he would not get past her defenses.

"There's no such thing as magic. Not in this world. Not anymore," she said firmly, and reached for her coffee. She had said it to herself over and over again for the past three years, she'd believed it wholeheartedly, and had never had the smallest doubt that she was right—until now.

Shannon and Ian walked together into the cool quiet night, each of them carrying a slice of Black Forest cake carefully wrapped in a pink napkin. They turned off the main campus road into the well-worn neighborhood of small houses and student apartments and cracking, tree-lined sidewalks. It was not far to the little white house on Second Street which Shannon shared with her parents, though she found herself wishing that it was farther . . . much farther.

Ian walked close at her side, close enough for her to feel the warmth of him, close enough to make her wonder if in a moment he would reach for her hand, or even place his arm around her shoulders. She grew increasingly tense, waiting for something—anything—to happen. But he only walked beside her with long, sure strides, appearing to be as relaxed as she was nervous.

Just as she was searching for something to say to break the silence, Ian spoke. "You have not yet told me why, Shannon."

She gave him a quick glance. "Told you why—what?"

He shook his head, and she could see the look of curiosity as they passed beneath the glare of a streetlight. "Everything you know, all your family and friends, are here. Why would you leave it behind, perhaps forever, for a strange land where you have nothing and no one?"

Shannon slowed as they reached the shadows, and closed her eyes. "Because—there is nothing left for me here. I really don't fit in, and I'm not a child to live at home anymore. My parents are retired, my older sisters are married and moved out. When I leave, my parents can begin the travels they've always wanted to take—maybe even move to the south. The winters are so cold here."

"You feel you must leave, that your parents want you gone?"

"No, no, it's not like that at all. It's just that they deserve freedom and time to themselves now, after—all that has happened to them. I have to move on and find my place, wherever that might be."

"It is very difficult to be wealthy one day, and not wealthy at all the next, isn't it." His Irish voice was so soft, so gentle.

At first she simply stopped and looked up at him in

shock. She reached for his arm and turned him around to face her, forcing herself to ignore the smooth warm skin and silky black hairs.

"Who told you that?" she whispered, her voice shaking.

"You told me yourself," he answered.

Again she was stunned. She let go of him. "What are you talking about? I've never talked about this to anyone. Someone who knew my family must have said something to you." A former servant? A business partner with an old grudge? When she found out, she would—

"You told me, Shannon. You told me, and all the rest of the world, with everything you do—the way you carry yourself, the way you answer my questions."

He waved his arm toward the old houses, with their bare yards and sagging porches. "You did not grow up in a place like this. I have seen the fine neighborhoods of America, I know what they are like. You are aware of so much of the world. How many girls growing up in a small farm town like this would think of studying an ancient language in a faraway land, or long for the paintings of Cezanne and the dances of Pavlova?"

Shannon stared at him, trembling, her face hot. She struggled for words but could think of none.

The shock of it was that everything he said was true. She had not grown up here, had never lived anywhere remotely resembling this place until three years ago.

Life had been very different before that.

She had never talked to anyone about her previous life. She had kept to herself and tried to think only of the future, her future in Ireland. But in just a couple of hours this man had drawn her out like no one else ever had. Thinking back over their conversations, she realized that he had played her like an instrument . . . skillfully, and beautifully, coaxing the truth from her without her ever realizing it.

Shannon longed to turn her back on Ian and flee, to race home, slam shut the door, and forget she had ever met him. But she knew, with terrible certainty, that as of right now the days and months and years of running away and hiding were over.

She had no choice but to tell him. He needed to know what had happened to her three years ago that had changed her life forever, no matter how shallow or vain or foolish he might decide she was. He must know exactly what had happened, because if there was any man in the world who could hurt her in the same way again, Ian Galloway was that man.

Shannon looked away from Ian and began to walk slowly up the sidewalk. She could hear his footsteps as he followed her, could feel his nearness even though she could not see him. As she walked, she crossed her arms tightly in front of her, and began to speak.

"You are right. I did not grow up in a neighborhood like this one. My family was wealthy. Very wealthy. My older sisters and I had everything any child could ever wish for. All of us were very much sheltered and protected from the rest of the world. That's what having money does to you, whether you intend it or not."

"And you found it too limiting. You longed for a simpler, more normal life."

She stopped again, but did not look at him. Why was he making this so difficult? And why was she bothering to tell him this at all? She should just hurry straight home and tell him never to speak to her again. But she drew a deep breath, and then went on slowly walking.

"I did not find it limiting. I loved it. I loved it all, and I miss it terribly today."

There. She had said it. Now he would think she was just a spoiled, shallow, formerly rich brat who only cared about money and had no idea what was really important in life.

"Then tell me about it, please," he said softly, close by her side.

Shannon raised her chin. "We three were Daddy's princesses. We were praised and petted and pampered, surrounded by beauty and luxury of every sort. We went to the finest schools, we traveled all over the United States and Canada and Europe, we rode our own horses . . . and yes, we had French paintings on our walls and tickets to the Russian ballet whenever it was on tour."

"I cannot blame you for missing such a lovely life," Ian said quietly. "Now I wonder if you will tell me what happened to change it so."

"A series of bad investments. A couple of dishonest employees. The combination destroyed my father's business and the legal battles drained the rest. It's all over now, and my father is retired. It will never be as it was before. Never."

"I see." Ian reached out to lightly catch her arm with his fingers. Shannon stopped in her tracks, unable to take another step. His gentle touch held her as surely as if he'd used all his strength. "But that was not the worst of it."

She looked up at him, going hot and cold all over as her sense of shock and bewilderment returned. "How do you know all this?" she whispered, with a slight shake of her head. "Who told you?"

He smiled down at her, his dark eyes bright even in the shadows where they stood. "Again, dear Shannon, you told me yourself.

"It is clear that you do not trust any man. You keep to yourself, you do not date, you guard your privacy fiercely;

27

yet it is just as clear that you are not merely waiting for someone who is, perhaps, only away for a time. You are lonely, and you long for love and companionship as any lovely young woman must. More than money was lost when your father's riches vanished.''

She made herself look directly into his eyes, refusing to give in to fear or embarrassment or even to the gentle look on his young and noble face. "Even during the worst of it, my parents stayed together. They helped each other and they are still together—and happy—today, even though their lives have changed so drastically. But—''

"That did not happen for you," Ian said.

"I was to be married," Shannon whispered, glancing into the shadows. "We were together for two years. I was certain that he loved me and that we would be happy. But when my father's money disappeared, so did he.''

"A shallow and foolish man who did not deserve you.'' He took her hand, careful of the cake she still held wrapped in the napkin. "I know it is difficult to hear. But surely you know that if he would leave you for such a reason, you are better off as you are . . . and one day a man will come who will make you glad you waited.''

She looked back at him, her gaze colder now. She withdrew her hand. "I've heard the same advice many times. I only know that I'm better off alone, and will be better off still when I get to Ireland and can start my whole life over." Shannon turned and continued up the street.

"I see," Ian said, following her once more. "But if that is so . . . why is it that on the third finger of your right hand you wear what can only be an engagement ring?''

Quickly she made a fist of her right hand and pressed it against her side. "It's just a ring."

"Yet it is beautiful indeed. I noticed it while we were

having coffee. An emerald set in gold, is it? It must be very valuable.''

She glanced at him, wondering what would make him ask such a gauche question. ''I don't know. I've never had it appraised.''

''I see. Then perhaps its value lies elsewhere. You wear it to remember him?''

''No. I wear it to remember what he did.''

''Why would you want to remember something that only brought you pain?''

Anger began rising in her, anger and pain at the fact that he would probe so insistently—but she felt compelled to respond to his question. All right, then. If he truly wanted to know, he would hear it all, and it might prove to be more than he'd bargained for.

''I want to remember that people are only interested in me for what I can provide for them. They are not interested in what or who I am—only in what I have and what I can give them. It is an important lesson to learn and I have learned it better than anyone.''

Ian whistled low. ''That is a very deep river which you have dredged for yourself, dear Shannon. I am not sure any man could learn to swim in such a depth.''

''I am not inviting any man for a swim. Until I find one who can be trusted—one who will not lie to me—I will find my place all by myself, in Ireland, and I will make my own happiness there.''

Now surely he would simply say goodnight, and leave her here alone, and never come around again. After what she had just said, what else could he think but that she was nothing but a selfish, spoiled child? But all of those things had to be said—she had to get it all out in the open, here, now, right at the very start, before . . . before . . . what?

To her amazement, his eyes were still as gentle and bright as before, and he reached for her hand once again. "I thank you for telling me what is in your heart. I know that what I have heard here tonight you have not said before, to any man or woman.

"I still believe that what you seek is magic—the beauty and magic that life can sometimes offer if we search for it in just the right ways. You had a taste of it in your earlier life, when your father's wealth could buy you the time and the solitude and the beautiful things and experiences you still long for.

"But wealth is not the only way to find the magic and beauty in life. And before you can protest—I do not think you vain or selfish for thinking so. It is only that there is more to the world than even you have learned, and it waits for you, now, even as I do."

She could only stare at him and wonder why he still stood there smiling down at her, why he had not turned away and dismissed her as selfish or neurotic or simply quite boring and self-centered. But he went on talking to her as if they had discussed nothing more momentous than the weather.

"So, Shannon Rose, we come back to the original question. Will you help with the Renaissance Faire?"

She blinked, and finally looked away. "Well—I told Abby I would—but it's a big commitment, and I have a lot of classes and other things going on right now, and I've been so busy planning my trip—"

"Of course. I understand. Then I will not be seeing you at the meetings. Not until after the Faire, or whenever you might be free—if you have the time, of course—"

"No." She stopped him with a word. "No, I'll be there.

I'll be at the very next meeting. I did promise Abby. I won't let her down.''

Even in the shadows of the streetlights she could see his smile. "I knew you would not," he said, and smiled again.

They walked for a few more moments in silence, Shannon's mind spinning, both appalled and relieved at the way she had revealed her innermost thoughts to him. "We're here," she said, and stopped before the small white house with the black wrought-iron porch and old overhanging trees.

"Thank you for walking home with me, and for a lovely evening," she said, glad that she'd at least remembered her manners. "Would you care to come in? My parents are home, I'm sure they would love to meet you."

"Thank you, but I must be going. Perhaps I can accept your offer some other time. And—here. Do take this for me. I give it to you in the hope that there will be another occasion for us to go to Isabella's, and get another." And he carefully handed her the slightly squashed piece of Black Forest cake, still wrapped in its pink napkin.

"Perhaps we will," she whispered.

Now he stood above her, gazing down at her, and all she saw was his serene and noble face, leaning down. . . .

"Goodnight, Shannon," he said softly. "Sleep well. It has been a lovely evening, and I look forward very much to the next meeting of the Renaissance Faire committee." And he turned and walked away, his tall, black-clad figure disappearing into the shadows between the glaring streetlights.

Shannon stood for a long time and watched him go. She breathed deeply of the damp night air as her heart gradually slowed to something like its normal rate.

Well.

Mr. Galloway had certainly managed to make an impression. Already it was clear that he was going to be much on her mind for a good long time, no matter how she might try to resist the idea.

But if she was going to help with this Renaissance Faire May Day celebration, she would have to think about something else for at least a little while. It would be no small task—it would require many hours of digging and research—but maybe it would help her learn even more about Irish history. And if it would help her to focus on something, anything, besides Ian Galloway, it would be well worth doing.

She would start with Beltane.

Chapter Three

Early the next evening Shannon walked across the busy campus to the university library. It was a familiar and comfortable place, but this time she began searching through shelves where she had never looked before. She reached for book after book, stirred as she had not been in a very long time. Finally she sat down at a far corner, opened the first book in the stack, and began to read.

Hours later, her mind buzzed with strange facts and fascinating history concerning May Day and its mysterious pagan predecessor called Beltane—and to Shannon's surprise, she found herself spellbound.

Yes, she had planned to go to Ireland to live, attracted by her family history and the promise of escaping to a brand-new life. But here was more than the dry recent history she had dutifully studied; here was mystery and magic. The more she found, the more tantalized she was. Her curiosity grew with each new legend she uncovered, as layer by layer the old ways began to reveal themselves to her.

The hawthorn tree is the one cut down for the maypole, but it is very unlucky to cut any part of it at any other time.

The hawthorn is a solitary tree belonging to the fairies. Never bring hawthorn flowers into the house.

It is unlucky to marry in May.

It is unlucky for a bride to wear green.

She sighed. It was great fun discovering these things, and she was vaguely aware of having heard some of them before. But her curiosity was not satisfied. She wanted to know the why of it, she wanted to know how such ideas had begun . . . but she supposed it had all been lost in the mists of time.

The days of April stretched into weeks, weeks which Shannon spent immersed in fact and mythology regarding the ancient Celtic festival of Beltane. But they were also weeks spent growing slowly, and cautiously, closer to Ian.

She never knew when he might appear. Some mornings he might come striding around a corner and walk with her to class; afternoons could find him waiting beneath a shady tree with a picnic lunch to share. Evenings were often as not spent in conversation and laughter in a place like Isabella's, or simply out walking together in the twilight.

The days passed in a kind of soft glow. It was nearly enough to make Shannon forget both her long-lost past and her uncertain future. And then, one night, Ian brought her a gift.

They had walked home together after a fine dinner and an outdoor concert of harp music. Ian stopped beneath the streetlight in front of her house, as he always did, and Shannon turned her face up to him to say goodnight. But instead of reaching out to touch her hair, as she had expected—he had never kissed her, much as she had begun to long for him to do so—he took down from his shoulder the leather knapsack he had carried all evening, and reached into it.

Slowly he drew out a long cylindrical object, perhaps a foot in length and a few inches in diameter. Its coppery surface shone in the glare of the streetlight. Hardly realizing that she was doing so, Shannon reached out to touch the magnificent piece, her fingers tracing the curving and intertwining patterns which covered its surface. They were Celtic patterns, she was certain, but very primitive ones, strange-looking leaves and birds and beautiful rippling lines. . . .

"What is this?" she whispered. "How old is it? Where did you find it?"

"It is yours, Shannon Rose," he answered. When she looked up at him, he only smiled. "It is yours and no other's. I can tell you, with great certainty, that this lovely antique is a family heirloom of yours and it belongs with you."

Now she could only stare at him in bewilderment. "What are you talking about? I've never seen this before. I've never seen anything like this before."

"Yet you recognize it, do you not? You see it for the special thing it is. It speaks to you, when you touch it; it holds meaning for you where it would be naught but a curiosity for anyone else. It is yours, and at long last it has found its way to you, and now," he went on, placing the copper cylinder in her hands and gently folding her fingers around it, "you must take it home, and keep it very safe."

"Take it home," she repeated, shifting the surprisingly lightweight piece in her arms. Gazing down at the shining copper, she shook her head. "I must admit, you are right.

This is something very special. And while I don't see how it could possibly be a family heirloom, if this is yours to give, I will accept it.''

''It has always been yours. I, and others, have merely kept it safe for you for a time.'' Ian smiled down at her, and reached out to brush a strand of hair from her eyes. ''Yet there is one other thing you must do with this, Shannon.''

''Oh? And what is that?''

''Open it.'' His voice was dry, hardly more than a whisper.

''Open it?'' She frowned, and turned the cylinder over, examining it closely. ''How does it open?''

''The ends are sealed, but they can be opened by one who has the patience to try. They will open for you, of that I have no doubt.''

She sighed. ''Open it. And what will I find when . . .''

The words left her as Ian leaned forward and his lips brushed her forehead. ''Good night, dear Shannon Rose. Good night.''

He turned and walked away, disappearing yet again into the night, leaving her alone with his strange and beautiful gift.

For a time Shannon felt happier than she ever had since her life had changed so dramatically three years before. The beautiful copper piece stayed out on the desk in her room, where it tantalized her and aroused her curiosity even as Ian did. What did the cylinder contain? Could she ever hope to get it open without harming it? And what had Ian meant when he'd said it was a ''family heirloom?''

She could hardly wait to see him again. Perhaps he could

help her open it. And he could be there when she discovered what, if anything, it held.

But as the month drew to its close, and the Renaissance Faire committee begged for more and more of Shannon's time, she began to realize that she was seeing less and less of Ian. Of course, he was busy with his studies, and planning for the Faire, just as she was. She could not expect him to spend every moment of every day with her. . . .

After a time, she hid the copper cylinder away.

Yet she was at a loss to explain his increasing absences. Try though she would to deny it to herself, she felt her heart sink whenever she walked to class without seeing his tall, broad-shouldered form in the distance. Any afternoon which did not bring his beautiful smile and lively presence was a lonely, empty time.

And night after night when at last she fell asleep, always very late, without having heard his gentle Irish voice or felt the touch of his fingers on her cheek, she would dream that he had walked away from her and vanished into a mist, as though he had never been, and she would awaken suddenly with a pounding heart and a terrible emptiness within.

Finally came the day before the Faire. Shannon, sitting in the shade on the small back porch of her parents' house, felt only relief that it would all be over soon. Then she could go back to her solitary life without having to worry about Renaissance Faires or maypoles or Beltane or anything else.

There was a rapping at the gate. "We're here!" cried the laughing, merry group as they spilled into the backyard, followed by her father. "We're here for the maypole!"

The nine members of the Renaissance Faire committee

quickly gathered around the solitary tree at the center of the quarter-acre yard.

"Oh, it's gorgeous!"

"Look at those flowers! White as snow!"

"And the smell of them! Heavenly!"

Shannon walked out to the group and stood beside the lone hawthorn tree, cautiously resting her hand on its red-brown bark beneath the glossy green leaves. "The branches are covered with thorns. Be careful," she warned.

"Are you sure you don't mind if we cut it down, Mr. Grey?" said George. "It seems like a crime to take an ax to such a beautiful tree."

"Yes, I'm sure," said Charles Grey. "I've been talking about cutting it down ever since we moved here nearly three years ago. It's sitting right in the middle of the yard, and Shannon's mother has been wanting to put a garden there. You'll be doing us a favor if you take it out for us."

"All right, then! Let's go get the ax!"

The happy group turned and headed through the gate once again, all except for Abby. "Ian asked me to give you this," she said, and handed Shannon a small white envelope before hurrying off to join the others.

Inside was a note on a folded white card, written in a large clear hand:

I cannot see you for a time, Shannon. I am, of great necessity, otherwise engaged. I promise you that very soon you will understand.
Your friend
Ian Galloway

Quickly, making sure to hide the trembling of her fingers, she replaced the note in the envelope.

Of course. He was otherwise engaged. But he had been mistaken about one thing: She would not have to wait to understand what was engaging him. It could only be one thing. She gripped the envelope tightly for just a moment before hiding it in the pocket of her jeans.

She told herself to put the note, and anything to do with Ian, completely out of her mind. Was she surprised? Had she expected anything else? Where did she think he'd been spending his time, all those mornings and afternoons and evenings when she looked for him and he was not there?

Had she really thought he was different from any other man? If she had, she'd just been quite strongly and unmistakably corrected.

Before she could escape back into the house, the committee returned with the ax, still engaged in happy chatter about the tree. Shannon let them sweep her along, doing her best to forget about the cool white note in her pocket.

"Well, I guess it will be okay. I mean, that's what they did back in the old days, didn't they? Cut down a tree for the maypole? And you'll be planting a lot more things in its place."

"Hey, I can tell you that this is going to make the perfect maypole. Trim off the branches, we'll have a ten-, maybe twelve-foot trunk. Perfect!"

"Those branches won't be wasted, either. Every last one is covered with flowers! We can decorate half the site with them."

"And it's the real thing! That's what I like. I thought we'd have to settle for using a flagpole or something. But we've got a real hawthorn, just like they used in the old days!"

"Well, that's what they used as far as we know," said Shannon, just as George raised the ax. "There isn't much written down, but the legend of the hawthorn tree kept coming up. And the stories always emphasized how unlucky it was to cut one down.''

George stopped in mid-swing. ''Unlucky?''

''Why?'' added Abby.

Shannon shrugged. ''I don't know. But there was one exception: the day before Beltane.''

''The day before—what?''

Shannon smiled politely. ''Beltane. The pagan festival celebrated on the first of May.''

Abby sighed with relief. ''Well, lucky for us, May first is tomorrow. I guess we're safe!''

''Good thing the RennFaire Saturday just happened to fall on May first this year,'' said George, taking up the ax once more. ''But what will we do next year?''

''I don't know, George. I don't know.'' *And I won't have any reason to care, either,* Shannon thought, as the ax struck the tree again and again. *I'll be far away from here this time next year . . . far away in Ireland.*

The wreath of flowers dropped onto her head and fell forward over her eyes. Shannon pushed it back up.

''Careful!'' said Abby, hastily placing her needle and thread in her mouth and fussing with the rapidly wilting daisies and white hawthorn blooms. ''They'll fall apart. They've got to last at least through the afternoon!''

''I never thought I'd end up being Queen of the May,'' Shannon muttered, fidgeting in the hard classroom seat as Abby twisted and tied the daisies. ''I thought you were going to be the Queen. I know how much you would have enjoyed it.''

''Well, you deserved it! We all agreed that it should be you. You've helped us so much with this project, even giving us a real tree out of your parents' backyard for the maypole. It's going to be great! And you're so pretty, Shannon, you'll be terrific as the Queen of the May!''

Shannon lifted the too-long hem of the makeshift gown, fashioned from a lime-green bedsheet, and stood up. Abby tied a bright yellow sash around her waist. ''There! It's perfect. Now, let's go—everyone's waiting for you!''

''All right,'' Shannon said, pushing back the flower wreath a bit more carefully this time. ''But—like a lot of things about May Day, the old stories were kind of vague. I'm still not exactly sure what the Queen of the May actually *did*.''

''Well, uh . . . as far as we're concerned, she's just the Queen, that's all! She leads the procession to the maypole, and leads the maypole dance, and is the prettiest girl there! And, as I said, you are perfect for the part. Now, let's get going!''

Shannon lifted the skirts and made her way down the hallway, hoping she wouldn't trip over the dragging bedsheets. How had she got herself into this? Ah, well, it would be over soon, and she supposed it might be educational to actually go through the maypole ritual.

Yet one thing nagged at the back of her mind. What had been the role of the ''Queen of the May'' back in the ancient days? The only accounts she'd found were of mere symbolism, just as Abby had said—the prettiest girl in the village was chosen to lead the maypole dance.

But how had it all started? How had it begun?

In and out, over and under, the laughing, skipping dancers wound the long strips of bright-colored cloth into a tight interlocking braid all the way down the severed trunk of her parents' hawthorn tree. With only a few brief halts to untangle the inexperienced dancers, it was not long before the maypole was completely encased in yellow and white and green and purple and blue.

It was fun, Shannon had to admit, breathless from the long dance. And since she was not the only one clad in sheets, she did not stand out in the crowd; the spectators just considered her part of the show, like an actress in a play. And so she did not mind too much when a couple of costumed committee members escorted her to a small platform stage in order to hand out the prizes to the winners of the day's games and contests.

The day was the loveliest she could recall for quite some time . . . clear blue skies with just a few puffy white clouds, the grass thick and green, the trees covered with pink and white blossoms. And everywhere was the soft perfume of the hawthorn flowers, coming from the branches decorating the maypole site and from the wreaths Abby had made—one of which rested on her brow.

She climbed up on the stage, careful not to catch her plastic sandals on the rough wooden planking. As she waited, the announcement was made, and the winner of the mock sword-fighting tourney was brought before her. He was quite a handsome young man, really quite striking in a surprisingly good replica of chain mail armor, brightly colored tabard, and beautifully painted shield.

It was a shock to realize how much he made her think of Ian Galloway.

Not that he looked like Ian. It was simply the same primal reaction to a handsome, well-muscled male presence, the same warm joyous feeling she got whenever she saw Ian in the distance and knew he was coming to join her.

Shannon found herself smiling at the young man as she placed the wreath on his head. He bowed to her with great courtly style, smiled back at her, and then walked away to rejoin his lady.

And now that she looked out over the crowd, it seemed to be filled with happy courting couples, young men and women paired off together celebrating May Day, surrounded by the sweet scent of warm sun and hawthorn flowers, watching as the Queen of the May gave her prizes to all the winners.

But who was the match for the Queen? On whose arm would *she* walk, when all of this was over?

Shannon made herself stop. She told herself not to think of it, as the winner of the chess tournament was brought before her to receive his wreath. This whole thing was just a very silly game to raise a little money on a pleasant afternoon in early summer. There was nothing else to it. She'd be home with her parents very soon and life would return to normal. She had far more important things to worry about than—

Ian.

There he was, standing at the edge of the crowd, watching her. And as he caught her eye, he gave her a little wave and made a small bow. Even at this distance she could see that devastating smile, see his dark eyes sparkling with amusement and—and something else.

Hope surged through her. He had come for her, after all! She would not have to leave here alone, she would not be the only one here with no partner.

She knew that the last thing she ought to do was leave with him—she should first demand an explanation as to why he had ignored her for so many days, up until now. But at the moment she did not care. It was enough to know he was here, she could not have stopped herself from going if she'd tried!

But just as she smiled back at him, a small woman hurried through the crowd and caught his arm. Shannon could not see her face; she was cloaked in gray with the hood pulled up. But Ian clearly knew her. He turned his smile on her, and hugged her close, and together they left the Faire.

Somehow, Shannon made it through the rest of the afternoon. She turned her pain and anger on herself, berating herself for ever allowing Ian to get so close to her and become so important in her life.

Whatever had she been thinking? She had no claim on Ian Galloway, and he certainly had none on her. Something like that was the last thing she wanted. She ought to be glad that he obviously had a real girlfriend, a girl who was no doubt beautiful and bold and fun and adventurous—nothing like herself. She should be quite relieved and happy to find that her relationship with him went only so far as their work together on the Renaissance Faire and no further.

Yet when she finally reached home, she could summon up the will to do nothing more than lie back on her bed in the darkness, still breathing in the scent of the hawthorn blooms from the wreath she had worn in her hair.

A few days drifted past, and a week, and it seemed to Shannon that the scent of the hawthorn still lingered in the air about her. But the faded flowers were long gone, and the May Day celebration was long over.

So why couldn't she forget about it and move on? Her move to Ireland was rapidly approaching. There was still a great deal that had to be done and it had to be started now—she had to get a job and a place to live, and of course there was the question of citizenship. Giving up her United

States citizenship to become a permanent resident of another country was a terribly big step. She would have to set it all in motion very soon.

Yes, it was a wrench, it was a loss, but what was there to keep her here now? She needed to start again, start completely over, and this was the only way she knew to do that. Everything would be new and fresh and different; every part of her past would be left far behind.

Except Ian.

The thought kept pressing at her mind. She closed her eyes. No. No, she had sworn that no man would get his fingers around her life again. Hadn't she learned anything from the last time? Shannon was absolutely determined that no man would ever have that kind of control over her again—not even a man like Ian.

Chapter Four

"Shannon, I know the costume wasn't your favorite thing to wear, but would you put it on once more for me?"

Shannon looked up and smiled. "Daddy, you know I could never say no to you."

"We want to have as many pictures of you as we can before—before you leave on your trip," her father went on. "And you were so pretty as the May Queen."

"Well, I suppose I could put it on again—so long as you promise not to hang the pictures on the walls."

"I promise. Now, I told your mother I'd help peel some potatoes for dinner, so I'll meet you in the yard in about forty-five minutes. We'll get the pictures in front of the hedge. Agreed?"

"Of course, Dad. Forty-five minutes. I'll be ready."

In her own small room, Shannon opened the bottom drawer of her dresser and reached for the lime-green gown and yellow sash. She'd slipped away from the Renaissance Faire at the first possible moment, not caring that she had to walk home dressed in bedsheets, and had not had a chance to ask Abby if they wanted the costume back.

Since the Faire had ended, she had seen none of the committee members. She certainly had not seen Ian.

As she lifted the gown, something glimmered briefly in the wooden drawer. Reaching down, she found the copper cylinder with the beautiful patterns on its surface—the gift Ian had given her on the same night he had given her a gentle kiss.

It had been one of the last times she had ever seen him.

She started to close the drawer, then paused. So many times she had tried to forget the strange piece of art that he had given her, just as she had tried to forget Ian himself.

Both had proved equally impossible.

Open it. . . .

The voice was so clear that it almost seemed he was in the room. *Open it, Shannon Rose. . . .*

She raised the gleaming, polished cylinder into the light and examined it closely, looking for a way to get inside. The ends were sealed with disks of copper, bent and hammered to close it tight. How could she ever hope to get it open? She took hold of one of the disks, turning it a little and trying to see if it might bend even the slightest bit.

To her great surprise, the disk came off in her fingers.

The cylinder was so light that it seemed it must be empty. But as she peered inside, she could see that there was a scroll—or something—rolled up within it.

With the greatest care, Shannon reached in and drew it out. It was not a scroll at all.

It was an irregular piece of very thin, very fine leather, deep tan in color. It was clean and soft and finely made, with the faint warm scent that good leather has. The edges looked natural, almost ragged, and on one side were traces of fine white hair. Like the copper cylinder this was clearly something unique, something made most carefully by hand.

With the utmost care, she smoothed it out, trying to get the rolled-up leather to flatten out so she could see it. There were fine black marks on it—writing of some kind? It was hard to tell; the marks had gotten rather smeared. Charcoal, most likely. But wait—those marks weren't words. They were music.

A set of musical notes.

She knew how much Ian loved music, especially in the traditional Celtic styles of harp and drum. Perhaps this was something he had written himself. How lovely it would be to play music that had come from his own heart, music he had given to her. . . .

Instantly she stopped herself. If he had wanted to give her something from the heart, he would have stayed with her instead of slowly fading away into the dull, gray, ordinary world.

She placed the cylinder back in the drawer and started to toss the leather sheet back in with it—but as she gazed at the painted notes, she could almost hear them in her mind, could almost picture Ian playing them and writing them down.

It didn't take long to slip on the gown and tie the sash. Shannon simply brushed out her hair and let it lie on her shoulders; no flowers this time. While she waited for her father, she picked up the fragile leather piece gingerly in both hands and walked out to the quiet den where the piano stood.

She was almost afraid to try to play the notes. What sort

of music would Ian give her? How could she listen to it, knowing that she would probably never see him again?

Yet she found that she could not resist. It was impossible to set aside Ian's music and never hear it for herself. After a brief hesitation, she touched the keys, and listened to the song for the first time.

It was a gentle melody, happy and sweet; easy to listen to, easy to play. She wondered what it would sound like on a harp. The individual notes, so clear and cadenced, seemed perfect for the harp.

She played the notes through again, and then once more, and then reached for the leather sheet to put it away—but as she lifted it, it fluttered, and trembled, and crumbled away to dust.

Shannon sat in shock for a moment. It seemed unreal that the leather would simply vanish this way, the way the music she had just finished playing had spun away to nothingness on the air.

Oh, why hadn't she been more careful? The leather must have been old, much older than she'd thought. She had been lucky it had not fallen apart before then.

Slowly, gingerly, she swept the dry dust into one hand and carried it outside. She could not leave it on the piano, but neither could she bring herself to simply discard it in the trash. Perhaps she could scatter it over the garden, over the spot where the hawthorn had been uprooted. That would give a little something back to the earth in return for the tree they had taken from it.

She walked outside to the garden, into the cool damp evening. The quiet yard had long ago become her favorite place at her parents' home. It was large enough, and walled off with enough hedges and tall trees, that it could almost seem like—she could almost feel that she was back at—

But no. That life was long over now. This small college town was the only reality now, until she could move away and change it all forever.

She felt a sense of peace return as she stood in the newly fallen darkness, watching as the stars gradually increased in number, the sky above her filled with their brilliance. And there on the horizon, just peering up through the tops of the trees, was the giant yellow moon, full and round and perfect.

She thought idly of how nice it would have been to have had a full moon last Saturday. That would have been the cap on the Renaissance Faire, since the ancients had always celebrated their festivals during a full moon. She clearly remembered reading that Beltane was always held during a full moon. . . .

Shannon caught her breath.

The full moon!

She had told the committee it was safe to cut down the hawthorn tree because it was the night before May Day— but that wasn't true! *Tonight*, the first night of the full moon, would have been the night before May Day!

Or no—not May Day.

Beltane.

After a moment, Shannon shrugged and walked briskly into the yard, chiding herself for falling victim to such silliness. What was she so shocked about? It was all just superstition, very old and very dead superstition. It meant nothing anymore, nothing in the modern world.

In the center of the yard stood the familiar hawthorn. The moon certainly brought out its beauty; it looked shining and ghostly, with dark and glossy leaves and heavy blooms gleaming white out of the darkness.

With a great start, she fell back several steps. She kept

on backing up until she was up against the hedge.

How could the hawthorn still be there? The committee had cut it down for the Renaissance Faire! It was gone, destroyed, its trunk used for the maypole and its branches and leaves and lovely white flowers scattered all around the site of the Faire.

She touched her forehead. Some of those blooms had even decorated her own hair. . . .

The tree was gone! How could another one be there in the center of the yard?

Shannon frowned. Had her father found a new hawthorn and planted it? But why would he do that? He'd wanted the old tree gone so he could start digging her mother's garden. Had Abby and her friends on the committee replaced the tree? But they'd had enough trouble finding this hawthorn to cut down. Where would they have found another just like it?

Maybe it was someone's idea of a joke. It probably wasn't even a real tree. No doubt it was some kind of paper-and-plastic fake, like the ones decorator stores sold for windowless offices.

She raised her chin. Yes, it had to be a fake tree. The plastic leaves shining in the moonlight were giving it that strange ghostly look. She would just walk right over to it and see for herself—yes, she would—

After a long moment, Shannon took a hesitant step toward the center of the yard.

There was nothing she would have loved more than to find something magical, truly magical and otherworldly, right here in her own backyard; but it was impossible to believe . . . impossible.

Yet the sight of the tree was so beautiful that it was equally impossible to turn away from it. Though it could only be a trick of the light, or the moon, or her overactive imagination, or someone's idea of a joke, she simply could not turn away.

Shannon walked the remaining few steps to the center of the yard and stood right in front of the hawthorn. The sweet scent of the blooms was nearly overpowering there. The tree remained, shining and ghostly, its leaves and flowers moving gently in the night breeze.

How could it not be real? The look, the scent, the quiet rustling sound its leaves made—they were the same as they had ever been. Slowly she reached out to touch the shining glossy leaves and see for herself.

Her hand passed right through the branches.

She snatched it back and hurried backward a few steps, heart pounding. She could see it, but it wasn't there. It simply wasn't there.

But how could it not be there? Much as she might like to, she'd never seen a ghost, and certainly not a ghost tree! And she refused to believe she was seeing something that didn't exist—like a tree she knew for certain had been cut down.

But this tree had been cut down at the wrong time. *It is unlucky to cut down a hawthorn tree on any day except the eve of Beltane. . . .*

Except the eve of Beltane. And this tree had been felled many days before. Whatever magic it held, whatever power it possessed, had been released uncontrolled by hacking it down on a random afternoon.

Shannon summoned her courage. Reaching out with her left hand, determined to feel the shining leaves and moonlit flowers which her eyes insisted were there, she began to walk around the ghostly tree. Yet her outstretched fingers felt only air.

She stopped, but now her fear began to merge with a rising thrill of excitement. Could this really be magic? True magic? For her, magic existed only in the legends of Ireland, in the ancient times when the island was known only as *Eire*. How could such a thing exist in the modern world? She'd stopped believing in any kind of real magic a long time ago.

The dust which had been the leather sheet remained in her tightly clenched hand. Now she flung the dust into the air and watched it vanish, sparkling, onto the shining tree. And into her mind came the song she had found on that same leather sheet, the song she had played on the piano in the house just a little while ago.

It seemed quite fitting . . . a lovely, mysterious song for a lovely, mysterious sight. The leaves and branches seemed almost silvery, translucent now, and the scent of the white blooms was sweeter than ever.

She hummed the song, and closed her eyes. The gentle melody ran through her mind and filled the air around her, whispering along the gently swaying branches of the ghostly tree. Now it seemed that she could hear the notes played as they should be played, on a harp, by someone who loved the music enough to play it to perfection.

The delicate sound of the harp took over all thought, and all feeling, and all sensation, until all she knew was the sweet scent of the flowers and the beautiful notes of the harp.

Lasairian lay resting on his island, motionless in the first rays of warm summer sun. The faint heat was intoxicating after the long damp chill of winter. Adding to the warmth were Keelin and Keavy, two of the loveliest young women of Abhainn Aille, lying close on either side of him.

He was surrounded by beauty of every sort, but closed his eyes and allowed his other senses to take over. He was soon lost in the quiet sounds of the waters of the lake, lapping at the edges of Abhainn Aille. . . . the feel of cool fresh air playing over his face . . . the smell of water and new grass and fresh damp earth . . . the gold-finished harp near his feet, its sensitive bronze strings singing faintly in the breeze . . . the soft heavy warmth of the two girls who lay beside him.

What a lovely song this day would make. How to put it into words? Perhaps if he lay here long enough, the words would come to him. Fortunately for his craft, there was nothing he liked better than to lie in a beautiful spot and wait for words to come.

It was, he told himself, one of the very best things about being a bard.

Beside him, Keelin shifted ever so slightly. "Please, do quiet down," Lasairian murmured, eyes still closed. "You're far too lively for such a day."

"Lively?" There was a faint giggle. "Not out here, thank you! Not with the houses close enough to touch and the people in them well within calling distance!"

Lasairian grinned. "Ah, that's right. You're the one who prefers the deepest forest when the moon is full. I'd almost forgotten."

From the other side, a small fist bounced off his arm. "Lasairian! How can you say that! I'm the one who likes the forest—" Keavy paused, and frowned at him. "Aren't I?"

"Of course you are," he said smoothly, still lying motionless. "You are the lady of the forest, where the trees create their own great hall . . . and of the clearing, where the grass grows thick and soft . . . and of the hillside, where the sun shines warm and the softness of the mist rolls in. You are in all those places, in every place that is made for beauty and sweetness and love."

Keavy sighed, and Keelin sat up. "You always know what to say."

"You're so good with words," added Keavy. "It's a pity you don't—"

She stopped at a quick glance from the other girl. "A pity you don't have more time to sit out here with us," finished Keelin. "Here comes your father."

By the time Lasairian could sit up and turn his head to look, the two girls had gotten to their feet, lifted the hems of their long linen skirts, and hurried away. The only person he saw now was his father, Fergus, striding toward him along the shoreline, his hands clenched into fists and a terrible scowl on his face.

A pair of magnificent white swans rested in the long green grass at the water's edge. This same pair had lived there for at least ten summers, usually as safe and protected and free from worry as Lasairian himself; but now the two birds suddenly stirred and moved apart in a great slow flutter of wings, hissing their displeasure as the man marched right in between them.

For a long moment Fergus stood and glowered down at his son, quivering with anger. The older man's long rough hair, red-brown and streaked with gray, stood out from his reddened face. Lasairian peered up without raising his head, and waited. When his father only maintained his furious silence Lasairian got slowly to his feet, smoothing the fine wool of his soft blue tunic as he did so.

"Oh, do be careful, there," growled his father. "I would not want you to strain anything, what with actually having to stand up."

Lasairian merely watched with a noncommittal expression. He knew that all he had to do was wait it out, and weather the storm, and allow his father to vent his anger until he was satisfied. Then Lasairian could go back to doing as he pleased, and all would be well.

It was a small price to pay for living such a carefree life the rest of the time.

"Oran has been waiting for you since the middle of the morning. You knew he would be. Why, if you have any excuse left that I have not already heard twenty times, and that is enough to fool a day-old trout, did you not arrive for the training?"

"I have no excuse, Father. I simply forgot."

"You forgot?"

"I did."

"Well, then! Why did I even bother to ask? And why do I bother to ask now what you have been doing all morning long?"

"I've been working."

"Working."

"I've been memorizing songs and practicing with my harp, as a bard should. I've even begun composing."

"Memorizing! Composing! How can you hope to do that out here on the water, with the breeze playing on the trees overhead and a girl tucked under each arm? You should be in Oran's house with the other young men, lying in the dark with a stone on your belly! That's the proper way to concentrate, and learn, and memorize!"

Lasairian's mouth tightened. "I love my music, and the words sung with it, but I cannot bear the methods Oran uses! Smoke and darkness and silence, broken only by his endlessly droning voice!"

"Those methods have been used to train every bard in

Eire since the time it formed out of the mists! Every bard, every poet, every druid! Brilliant men were created in just this way. Explain to me why it's not good enough for you!''

Lasairian sighed. ''It isn't training. It's punishment. Lying in a tiny closed-up house on a hard floor in the dark and gloom, with nothing but five other men for company— smoke filling the air—Oran's voice droning on and on, and that wretched stone pinning you down—''

''The stone's to keep you from falling asleep!'' Fergus said, with a fierce glare. ''Now, you said long ago that you did not want to be a warrior. No matter what I said, I could not dissuade you, and neither could my brother, though I can understand that—he's only the *king*, after all.''

Lasairian frowned, but said nothing. He reached down to get his harp and settled it carefully in his arms. Just a little longer, and then . . .

''You have nothing to say to me? You do not intend to go to Oran's house today?''

''Not today, and not any day. I will be a bard, but I will learn by my own methods—not Oran's.''

Fergus's jaw clenched tight, and his face turned as red as his beard. ''You refuse to finish your education with Oran?''

Lasairian looked off into the distance, studying the way the tall pine trees on the mainland moved gently in the soft breeze. ''I do.''

''Of course, I have no way of forcing you.'' His father's voice suddenly became so soft that Lasairian glanced back at him. ''I suppose I have no choice but to let you train in your own way, in your own good time.''

Lasairian studied him, not quite believing what he was

hearing. "I promise you, Father, I will finish studying, and I will become a bard," he said cautiously.

"Oh, that you will. You will finish studying. You will finish studying with Oran just as the other young students are doing. You will do this," he said his voice rising as Lasairian started to protest, "or you will marry Clodagh."

Lasairian blinked. "I will—what?"

"You heard me! I am giving you a choice! You will either return to your training and submit yourself to Oran, or I myself—*and the king*—will *order* you to marry Clodagh! And if you refuse to do either, you will no longer be a part of Abhainn Aille!"

Shocked, Lasairian stared back at him. Never had his father offered him any sort of ultimatum—nothing like this! "No longer be a part of Abhainn Aille? You would exile me? You, Father, would do this to me?"

"You have done it to yourself! You cannot stay here, a grown man, and refuse to work or study! You tell yourself, and me, that you are 'training,' when you know as well as I do that you are merely wasting your time in laziness!"

Fergus shook his head, his fierce gaze never wavering. "So there it is. If you do not want to face exile, you can either put in the work to become a proper bard or you can marry Clodagh and at least give that woman a husband. If you can manage no other task, I am sure you can manage that!"

Now Lasairian saw which way the wind was blowing. It was true that the last thing he wanted was to leave Abhainn Aille; his beautiful island home was one thing which did have a certain hold on him.

And there was good reason why Clodagh was unmarried. No doubt his father thought he would back down in horror from the very idea of marrying such a woman, and go meekly back to Oran and his awful, stinking little house.

"I only want to please you, Father," he said, with an easy smile. "It's settled, then. Please inform Clodagh that I will marry her tomorrow."

Chapter Five

Fergus glowered at him, his eyes narrowing in suspicion. "You are telling me that you have no objection to marrying Clodagh. That tomorrow you will make her your wife."

Lasairian shrugged, "I have no objection. I hear she is a fine cook. I am sure we can come to an arrangement that will be satisfactory to us both."

"Good." Fergus gave him a slight nod, and Lasairian saw his father relax ever so slightly. "I will speak to Oran, and the king. And it will be done tomorrow."

"Of course. I look forward to it. Thank you, father." He smiled in gratitude and shifted the harp again, waiting for his father to leave.

Lasairian felt no worry over the prospect of marrying Clodagh. He had quickly assessed the situation and realized that it was the simplest way out of his dilemma. If his father and the king would be satisfied by his providing for the woman, and allowing her to keep his home and cook for him and occasionally weave him a fine new tunic or *brat*, he had no intention of protesting.

And no intention of changing anything else about his life. It was almost too easy.

His father seemed about to go, but hesitated. Finally he reached beneath his woolen cloak for something at his belt. "If you are to be married, you will need a bride-gift. You may give this to Clodagh." Fergus paused, and his voice became low. "It was a gift I gave to your mother when she became my bride."

Cradling the harp in one arm, Lasairian reached out for his father's offering and examined it closely. It was a copper container, polished and gleaming and as long as his forearm, made from a single sheet of metal rolled up and then sealed at each end with a flat copper disk.

Turning it over, he saw that the entire surface was decorated with lovely curving patterns—intertwining willow leaves and swans, and long rippling lines which he recognized as representing water.

He looked up at his father. "I have not seen this before," he said. "It was my mother's?"

Fergus started to speak, but only nodded instead. "It was a favorite of hers," he said after a moment. "As were you. Did I ever tell you . . . that you have her eyes, the same dark hair?"

Lasairian smiled, with the same patience he always felt when his father spoke of the long-dead mother he himself had never known. "You have, Father. But I don't mind hearing it again." He looked again at the copper container, shining, perfect, its designs seeming almost to move on their own. "You are sure you want me to have this? You want me to give this to Clodagh?"

"I want you to give it to the woman you marry, in the hope that she will make you as happy as your mother made me. That is what I want." And with that Fergus turned and strode away, as though he were afraid he might change his mind.

Lasairian stood for a long moment, holding the shining copper container. With one nail he gently traced the interlocking designs. And then he turned and started down the shoreline, away from where his father had gone, and walked until he reached the farthest end of Abhainn Aille.

He set down the harp. Now he stood at the point where the river met itself once more, after dividing to flow around the island. The water rippled and splashed white as strong currents pulled it along and sent it rushing away.

He stepped onto a rock, held out the copper treasure, and began to speak softly, whispering the way the spirit of the waters always did.

"Keep this thing of beauty for me, mistress of the waters, for I cannot. It is meant for the woman I should marry, the woman I should love above all others—but I know too well that no woman lives who could persuade me to close my eyes to all the others.

"I would not dishonor my mother by simply hiding her gift away. Therefore I will give it to you, ever-changing, ever-lovely lady of the rivers and the streams and the lakes, who sees not, and scolds not, but always travels on, and sings gently."

Lasairian dropped the shining copper into the swiftest part of the water. It flashed once in the light of the sun and vanished.

The river took no notice, but flowed on.

*   *   *

Two fortnights passed—fourteen nights once, and then again. And one late morning found Lasairian sitting alone on the mainland, not far from the water's edge, quite comfortable in the dappled shade beneath the willows.

With infinite care and gentleness he caressed the metal strings of his harp with the long fingernails that were his pride. The playing was a bit hesitant, a bit tentative, for it was a new piece of music. As he had promised his father, he was indeed composing. In the days since his marriage to Clodagh he had nearly finished the little song he practiced now.

He knew well that such a leisurely rate of composition would hardly be satisfactory to the druids. But since he had kept his part of the bargain by getting married, his father had kept his too; Fergus had made no further attempt to force his son back into Oran's school. But just to make certain that he could indeed work as he pleased, Lasairian now made it a habit to leave Abhainn Aille and pass the days with his harp beneath the oak and tall pine trees.

Although, most days he had not only his harp for company.

He heard soft footsteps behind him, coming through the woods. It was not his father's heavy tread nor Clodagh's determined pace. These steps were lighter, happier—

"Morrin?" he called, his attention still on his harp.

There was an exasperated sigh from behind him. "I should turn around and go back!" said a young feminine voice.

He twisted around to see Monat. "Ah, but I was hoping it was you," Lasairian said. "I was just being polite."

She laughed and sat down beside him, pushing him down to earth, rolling atop him. "Good," she whispered, and began to kiss him.

Lasairian lay back and let her do as she wished. It did not matter to him whether Morrin or Monat or Keelin or Keavy had come into the forest to seek him out, so long as at least one of them did. . . . But he was wise enough not to say so.

Suddenly she stiffened and sat up. In a moment she was off of him. Puzzled, he raised himself up on one elbow. "Monat! Where are you going? What's wrong?" But as he turned around to look for her, he saw no one—no one but his father.

And behind him, King Irial, Lasairian's uncle, young and strong and the image of a powerful warrior.

Never before had his father gone to the trouble of trotting out the king to chastise him. He began to feel the first touch of worry.

Lasairian got slowly to his feet. "I'm surprised to see you here, Father," he said, carefully controlling his temper.

"Would you rather I sent Clodagh?"

Lasairian's jaw tightened. "She has no reason to come here and seek me out. She is well cared for and has plenty to do in our house. I have kept my part of the arrangement."

Fergus only glowered at him. "You did indeed marry Clodagh—for all the pleasure it's brought to either one of you."

"Marriage is not about pleasure, or so I'm told. It's about duty. And I have done my duty as you have asked me to do, and married Clodagh. What more do you want from me?"

"I want you to keep the rest of your promise! I want you to train to become a bard, as you told me you would!" shouted his father. "I want you to be a man, not a lazy, spoiled boy who will do nothing but lay on his backside under a tree all day long!''

"My life suits me to perfection as it is," Lasairian answered, through clenched teeth. "I play my music and perform for the people, as any bard is expected to do. I have married Clodagh, a woman no one else would have, and given her a home and a place. And if I choose the solitude of the forest to do my composing, why should anyone object to that?''

He expected another angry outburst. Shouting and swearing would have been easy to weather, as always. But his father only shook his head and spoke in a low, deadly voice.

"You think of no one but yourself, Lasairian," he said. "Your promise to study meant nothing. You are not a bard and you will never train yourself to become one. No one can train himself in such an art. This 'training' you speak of consists of dozing in the forests all day, when you are not busy with Monat or Morrin or any of the rest of them.

"I blame myself as well as you. I have allowed you to do as you wished ever since your mother—since you lost your mother. I let you grow up petted and pampered, thinking to make up the loss to you; but I have succeeded only in raising a lazy spoiled prince, not a strong and worthy man.''

At first Lasairian felt only anger at the insult. But the emotion was quickly tempered by something he scarcely recognized.

Shame.

He looked down at the soft grasses waving along the bank of the river. "I have no wish to disappoint you, Father," he said. "I simply wish to live in my own way, in peace and freedom.''

"Then perhaps we can arrange for you all the peace and freedom you desire," said King Irial, stepping forward.

Lasairian held very still. This was different from all the other times he had clashed with his father. These two had something planned for him, something he was quite certain he would not like at all.

Fergus spoke again. "Even Clodagh was not able to convince you to return to Oran and finish your training."

Lasairian's temper rose again. "Did you hope she would drive me out of her house and into Oran's? Do you think any woman, even my wife, could ever control me? Could force me to do anything at all?"

"I hoped that marriage might change you," Fergus went on, his voice still low and steady. "Especially marriage to Clodagh. But you are right. I was a fool to think that even she could do that."

"That you were." Lasairian waited for the outburst, but it never came.

"A decision has been made," his father said. "Your uncle the king will be pleased to tell you."

"You have shown a fondness for solitude in the fields and forests," said King Irial, eyeing him coolly. "You refuse to go to the houses of learning or the training grounds of the fighters. The only activity you seem to find agreeable is spending time alone with your harp—and with the youngest and most frivolous of the women of Abhainn Aille.

"I will not allow a fit young man to idle away his days, and neither will the rest of the free men. You have caused a great deal of ill-feeling, Lasairian, with your rejection of anything resembling work or study, though I doubt if you know or care. But I tell you, it will continue no longer.

"When the cowherds take the cattle to the high pastures after Beltane, you will go with them. You can still spend your days sitting in the fields, as you do now, but at least you can perform some useful service by keeping watch on the cows as you sit. And I doubt if the other herdboys will take kindly to it should you refuse to do any work while you are up there with them.''

Lasairian stared at the king, aghast. ''You are making me a cowherd?''

''We are,'' growled Fergus. ''Since you refuse to study so that your playing is fit for men and women, you can play your harp for the cows.''

He simply could not believe what he was hearing. A great sense of outrage flooded through him. ''You are banishing me? Exiling me? Sending me away like a common criminal? Father! How can you do this to me?''

The anger was genuine this time. The last thing Lasairian wanted was to leave his comfortable life at Abhainn Aille for the life of a lowly herdboy up in the windblown hills. ''What will happen to my fingernails?'' he cried. ''They will be broken, ruined!''

But both his father and the king stood unmoving and stared him down.

''You will leave with the herds on the morning after Beltane,'' said the king, ''and return with them at the end of the season. No more will be said. The matter is ended.'' The two of them turned and walked away, leaving Lasairian standing alone with his harp.

He was angry. He was outraged. He was filled with disbelief. But even as the men's footsteps faded, the shock of the king's decision began fading also.

There was nothing he could do to change it. With a sigh, he told himself that perhaps it wouldn't be so bad. At least he would not have his father or his wife constantly at his elbow, pressuring him to do this or do that. The herdboys would not dare try to order around a man of his station.

Surely he could do as he liked even more easily than he always had at home. It was only for a few months, until the end of the year, until Samhain. Then he would be home and life would go on as it always had.

And if Keelin or Keavy or Monat or Morrin could be persuaded to spend some time in the hills with him, so much the better.

He would never let anything change the way he wanted to live his life—not his father, not his wife, not even an order from the king.

He looked forward to a long, peaceful summer.

At first there was only the sound of slow rain falling.

It seemed to Shannon that some time ago she had been listening to the playing of a harp. Yet now, as she walked over the soft grass, the notes faded away and became the gentle, natural sound of water falling, a quiet rain falling into a river or a lake.

Perhaps she had only imagined the music of the harp. But the sounds of the rain and the cool air touched with mist were nearly as soothing as the playing had been. She was reluctant even to open her eyes, so much was she enjoying her pleasant walk. The delicate scent of lush green grass and spring wildflowers floated on the damp breeze, lingering like the notes of the harp, surrounding her with a natural beauty no artist could ever duplicate.

She almost smiled. With her eyes closed she could imagine that she was not in her modest yard, but back on her parents' beautiful wooded estate, years ago, before it had all disappeared forever.

She quickly banished all such thoughts and memories, just as she always did whenever they crept up on her. There was nothing to be gained by longing for things that were gone and could never be again. She should be going in soon; her mother and father would be sitting down to dinner and she did not want to keep them waiting.

With a little sigh she opened her eyes, blinking. It was strange how the sky seemed brighter than it had when she had first come out. Twilight had fallen, or so she had thought, but the light surrounding her now was that of a soft gray afternoon.

A glance upward showed her the branches of a tree covered with perfumed white flowers. At the base of the tree, right at her plastic-sandaled feet, a spring of clear water bubbled up from beneath a rock. From there the water ran over a tumble of rounded gray stones, stones which guided the water into a white and foaming fall which ran and rushed down a hill, a very wide, steep hill leading far, far down to a distant sparkling lake.

Shannon reeled at the unexpected sight and instinctively grabbed for a branch of the tree—a tree which, she was very thankful to discover, was quite real and substantial. Holding on to the rough, thorny branch in an effort to regain her balance, she glanced wildly around her and tried to determine just how she had come to be on the side of a hill in wide-open country, with a lake at her feet and a meadow above her head, all of it completely surrounded by forest, dark and green and seemingly impenetrable.

She was quite certain that there had been no meadows or lakes or thick wild forests around her parents' little white house in Bowling Green.

What should she do? She was afraid to speak, afraid to move. What was she doing here? How had she come to this place? And what place *was* this?

Yet even as she asked herself those questions, she knew

the answers with perfect clarity. She was here because she had wanted to be here—because she had dared to believe that very old legends and even older tales of magic just might be true. She'd made a deliberate attempt to open a door to another world, circling a ghostly tree and offering it the dusty remains of a mysterious song.

The last thing she'd expected was that she would succeed. And as with most dreamers, she had never thought about what she would do if the magic actually worked. But now she was here, in the place she had been thinking of for so long, the place she had been dreaming of when she began her innocent ritual. This beautiful place could only be Ireland, her Ireland, the mystical and magical *Eire* of the faraway past.

This was the place where magic still existed, in a time long before anyone had ever heard of May Day. A place where a traveler from another, grayer era might still find refuge if she discovered just the right elements and found the courage to make the leap. . . .

As she stood on the side of the hill, slowly easing her grip on the tree branch, there came once again, unmistakably, the sound of a harp. Someone very close was playing the same familiar song on a harp, the same lovely music she had heard while circling a silvery, ghostly, otherworldly vision of a hawthorn tree, just like the real one which waved gently above her head right now.

Almost as if for reassurance, she reached out to touch the hawthorn. The leaves fluttered against her fingers. The rough bark brushed against her skin. She reached for one of the white flowers, wanting to breathe its very real scent and hold the soft petals in her hand, and broke it off with a small snap.

The music stopped. From behind a rock just on the other

side of the tree, a man got to his feet, looking all around. After a moment he walked to the tree and parted the branches, peering through the leaves at her.

To her complete astonishment, she found herself looking at the face of Ian Galloway.

Ah, now, this was more to his liking. Lasairian had been wondering if any of the ladies would slip away from all the preparations and come up here to join him. Ever since his father and the king had ordered him to serve as a cowherd for the summer, most of the other young men and women had carefully avoided him. None wanted to be associated with the target of the king's displeasure.

Lasairian had even put away his fine clothes and gold and taken to dressing in the plain coarse wools and simple copper ornaments of a herdboy, hoping that his father would be so appalled by the sight that he would intervene and persuade the king to change his mind. . . .

He had to admit that it did not seem likely.

Of course, most of the people of Abhainn Aille would be quite well occupied getting ready for tonight's ritual, even as he was—practicing his new music. But he had hoped he would not have to pass the whole afternoon alone.

He looked carefully through the branches of the hawthorn, where the lady stood hidden behind the leaves and flowers. Which one was it? He couldn't be sure. He saw only a slight and slender figure dressed in a very unusual shade of green—a very pale, almost unnatural shade which he'd never seen before, with a wide belt as yellow as a *samhaircin* flower wrapped around her waist. On one finger he noticed a gleam of gold and the glimmer of some fine stone.

Lasairian smiled. "Keelin? Monat?" he called, peering

71

through the branches and trying to move them out of the way. He still could not quite make out who his visitor was. Well, if she wanted to play a little hiding game, he would be happy to oblige—yet his curiosity was growing.

Behind the rustling leaves he could see pale shining hair, long and fine, almost like a child's in the way it fell down loose past her shoulders; it was yellow, as though she had borrowed a touch of color from her sash. Her skin was smooth and fair as milk, with a faint blush of pink. Her eyes, clear blue, were enormous and staring.

"Ian," she said, in a voice little more than a whisper. *"Ian?"*

He stepped out from behind the tree, and smiled at her. "That is not my name, beautiful lady," he said. "Though it could be, if you wish it so."

She stared up at him, and up—she was not very tall, he noted, her head would just come up to his shoulder—and shook her head slightly. She kept her frightened gaze fixed on his face, as though she feared to look around.

She spoke again, more rapidly this time, and he could not catch a word of it. "I am sorry, but I do not understand any of what you are saying. Do you not speak the language of Eire?"

"Eire . . ." Now, though she did not move, her glance darted left and right and then back at him, as though she could not believe what she was seeing.

And at last she spoke to him in words that made sense. "Who are you? What is this place? Why am I here?"

She spoke haltingly, and with a strange accent, one he had never heard before. But he was most concerned about her demeanor—trembling and pale, eyes wide with wonder, lips parted as though she wanted to speak again but didn't know where to start.

After the briefest of glances left and right, she stared straight into his eyes. "Is this—is this Eire?"

Lasairian felt a chill. Just exactly what had he encountered here? He was certain he'd never seen her before. He would never have forgotten so pretty a young woman. "Why do you doubt that you are in Eire?" he asked gently, moving another step closer. "What has happened to you?"

"I don't know," she said. "I remember only walking around the tree behind my home—and singing the song—and it all faded away, and all I heard was the music, and then I was here . . . here with you."

Lasairian smiled, feeling certain that he could reassure her, win her over as he had always been able to do with every woman he'd ever encountered. "I can tell you that you are not from anywhere within a day's ride of here," he said. "But I can also tell you that no matter where you may have come from, you are indeed in the land of Eire."

When she continued to stare up at him, wide-eyed, he tried again. "Do you remember nothing of where you lived? Who you were?" He knew stories—true stories, not the ones woven by bards like himself—of people who had been injured, or desperately ill, and then lost memory of their past. Perhaps something like that had happened to her.

She only blinked, and then slowly, cautiously, looked around her. She said not a word, but her eyes grew even wider and her breath caught in her throat.

Lasairian approached her, and before she could move he placed his hands on her slender shoulders and gently turned her toward the countryside.

Chapter Six

The warm touch of those hands caused Shannon's wild emotions to still themselves, and allowed her rapidly beating heart to slow to something like normal. It seemed that up until now she had been lost and floating in this strange and surreal place; but the strong yet gentle hold on her shoulders brought her back down to earth, and anchored her here, to this time, to this place ... even to this man who she could have sworn was Ian.

"Here, lady with no past," he said, "here is where you are. If there is a more beautiful place in Eire or in any other land, I have not been able to imagine it."

She braced herself against him, increasingly conscious of his warmth, his strength, and took another look. The world fell away beneath her feet, sweeping down from the single hawthorn tree into a steep hill, almost too steep to climb. The little spring at the top tumbled down the center of the hill to a wide plain below, a lovely flat grass-covered plain perhaps a quarter mile across which ended at the edge of a beautiful lake.

She could not take her eyes from the lake. The glassy surface glittered in the late-afternoon sun. The breeze from the west brought to her the wonderful smell of cool fresh water. But now she was calm enough to take note of something else: There, perhaps a hundred yards from shore, was an island—an island large enough for a house, for a mansion, for a castle.

But this island was thick with trees, and within their shadows she could just make out the dark wooden walls of buildings. At the surrounding shores were two small boats, with a third one resting on the bank of the mainland at the foot of the hill. This was not just an island. It was a home.

So beautiful . . . She who thought she knew what beauty was, and could appreciate it as few people could, now saw what beauty truly was.

She started to turn toward the man who still held her so gently, but kept her gaze on the island. "Do you live there?" she asked.

"That is Abhainn Aille," he said. "That is my home."

"Yours?"

"Mine. And many others. My father, my brothers and sisters, my—" He stopped, and reached out to her, placing his finger beneath her chin and drawing her around to face him. "If you have nowhere else to go, then please—allow me to offer you the hospitality of our house."

She looked up at him, and then glanced at the wild and open—and very empty—expanse of territory around her. "I have nowhere else to go," she said quietly.

"Then stay with us." He smiled, and Shannon stared

transfixed at him. "What is it?" he asked, still smiling but with his confusion evident on his face.

"I know you," she whispered. "I am sure that I know you. You are—you were Ian Galloway. I knew you at the university. We worked together on the Renaissance Faire committee. We went out for coffee and chocolate at Isabella's."

"Issa-bell-ahs." He shook his head. "Lost lady, I can only tell you that my name is not Ian; it is Lasairian, though I must admit that you do have correct the very last part of my name. And as I said before, if it pleases you, I will be happy to have you call me by the name of Ian—or by any other name that you might wish to say."

He spoke to her not in English, but in Gaelic, with a strong accent she found difficult to follow. Yet she was struck by the beauty of it, of listening to someone speak the language who had spoken it from the first and knew every nuance as no non–native speaker ever could.

And it was not the first time she had heard someone speak so.

If she had doubted it before, she doubted it no longer. The lovely words, the mesmerizing voice—it was Ian exactly as she remembered him. The beautiful dark eyes, the fine skin, even the touch of color at the cheekbones—it was all there.

It was true that the dark curling hair was longer now, falling to his shoulders, and there was one very strange thing: His fingernails, all of them save the ones on the little fingers, were long and thick and curved longwise; it was as if he had the tip of a quill pen attached to each finger. She could not imagine why any man would have such nails, but when compared to the other things she had experienced this day, it did not seem worthy of much concern at the moment.

The clothes were not so startling. He was dressed like a man who had walked straight out of a history book. He wore a simple knee-length tunic of cream-colored wool, with a belt made from thick brown leather and fastened with an iron ring. Over it was a wide wool cloak, dark brown in color, pinned just like a blanket over his shoulders and thrown back over his right arm. The pin itself was a circle of what appeared to be copper, as were the wide bands at both his wrists.

It was very simple, obviously the garb of a working man. Yet it all looked perfectly natural on him. These were clothes, not a costume.

Lasairian. He belonged here.

"Now, since I have told you my name, will you tell me yours? Though I understand that perhaps you do not remember it. Ah, but even that does not matter; we could think of one for you. You could be called *aille*, like my home, for your beauty; or *abhainn*, after the river, the lovely river which sings to us each night as we sleep—"

"Shannon," she said quickly. "My name is Shannon. Shannon Rose Grey."

"*Shah-non!* Shannon Rose," he repeated. "A lovely name. And so, dear lady Shannon Rose, will you come with me to Abhainn Aille?"

She smiled, lost in those dark and shining eyes, swept away by that voice. "I will come with you, Lasairian. I will come with you."

He ran his hand over her hair, smoothing it back from her face. "Wait here," he said, and walked back toward the rock from which he had come. Shannon watched him go. If the lake itself were to rise up and send a tidal wave rushing toward her, she would still remain rooted to this spot, waiting for his return.

When he came back he carried a large object in one arm, something carefully wrapped and tied in smooth brown leather. He offered no explanation of what it was, and Shannon felt no compulsion to ask; and so together they started down the steep slope beside the lovely waterfall.

Shannon's sandaled feet slipped on the wet grass and loose rocks. She quickly caught hold of Lasairian's arm, her attention divided between the world around her and the handsome man she walked beside. It was hard to decide which was more compelling, or more beautiful, or more magical.

Finally they reached the edge of the lake, where a small boat waited for them. Lasairian stepped into it, set down his leather-wrapped burden, and offered her his arm. Carefully she followed him into the boat and sat down on the single wooden plank which stretched across it.

Kneeling down, using only a single straight oar, he sent the vessel gliding across the water as the setting sun shone down on them. Shannon felt as though she were leaving behind the last vestiges of her drab former life and emerging like a butterfly from its safe, dark, imprisoning cocoon. This world, her world now, was bright and beautiful, as sparkling as the glitter of the sun on the water.

In just a few moments they had drifted across the lake. The little boat gently ran aground on the edge of the island. Lasairian got out, picked up the leather-wrapped object, and once again offered her his hand; and Shannon, feeling like she had been reborn, stepped out onto the soft grass on the shore of Abhainn Aille.

It was a magical kingdom of small wooden houses, their dark walls and steep thatched roofs nearly hidden from sight beneath the shade of the towering pine trees. Ringed with grass, its floor of clean dry earth cushioned with pine needles, the island sheltered a rustic city in miniature. Well-worn paths crossed and curved among the randomly placed buildings. One of the buildings was quite large, most were obviously homes, and the rest appeared to be places for storage and for work.

A little way up the shore, a flutter of white caught Shannon's eye. A pair of great white swans came up out of the water to the soft grass where the island met the lake, and seemed to gaze at her before settling down to rest.

"Home," she whispered, gazing back at them.

"It is my home," said Lasairian, from close beside her. "And I hope that it will be yours for a time, as well."

She looked up at him, and nodded faintly. "Please— show me."

He smiled, and once again his gentle hand rested on her shoulder. "Nothing would please me more, lady of the hawthorn tree," he said, and together they walked into the shade of the tall sheltering pines.

"How many people live here?" she asked.

He shrugged. "A good number. There are some fifteen houses; perhaps four or five people occupy each of them, perhaps more in the larger ones, such as the King's house. And there are servants who take shelter where they can, in the King's Hall or even in the armory or granary."

"A hundred people here on this island . . . yet it is so clean, so neat. Wait!" She looked around, carefully studying all the buildings she could see. "I don't see anything that looks like a barn or a pen. There are no animals on this island! How can you live so well without cattle or sheep?"

"Now, that is an easy question. All of the animals are

kept by the farmers in the fields and forests, there, along the river. Horses nearby, then the cattle herds, and then a few sheep. They are brought here only as needed. Abhainn Aille remains clean and untouched, a fine place for her people to live.''

"There aren't even any chickens," she marveled.

"Any—what?"

"Um—chickens?"

He looked closely at her. "I must apologize to you. I do not know what sort of animal that is. Perhaps it is something that lives only in your land, or you had a different name for it. Do you know it by another name?"

She searched her memory. "*Sicin*—that is the only word I know for 'chicken.' Are you sure you don't have them here? Tame birds, not so big as the swans, good to eat, lay eggs?"

"I have heard of no tame bird such as that anywhere in Eire."

Now her face burned with embarrassment. Maybe they really didn't have chickens here. Maybe the birds weren't native to this part of the world. Now that she thought about it, she didn't have the first idea as to where chickens had come from or when they'd been brought to Ireland.

A cold and disorienting fear began to grip her. If she was in the dark about something as trivial as chickens, what else did this world possess that she knew absolutely nothing about?

Lasairian reached for her hand, and leaned down so that he could catch her eye. "I know that this is all very strange to you, but I promise, I will help you in every way I can. I hope that you will know this, and that you will trust me to care for you until you can once again care for yourself. Will you do this, Shannon?"

Of course I will, Ian . . . of course I trust you. She drew back a little, yet still held his strong warm hand tightly in her own. "I thank you. And I am grateful for your help." She offered him a little smile, and felt warmth return to her skin as his dark eyes glowed in return.

"You will have nothing to fear while you are here with me. That I promise. Now, come with me, and allow me to take you to my house."

They continued down the path, and Shannon quickly became aware that she was being watched. From inside every building and behind every tree, at least one person stared openly as she walked past. Well, she could hardly blame them. She must seem as strange to them as they did to her, yet it was still disconcerting to be the object of such hard curiosity.

At least they did not stop and stare for long; everyone seemed to be quite busy and preoccupied as they hurried back and forth along the shady little paths, carrying loads of what appeared to be firewood and food. Though she knew nothing about this place, this seemed too tense and rushed to be the usual everyday routine. "Is something happening here?" she asked.

"All of the folk are getting ready for the ceremonies tonight," Lasairian said. "Many have gone into the forest, while some remain here to do what needs to be done."

"Ceremonies?" Her heart beat a little faster. She knew, she *knew*, what he was going to say—yet she could not believe it.

He led her to the edge of the island, near the place where the swans rested, and pointed to the sky. "Do you see the full moon? There, just beginning to show herself above the trees. This is the second full moon since the spring equinox.

And that, lost lady, means that tonight is the night of Beltane.''

Shannon closed her eyes. Of course. It could have been nothing else. On the evening that would have been Beltane in her world, she had walked around a ghostly hawthorn tree—a tree cut down at the wrong time, a dangerous time, as all the old legends said, and so its wild and ancient power had been released. That power had enveloped and overwhelmed her, drawing her back to another Beltane in another place and another time.

She had made it. She had been successful in her escape from the gray and hopeless modern world, and had found her way to ancient Eire. Beautiful, magical, long-ago Eire, the home of Lasairian, a man she had only dreamed of back in her own world—until the day she had met Ian Galloway.

But Ian had drifted out of her life and now that life was far behind her. She had found the same magic all over again here in Eire and she was determined that she would not lose it again this time—not now that she'd found both the escape she had longed for and a man who seemed to have the power to fulfill her wildest dreams.

Lasairian led her to the doorway of one of the smallest of the neat wooden houses, sitting almost at the shore at the far end of the island. She shivered as she lifted her long lime-green skirts and stepped over the threshold. This was no museum re-creation or quaint textbook photo. This was the real thing. This was someone's home.

Lasairian's home.

Inside were smooth, dark wooden walls, built high to allow plenty of headroom for these tall men and women. There was a steep roof of tightly thatched straw with a small neat hole cut in the center, directly above the stone-ringed firepit in the center of the floor. The smell of wood smoke and something like fresh-baked bread filled the little house. The single window at the back of the house had its shutter pulled open and the light wind, fresh from the lake, made a pleasant cross-breeze through the house.

The walls were hung with heavy iron implements and utensils, few of which she recognized. There did seem to be long two-tined forks, pokers for the fire, and carving knives. Scattered everywhere were woven baskets of various sizes. Near the back of the house, beneath the single window, was a long wide ledge strewn with soft heavy furs and what appeared to be neatly folded woolen blankets in all sorts of bright plaids.

Underfoot was an ankle-deep bed of soft green rushes, so thick they entirely covered what she knew must be a dirt floor. It was all rough and simple, but clean and sturdy and sheltering at the same time.

She followed Lasairian farther inside, staying very close to him, her glance darting everywhere as she tried to take it all in at once. She stood by the hearth, enthralled by the sight of flatbread baking on smooth stones set at the edge of the fire on the coals.

"Why, Lasairian! Such a lovely lady! Where has she come from?"

Shannon jumped at the shrill voice and looked behind her, blinking. Two women stood in the doorway, with two silent men behind them, all looking intently at her.

One of the women was smiling and grandmotherly in appearance, with an open, friendly face and bright eyes. At her side she carried something large and wet and dripping, in a sling made of linen. But the other—younger, not much older than Shannon herself, she judged, but tall and strong and formidable—was quite different. The woman only stared with a cold and sullen expression before walking silently past and attending to some task near the rear of the house.

"Her name is Shannon," Lasairian said, still facing the older woman. He seemed to be completely ignoring the younger one. "She is lost, and in need of our hospitality. Please give her whatever she requires. I will return for her in a short time."

"But—where did she come from? How did she come to be here? So strange, so strange," she murmured, looking Shannon up and down.

Lasairian only gave the woman a brief glance. "See to her for me, please," he said, his eyes on the men who still stood just outside. He did not look at Shannon, but as he moved toward the door she felt the gentle touch of his hand at her waist.

"Wait—who are these—" But he was gone.

She had no time to wonder where he was going, for the grandmotherly woman immediately set down her burden and came bustling over to her. "Well, now! Shannon, you are welcome here. My name is Bevin. It has been quite some time since we have had a visitor! I am always so happy when Beltane comes, for it means traveling and visitors again."

Bevin paused, and then peered up at Shannon with a merry little grin. "Of course, that's not all it means, isn't that right, Clodagh!" She laughed, first winking at Shannon and then trying her best to catch the other woman's eye. But the younger one refused to be drawn in. Her face was a taut, unsmiling mask, her eyes sullen and suspicious.

The laughter trailed off, and she gave a little sigh. "My daughter's first child will be born in the fall. She does not always feel well. Her husband—"

Bevin stopped as Clodagh shot her a fierce look. "Oh,

in the fall, in the fall, and I am so looking forward to having a new little one to play with and to hold." She turned her attention to Shannon. "But I have a guest to care for!"

The woman hurried over to the ledge and pulled off a couple of the soft furs, and then placed them on the rushes at Shannon's feet. "Please, do sit down. Now, then! Let me give you something to eat, and drink. Here—the very best bread, from the best of the oat flour, newly baked and still warm. Nothing is too good for Lasairian's house! There is honey for it, and a bit of butter. Sheep's butter, of course, though I think I prefer the butter of the cow. Which do you like best? And here is a bit of milk, fresh this morning, kept cool in the lake. Oh, but it will not be long now until we have butter and milk from the cow, so much better than the sheep, I have always thought!"

Shannon accepted the food, heaped on a small wooden tray, and the milk, sloshing in a flat, round cup of what appeared to be bronze. She tasted the milk cautiously; it was cool, as Bevin had said, and seemed to be fresh. The flatbread was a bit dry, but tasted quite good with the generous amount of pale, mild-flavored butter and thick golden honey that had been slathered over it.

Bevin kept up her one-sided conversation as Shannon nibbled at the bread. "We will be having a fine feast before the moon is high. A lovely trout Clodagh has caught for us today, how nice it will be rubbed with a little salt and honey and baked in the coals of the hearth. I do believe it is my favorite food of all, though I must say—" She paused, lifting her small iron knife from the trout. "I cannot think of one that I do not like at least a little!" She laughed merrily and returned to preparing the fish. "Oh, it's well you came when you did, before the fires are put out."

Shannon paused. "Fires put out? Why?"

"Why? Tonight is Beltane! Beltane!"

Chapter Seven

The older woman looked at Shannon with astonishment. "Did they never celebrate Beltane in the place where you are from?"

Shannon smiled wryly. "I suppose they did. They just didn't realize it."

"Didn't realize?" Bevin stopped, as though thinking better of asking, and bustled around to a corner of the house. Standing at one of the several wooden shelves, she rummaged for a moment and then took down what looked like a large folded woolen blanket, a beautiful plaid of green and yellow and cream. Shannon noticed Clodagh's cold glance at this.

"Here, now," said Bevin, "I can see that you have no *brat*. You will surely need one later on!"

"Do you expect that it will be cold?" asked Shannon.

Bevin laughed, throwing her head back in merriment.

"Oh, it will be quite warm, I expect!" Shannon wondered what she meant by that, but had no chance to ask. "You may take this. I do not doubt you will have need of it later." She set it down on the rushes next to Shannon, and then crouched down to study the lime-green gown. "And may I ask you, who has made this?"

"I'm not sure. Probably Sears, or maybe Wal-Mart." Of course these women would not understand the references, but it hardly seemed to matter. Her gown was cut very like the ones they wore—long and loose like a nightgown, and belted at the waist—but the bright yellow sash and lime-green bedsheets looked even more ridiculous now beside their finely made wool gowns.

Bevin's was woven in a soft plaid of yellow and cream and very dark brown, while Clodagh's was a magnificent work in a plaid of blue and green and yellow and cream. They wore linen undergowns beneath the plaid wools, and well-made belts of beautiful leather.

Shannon felt like a child attempting to play dress-up.

"But, this is the finest fabric I have ever seen!" Bevin could not resist reaching to rub the lime-green sheets between two fingers. "So very smooth, so very soft! And the stitches, so small I can hardly see them!" She shook her head, marveling. "I would love to meet this lady *Seers*, who can do such fine and perfect work. If you see her again, please tell her that her work is like a magic."

Shannon smiled at her. "I suppose it is at that, now that I think about it." Then she looked straight at Bevin. "But, please. May I ask you—who *are* you?"

Bevin paused. "Who am I?"

"I mean—are you part of Lasairian's family? Are you his mother?"

There was only shocked silence for a long moment.

Bevin started to speak, then glanced at the silent Clodagh and burst out laughing instead. "Why, you would not be wrong to say that! It is true, I am a mother to him."

Shannon wasn't sure she understood correctly—her Gaelic was getting quite a workout, especially with Bevin's nonstop delivery—but she felt certain that Bevin had said she was Lasairian's mother. Clodagh must be his sister, then. That would explain why they would all be sharing a house together, since it seemed clear that Clodagh no longer had a husband.

She took a deep breath. Now she was beginning to see how things fit together here, though she was certain that it would be some time before she had the entire picture. But it was a start—it was a start.

"Now, just one more thing." Bevin returned to the shelves once more, and from a wooden box lifted out something that looked to be made of intricate, gleaming gold. "Here's the one! Fine gold, just perfect for such a lovely—"

She stopped as Clodagh reached out and placed an iron hold on her wrist. The younger woman said not a word, but looked straight into her mother's eyes for a long moment.

"Why, of course, this one will suit you much better," said Bevin, after just a moment's hesitation. With her other hand she reached in and lifted out a second piece. Clodagh released her wrist, and moved away once more.

She gave Shannon a copper brooch, and Shannon accepted it, feeling almost dazed. It was completely unreal that these people were handing her priceless objects and talking about Sears as if it could work magic; but to her surprise she found that right now she was wondering about Clodagh, who was clearly so desperately unhappy in this beautiful place, and wondered what could have happened to make her so bitter.

"Who is this woman?" demanded King Irial. "Where is she from?"

"That's right. Who is she?" added Fergus, equally demanding.

Lasairian walked slowly along the shore, with the king at one elbow and his father at the other. It certainly had not taken them long to discover what he'd brought home. "Her name is Shannon, but I do not know where she is from. I have never seen her before. I was up on the hill, composing, and when I turned around, there she was, beneath the hawthorn tree."

"Well, did you *ask* her where she was from?" said Fergus, growing more exasperated by the minute.

"Of course I did. She said she did not know—that she could not remember."

"No doubt she is nothing but a servant," growled Fergus, refusing to be impressed by his son's latest find. "A noblewoman would hardly forget her origins."

Lasairian stood his ground. "She could be a noblewoman. She could have been captured, and held for ransom, and managed to escape, perhaps striking her head somewhere along the way. That would explain why she has forgotten where she is from."

The two men stood and looked at him as though he had suddenly sprouted fins. "If there's anyone who knows every female over the age of twelve within three days' ride of here, it's you," said Fergus. "Now, tell us—have you ever seen this woman before, or heard anything about her?"

He sighed, and looked away. "I have not."

"You have not. Did she wear any fine clothes? Any gold? Anything at all which would make her appear to be anything but a servant—maybe even a slave?"

Lasairian stiffened. "I cannot believe she is either one. Her hands are smooth and soft, and she wears a fine gold ring. She has not been doing the work of a servant."

Fergus snorted. "I have never seen a woman yet who did not wear whatever gold and ornaments she possessed, or who would wear a plain gown when she had fine wool and good embroidery to flaunt. Don't you see? This 'forgetting' of hers is just a ruse to fool a gullible man who can't see past a pair of pretty blue eyes, to make you think she is a kidnapped freewoman when in truth she's a lazy runaway servant just trying to get out of a bit of work!"

Lasairian clenched his fist. "So what do you propose to do with her?"

The king stepped up. "If we cannot find her family, then she can of course stay here. But if she is not a freewoman, she will stay as a servant."

"And if she gives us any trouble, she will stay as a slave," said Fergus, "and if she causes any major trouble at all, she will be sold."

"Sold!" Lasairian could not keep the shock from his voice. "I've only known one slave ever in my life here at Abhainn Aille, and that man was paying for a crime! Father, how can you talk of making an innocent stranger a slave?"

"And what is it to you? Why should you care what happens to her? You are already treating her as your own possession, the way you treat every woman you encounter. You will not own this one! You are no longer a bard, remember? You are a cowherd! I told you I would put you in your place, and I will start right now! You will be far away with only cows for company, and your fresh new prize will stay right here—untouched by you!''

"You cannot do such a thing to her," Lasairian pressed, determined to protect Shannon any way he could. "She does not know where she is from! She does not remember!''

"So, is she just wrong in the head? Lost her wits? What will we do with her then?" said Fergus. "She is quite lovely, to be sure, but beauty is not much use without a mind to go with it.''

"Oh, use can be found for even the most witless beauty," said the king, in a low voice. "And I may have a use for it tonight.''

Lasairian's blood ran cold. "Tonight—''

"Tonight," Fergus said. "The Beltane fires burn tonight, and beside them the king will take his queen. What better queen than this new young woman, so beautiful and strange that she might as well be from the Otherworld?''

Lasairian glared at his father, the rage rising within him. "You might make a cowherd of me," he growled, "but I promise you both that you will never make a slave of her. Or a queen." And with that he turned away from them and walked back toward his house, determined to find Shannon just as quickly as he could.

As the last light of sunset filled the house, Shannon raised her cup to finish the last of the milk—and quickly set it down when a sudden shadow at the doorway caught her eye.

"Shannon," Lasairian said, "come with me now." He held out his hand to her, and before she could even thank Bevin and Clodagh for their kindness, he had caught her by the wrist and hurried her out the door.

"Where are we going?" she asked, hastily gathering up the heavy wool *brat* and copper brooch and following Lasairian down the path across the center of the island.

He turned to her and smiled. "We are going to a place of magic, lost lady—to a dance of joy, and life, and renewal, and even ecstasy—a celebration of love. Will you come with me?"

He kept up his hurried pace, and she could feel the tension rising. Something was building, something big. She could feel it all around her. Lasairian was joyous, excited, filled with anticipation of—what?

"I will come with you," she said, catching a glimpse of his sparkling eyes. "Oh, I will come with you. . . ."

He helped her into the boat and quickly began paddling it across the stretch of smooth water. In a moment the little craft ran gently aground on the shore of the mainland, and they stepped out onto the wide grassy plain.

Lasairian took the rolled-up woolen *brat* from her and tossed it aside on the grass. Just then the forest came alive with shouting and laughter, and with the crashing and tearing of brush. Shannon held tight to Lasairian's hand as a great crowd of laughing, shouting, dancing young people came out of the dense wood and into the soft golden light of the grassy plain. At the head of the riotous procession were two long lines of men, side by side, each line of them dragging a fallen tree, freshly cut, with green leaves still fluttering from the springy young branches.

The men hauled the trees out onto the grass. Behind them came a mob of laughing, dancing women, all of them tall and strong and lovely, with long hair of red or blond or light brown. Each one, barefoot in a long simple gown of linen, and bright with touches of gold, carried an armload of leafy green vines and bunches of tiny white and yellow wildflowers. The spicy, musty scent of fresh-cut leaves and flowers reached Shannon on the breeze, and instinctively she began to step toward them.

Lasairian stayed close beside her, and the men and women began shouting a greeting to him—but then paused when they saw Shannon.

The men dropped their ropes. They and the women gathered in a little circle around Lasairian and Shannon, and she was able to get a closer look at them. These people were all tall, strong, fresh-faced, and vital, a bit damp and flushed from their exertions—and not all of them so young as she had thought at first. But every one was filled with the same tension and excitement and sense of wild magic that had swept up first Lasairian and then herself.

They all seemed to talk at once. Shannon could follow most of what they were saying, but quickly discovered that some words were not taught in the Gaelic classes at the university. She could only listen closely and try to let body language and gestures fill in the gaps.

"Lasairian! Who is this lovely new lady? We've never seen her before! Have you kept her a secret all this time? Where is she from? What is her name?"

Lasairian placed his arm protectively around Shannon's waist. "This lady's name is Shannon," he said, "and she has come to visit with us for a time, and she is my guest. And that is all that I will tell you for now."

"Oh, ho!" someone said, and the whole merry group erupted into laughter. "So, you think you will keep her for yourself? Remember what night this is! Are you sure she is meant for you? The Lady might have other plans for her!"

His arm tightened around her and he pressed her close to him. "She is for me! I am certain of it," said Lasairian. And before Shannon could respond, he turned and began walking off with her, toward the plain. "Why are you all standing there? Come on, we have work to do! It's Beltane! It's Beltane!"

Someone began to play on a small, flat, handheld drum, and its lighthearted rhythm floated out over the evening and set them all into motion once again. Cheered on by the women, the men resumed their pulling, and in a moment had dragged the fallen trees to the two bare circles on the grassy plain.

Two of the men made short work of the remaining branches, quickly stripping them away with small axes and piling them up on the grass between the circles. As soon as the trees were clean and bare, the men dug out the holes at the centers of the circles and used their rough braided ropes to begin pulling the trees upright.

"Oh, is that the best you can do, Donnan?" cried one of the women, with laughter in her voice. "Your pole doesn't seem to be going very high!"

"Shall we help you there, Cormac?" shouted another, as the men struggled with the wobbling trees. "Are you having trouble finding the proper place for your pole?"

"Everyone knows that women are best at raising poles," called yet another, and the whole group fairly collapsed in hilarity. "I never understand why such a task is left to men!"

Shannon understood the crude exchange only too well. Her face reddened, but she began to smile in spite of her embarrassment at finding herself among a crowd of very bawdy strangers. The remarks seemed to be flung in a spirit of fun and teasing, and the men were all grinning broadly at the women's observations.

"There!" shouted one man, as the first of the poles

dropped down into the hole and settled into place. "Is that what you wanted?"

"*Ahh*, that is much better, though it certainly took a long time!" answered the group of women. "And *ohh*, there is the second one, in place at last! Finally you men have done as you ought!"

"We have not yet started!" the man shouted back, as he climbed on top of another's shoulders and hammered the pole down securely into the hole dug for it. "I should say that you women still have much to look forward to!"

"Oh, do we now?" cried the women. "We shall see, we shall see about that!" With that the women moved to the great stack of branches and began stacking them up on the bare ground around each pole.

Now the men stood back to watch the women work, and it was their turn to keep up the commentary. "Do get those bushes of yours nice and close about the poles! How do you expect them to stay up if not for the softness surrounding them? And throw on a few of those lovely flowers! Though beauty is not necessary to hold up a pole, it certainly does no harm!"

As wave after wave of laughter echoed through the crowd, the women finished stacking up the green-leafed branches. They covered the top of each stack, and each other, with the vines and flowers they had brought from the forest. Soon each of the revelers was draped with greenery and wore flowers in his or her hair—including Shannon and Lasairian.

She remained in the shadows, pressing close to Lasairian as she took it all in and struggled to follow the words; but as darkness fell, Shannon found herself drawn up more and more into her surroundings and the strange actions of the people around her.

The real world began to fall away, gone with the day. The soft yellow-white light of the full moon behind the drifting clouds turned the night into a magical, shadowy twilight.

With the poles and brush in place, the raucous, merry, flower-decked group turned its attention toward the top of the hill. The drummer led them all up the steep grassy slope to the lone hawthorn tree beside the glistening stream, with Shannon and Lasairian following close behind.

The crowd seemed drawn to the tree, running the last few steps and crying out in delight. Even from her place at the rear of them, Shannon could smell the sweet scent of the hawthorn on the cool damp evening breeze, and she too felt drawn to the tree. But still she stayed close to Lasairian, holding on to his hand. He seemed content to stay with her, but she could feel the thrumming tension in his body, and all but hear the pounding of his heart. It was clear that he was just as caught up in all of this as the rest of them.

Now the laughing revelers reached up and began to strip away the soft white blooms of the hawthorn, pelting and decorating one another and breathing deeply of the fragrance. Then the drummer shouted out to them.

"Look here! We have taken the blossoms of the hawthorn, taken its powers for ourselves! What will we give in return? What will we offer to the Lady? What will we give as a gift to the Goddess, for the gifts she is about to give to us? What will we give to her?"

"Here! Here is something for her! I will give this, for the Lady!" And as Shannon watched, wide-eyed, the men began ripping off their tunics and the women reached down to tear off long strips from their bright linen skirts. They tossed the tunics and strips of fabric onto the tree, circling around it to find spots to hang them on, and soon the thorny little tree was covered not with blossoms but with ragged, colorful pieces of linen.

"It couldn't be," Shannon whispered. Was this how the maypole dance had started? Dancers making a moonlight offering to a goddess? She shivered. What else would this night show her about the quaint customs of the modern May Day?

There was a ripping sound close beside her, and she turned to see that Lasairian had torn away his own tunic and thrown it over the tree. His smooth skin glowed in the moonlight and his soft black hair ruffled in the night breeze. "Shannon!" he said, turning back to her. "Surely you will join them!"

When she only stared at him, he leaned down and tore a strip from her own bedsheet gown. "Give it to the Lady!" he said, handing her the strip, and without a word she took it from him.

Slowly, like a sleepwalker, she moved toward the tree. In the shining twilight it looked very like the ghostly tree she had encountered in her parents' backyard. But as she hung the long strip of fabric over one of its thorns, she knew for certain that this tree—and everything else she was seeing tonight—was very, very real.

Finally, the bare-chested men and ragged-hemmed women stood laughing and gasping beside the tree, each of them covered now with hawthorn petals and long strands of vines and green leaves and flowers. They gathered at the spring and lined up all along the stream, dipping up the clear water in their hands to drink and splash their faces and then flick the cold water at each other—men splashing women, women splashing men.

Shannon gasped as a few drops of water found her cheek, and she looked up to see Lasairian grinning down at her.

Immediately she caught up her own handful of water and flung it at him, laughing with him as the refreshing coolness ran down his neck and onto his bare shoulders.

He fairly glistened in the moonlight.

Oh, it was a beautiful world she had found, this place of lush grass and sweet flowers, of cool clear water and happy, laughing people . . . of Lasairian, who stood looking into her eyes, leaning down toward her, so close she could feel the heat of his smooth neck and soft dark hair . . .

His expression suddenly became serious. In a moment he had straightened and looked away from her. And then Shannon realized that all of the people on the hillside had fallen silent and turned to stare out over the lake toward Abhainn Aille.

As they watched, all the torches and firelights on the island began to go out. In a moment it became a shadow, lost on the silvery waters, and the only light in the world came from the shining of the moon on the lake and the tumbling stream.

Chapter Eight

Shannon felt a coldness descend over her. Everyone had been completely raucous and uninhibited one moment, and then deadly silent and serious the next. "Why have they put out all the fires on the island?" she whispered.

Lasairian stood close behind her and placed his hands on her shoulders. "Because it is time to relight them," he said.

"Oh." It was not an answer she understood, but she had little choice but to stand in silence with the others and wait for something to happen—though she saw nothing but the glowing twilight and heard nothing but the rushing of the stream flowing downhill.

After long moments, another sound began to reach her. There was a faint splashing from the lake, drawing closer and closer, and as they heard it the crowd of men and women started back down the hill toward the edge of the water.

A small boat ran aground. From it stepped five figures. Though it was difficult to tell in the darkness, Shannon thought she recognized the tallest of them. He had been one of the two silent men waiting for Lasairian outside his home earlier that day.

"Who is that?" she whispered over her shoulder to Lasairian. "The tall man?"

There was only the smallest hesitation on his part. "That is the king. King Irial. And the others, of course, are his advisors, druids all."

The king. Shannon studied him. He was surrounded by his four advisors, dressed the same as he was, in fine woolen tunics with heavy bands of intricately worked gold at their wrists and throats—but one wore a long tunic, so long it reached to the ground. When the figure shifted, Shannon realized that it was a woman.

The king approached the group of revelers and then stopped, with the druids standing in a half circle behind him.

"Your fires are out," said the king. "Are you ready to rekindle them? Are you ready to renew the energy and life of the fire, even as you renew the life of your people?"

"We are ready!"

He turned to the druids. "Kindle the flame," he said.

With a shout of joy the revelers all turned and ran toward the piles of brush surrounding the erect poles, sweeping Shannon and Lasairian along with them. But almost immediately the crowd separated into two groups, the men gathering around one pole and the women around the other. Shannon found herself alone, surrounded by the tall, strong women, strangers all.

The druids set to work. They knelt down in the grass between the two poles and began working very intently with a strange implement. Shannon edged her way to the front of the crowd to get a better look.

One, the female druid, steadied a small wooden piece which looked like a little hollowed-out log. One of the males used a device that looked like a bow—a slender curving stick tightly strung with something that she guessed was leather. The string was wrapped once around a slender wooden spindle, and the spindle placed vertically in the log. When the bow moved back and forth it forced the spindle to bite deeply into the small hollowed-out log.

Over and over the druid's hand flew, the spindle racing back and forth. Another of the druids quickly crouched down and held his hand out over the bow, apparently sprinkling something over it.

In another moment the tiniest red-gold light appeared at the juncture of the log and spindle. The crowd held its breath, but the light was gone almost as quickly as it had appeared.

The druids persisted. The little glow of light reappeared beneath their hands. It brightened, and faded, and flared up again, breathing like a living thing, and within a few heartbeats a flame flickered in the little wooden log.

King Irial dipped two torches side by side into the newly kindled flame and then stretched out his arms, one toward each pole. A male druid took one torch and started toward the gathering of men, while the female druid took the other and walked toward the women.

The crowd stayed very still, the tension rising, and it seemed that no one dared to breathe. The flame-bearing druids each stopped in front of the poles and raised their torches high, burning brightly now, to cast a flaring light over the group.

The king's voice came out of the darkness beyond the

torches. "You have all declared your intentions to take part in this ritual," he said. "I am your king. What do you want me to do?"

Both groups shouted out to him, the high female voices singing out over the deeper ones of the men. "Light the fires! Light the fires! Light the fires!"

The king walked out of the shadows and stood facing the two druids. "Light the fires," he said to them, and immediately the two torches flew through the air and fell on the piles of brush.

And now the high spirits and excitement of the two groups could be contained no longer. They burst into wild laughter and shouting and dancing around the poles, and Shannon was pulled along with them. With every shout, with every leap, the flames grew, helped along by the dancers, who kept reaching down to pull out burning twigs and sticks and throw them onto the bare sections of the pile.

They wove in and out, the flaming twigs arcing through the air, up and down onto the brush, up and down, up and down, streaks of light weaving around the fire as the dancers circled it, a maypole dance woven not of pale pastel cloth but of flying, living, glowing streaks of flame.

Now the fire took hold in the piles of brush. The flames swelled and grew and rolled in a smoky, billowing, orange-red ball through the piles of brush and greenery. The circling dancers moved outward, driven back by the heat and smoke, and in the center, between the two fires, found themselves forced together.

The men and women began to look at each other as they passed by, smiling and laughing and flirting and posturing. The men leaped high through the flames to show their strength and prowess, while the women danced and posed and tossed their long loose hair. Shannon danced along with them, laughing now, with eyes only for Lasairian, hoping to catch a glimpse of him each time she passed between the two great fires.

But just as the dancers began boldly brushing and touching each other at the point where the two circles met, Shannon heard a great rumbling in the distance. Something was fast approaching, but what?

She stopped in mid-stride, frightened, staring, hardly noticing as the dancers bumped into her; but they only laughed and dashed away from the center, the women pulling Shannon with them, to gather in two breathless crowds on the far sides of the bonfires.

"It is not yet your time!" shouted the king. "Where would we be without the cattle? You will have to wait for your own pleasure until the cattle are ready for the pastures of summer! Let this remind you of what is truly important, of how the good of your tribe must come before your own! What wealth will your children have if you cannot provide them with cattle? Make way for them now! Make way for them!"

And to Shannon's amazement a herd of small red-and-white cattle appeared out of the darkness, their herders working hard to force them to run between the blazing bonfires. The creatures stopped with legs braced and heads down, their eyes large and glittering, and tried their best to run this way and that to dodge both the flames and the herders.

But the herdboys were determined, and with long iron goads and much shouting and whistling they drove the herd of twenty or so cows between the smoky fires and back out onto the plain.

Shannon breathed a sigh of relief as the panicked animals disappeared back into the darkness. But she had no time to relax, for the men and women immediately rushed back to the bonfires and took up their lusty dance once more. Even the king and the druids leaped in with them, and it was clear that several of the women were especially interested in the tall and powerful king. He would have no shortage of partners to choose from.

But now, even as she searched desperately for Lasairian each time she moved through the point where the circles overlapped, Shannon realized that the dancers were no longer remaining separated into one circle of women and one circle of men. They were crossing over and joining each other's circles, finding partners that were to their liking and dancing ever more suggestively with each other.

"Lasairian! Lasairian!" she cried. But he was far on the other side of his bonfire, and there was little hope that he would hear her over the roaring of the flames and the shouting of the dancers.

She pushed her way to what had been the men's fire, hurrying through the dancers in an effort to catch up to him. Then, from behind her, a strong hand closed over her arm. For a moment she felt great relief. *He is here, he has found me!*

But when she whirled around, she saw with a shock that it was not Lasairian who held her so tightly.

It was the king.

Slowly, his eyes never leaving hers, the king drew Shannon into the bright glaring light between the two fires. She twisted her wrist in an effort to escape his grip, but quickly realized that it would be no use.

"What do you want?" she tried to say, but her throat had tightened so much that the words were barely a whisper.

He seemed not to have heard. He looked out over her head at the rest of the dancers, who now stood panting and glistening in the firelight. Most of them had found partners too, she realized, though a few of the women seemed to be frowning at her with something like disappointment on their faces. She ignored them and searched wildly for Lasairian—but he was nowhere to be seen.

There! There he was, at the back of the crowd, staring at her with a look of surprise and concern. She started to cry out to him, but her voice was lost in the shouting of the king.

"People of Abhainn Aille! Now, on this night of the Beltane festival, you have all done as you should! You have made your offerings to the Goddess, declaring to her your intention to participate in her ritual! You have driven the cattle through the smoke of the fires, to prepare them for the coming year! You have found your partners for the rites beneath the moon!

"I will tell you this: Your king has found his partner, too. His task is to be the mate of the Goddess, to be her husband and protector. And she whom he chooses to be the Goddess for him shall be as his Queen for this night, this night of Beltane."

He gazed down coolly at her. "This woman, new to us, small and fair, as strange as a visitor from the Otherworld, shall be the Goddess for your king tonight."

At this there was a great cheering and shouting from the dancers, who all began to catch hold of each other's hands and rush forward to gather around their king and his chosen partner. But a terrible surge of fear ran through Shannon. Now she knew what it all meant, now there could be no doubt!

"His task is to be the mate of the Goddess. . . ."

105

"She whom he chooses to be the Goddess for him . . ."
The king meant to quite literally take her as his mate. It was part of the ritual, the fertility ritual of Beltane. And in this place and time, being chosen Queen meant doing far more than just handing out prizes to the winners of a mock sword-fight.

She cried out something like *"No!"* and tried to pull away again, but he took no notice at all. Instead he began to lead her away from the fires toward the cool darkness of the shadowy forest, at the head of the procession of ragged, green-draped men and women.

"Lasairian!" Shannon cried out. "Lasairian! Don't leave me with him! Don't leave me!"

To her surprise, the king stopped and looked down at her. The crowd fell silent. "Did you not declare your intention to participate in the Beltane rite?" he asked. "You gave a shred of your garment to the Goddess at the hawthorn tree? You danced round the fires with all the others?"

He shook his head. "I do not understand. You are beautiful and strange all at once; for me, this night, you are become the Goddess. Any of the other women would be pleased to lead the procession and go with me into the forest."

"I will go with you, King Irial!" cried out one woman.

"Choose me, choose me!" called out another.

"So let one of them go with you!" shouted an angry male voice. "Leave this one to find her own partner! Leave her to me!"

Shannon twisted around to see Lasairian pushing his way through the crowd, fists clenched, his face burning with outrage, defying his king for the sake of a woman he barely knew.

*　　*　　*

Lasairian stood alone within the glare of the fires. The crowd stepped back, hushed and tense and expectant, and left him there to face down the king. Shannon could only watch them as her heart pounded and her wrist remained fast in the king's grip.

"She is to be my partner tonight," Lasairian said, his voice low. "She is for me."

The king regarded him as though from a great distance. "I have already chosen her. The king has chosen his mate for the Beltane fires. Tonight she wears the face of the Goddess for me."

Lasairian's fists clenched again, and then relaxed. "Ah. I see that you did not know! I was searching out the druids when you chose her. This woman and I are to make a marriage tonight."

The king's hold on her grew even more tense. "You intend to make a marriage with her." It was not a question.

Lasairian smiled at him. "I do. Here, and now, before the druids and this company. And the king." He turned and waved at the druids. "Niall! Maeve! Come forward, please, and complete the contract for us!"

The two druids, one male and one female, came and stood before the king with questions in their eyes—and a moment later, to Shannon's great relief, King Irial released her.

"If you wish to make a lawful marriage, Lasairian, I am not one to prevent it," the king said. The words were polite, but the voice was cold. "May you find the greatest happiness with all of the women in your life." He strode away from the light of the fires.

After regarding the crowd for a moment, the king walked to a tall red-haired woman. With a delighted smile she took his arm, and he turned to face the druids.

"At Beltane, beside the reborn fires, each man becomes the High King and each woman becomes the Goddess. Where King and Goddess embrace, new life is sparked, even as the new fire is kindled every Beltane eve. Now we are for the forest, to embrace one another. Lasairian and his chosen woman shall join us as soon as they have stated to you their intent."

Shannon tried to breathe, to speak, to stop the shaking of her hands and the racing of her heart. "What is happening here?" she whispered to Lasairian. "Did you say that you would marry me? How can you say that you would marry me? You don't even know me!"

"I know that you are beautiful, and lost, and in need of a companion and a protector. And I know that if you do not come with me tonight, the king will claim you once again."

She swallowed. "I . . . I cannot go with the king! But how can we be married? How can we swear to spend the rest of our lives with each other when we are all but strangers?"

"There is no need to swear the rest of your lives," said the female druid. "Only that you will remain together until—"

"Until we no longer love one another," Lasairian broke in. "And this I will swear to you, Shannon: I swear that if you wish it, on the next celebration of Beltane you and I will return here before the druids and reaffirm the love between us. Do you agree to this?"

Shannon looked up at him, at the shining dark eyes and gentle smile that were so like Ian Galloway's, even in this strange and far-off world—and she also saw, from the corner of her eye, the brooding visage of the king in the flickering shadows.

She tried to speak, and caught her breath, and tried again.
"I agree," she whispered.

Quickly the female druid reached for her right wrist and
crossed it over Lasairian's. The male druid caught up a
length of green vine and wrapped it around their wrists,
binding them together. "Yours is a marriage of the forest,"
he spoke. "Yours is a marriage based on affection alone,
not on price or contracts. Yours is a marriage of the fires."

Shannon's heart rose at the words she heard. *A marriage
based on affection alone . . . not on price or contracts.* She
looked up at Lasairian, proud and happy, a bride draped in
green, and reached up her face for him to kiss.

"To the forest now! All of us, to the forest!" King Irial
drew his red-haired lady after him, along with the crowd
of men and women, and Shannon and Lasairian followed
close behind.

The heat and glare and snapping of the great fires faded
away behind them as the Beltane revelers entered the cool
darkness of the forest. Shannon clung tight to Lasairian's
hand, bound to him by the druid's vine, and followed his
lead until he stopped beside an enormous tree.

Carefully he unwrapped the vine and tossed it away. He
turned to Shannon, stroking her face with both hands as
she stared up at him in the soft twilight. "Ah, lady of my
heart, we have come to the place where I hoped I could
take you . . . alone in the forest on Beltane eve."

His words were gentle and sweet, but she could feel the
tension rising within him, feel his heart pounding, and hear
the catch in his voice. Even his hands began to tighten on
her neck and on her shoulders.

And all around them, in the misty, silvery forest, came
the sounds of laughter and low voices, and sighs and soft

moans, and here and there a wild cry of ecstasy . . . and in the instant when Shannon realized what she was hearing, her blood caught fire.

Lasairian pulled her close and bent down to bury his face in the hollow of her neck. "The sounds of love are all around us," he whispered, stroking her back with strong fingers. He pulled her a step closer so that they were pressed together for the full length of their bodies, even as they stood. It seemed that his heart was her own, and every breath he took, she shared with him. . . . He was becoming one with her right here, right now, and she closed her eyes and began to surrender to it.

Now nothing existed at all except this strange twilight world where her lover held her so closely, where the others who lived here gave themselves over to the pleasures of lovemaking without any shame or inhibition. It was what she had searched for all her life, it seemed; complete escape to a magical world, lost in the sweetness of love and in this beautiful, gentle, very powerful man who lifted her up in his arms and laid her down on the soft forest floor.

He pulled her close, so very close, and there was not a single place on her skin that he did not explore and caress. She returned his pleasuring in kind, searching out all the smooth hard curves of his strong male body and pulling him close to her, deep within her, until there was no separation at all left between them, and she was no longer alone but forever bonded to the man she loved, to Ian, to Lasairian.

And when her surrender was complete, Shannon too cried out with joy, adding her voice to those which rose throughout the forest in the same way that the flames rose from the bonfires.

Chapter Nine

The sound was soothing, a gentle splashing of water over rocks; but now a very bright light began to shine in Shannon's eyes, leaving her blinking and squinting. With a groan, she raised herself up on one elbow, shielding her eyes with one hand from the sun.

Close beside her lay a man, a handsome dark-haired man. He was sound asleep with his face turned up to the brilliant sun. He looked like Ian—but he couldn't be, this was Lasairian, he'd told her his name was Lasairian, though she had been so certain he was the man she knew . . . and . . . whatever were they doing lying out here on their damp woolen *brats*, thrown down on the dew-covered grass?

She sat all the way up, suddenly wide awake. The sound came from the spring beside her, tumbling over the rocks and down the grassy hill. Down below, at the foot of the hill, the wide expanse of grass beside the sparkling lake held the charred and smoldering remains of two bonfires.

Now it all came rushing back. She remembered the wildness of her first night here in Eire, in this Ireland of the past: the ecstatic and frightening ritual in which she had taken part; the king who had wanted her for his own; and the night spent with the man who had rescued her, this man, Lasairian.

She struggled to her feet, feeling dazed and hungover, as though she'd spent the whole night drinking—but she had not been drinking. If only that was all! She'd done far more than that, oh, far more—

What *had* she done? And worse, *how* could she have done it? Making love in the forest with a man she barely knew, surrounded by strangers all doing the same thing, was not something that Shannon Rose Grey would ever have dreamed of doing.

Unless it was in dreams she would never even admit to having.

She had longed for magic and beauty, had been desperate for escape—but whatever had made her look for that escape in wildness and debauchery?

Even worse was thinking of what she would do now. She looked around again, and realized that even in the normal light of the morning the surroundings were the same: the wide plain, the rag-covered hawthorn tree beside her at the top of the waterfall, the beautiful island out in the lake.

It would have been wonderful under any other circumstances. . . . But the knowledge, the certainty, that she was not in the Ireland of her own modern time but had somehow found her way back to the ancient days, was almost too terrifying to contemplate.

Too terrifying . . . and too wonderful.

Now that the sun had risen, other men and women began

coming slowly out of the woods. They walked hand in hand or with their arms about each other, in little groups of twos and threes. They all moved slowly, and dreamily, back toward the island, going a few at a time in the small boats as the rest sat down on the bank to wait their turn.

There was a gentle touch at her ankle, a caress which reached to her calf. Lasairian sat up, smiling up at her. "Good morning to you, beautiful lady," he said. "Did you sleep well?"

Shannon could only stare at him, confused by his casual greeting. She had no idea what to say to him—*Where am I? What have I done? Will you call me?*

At last she just shook her head. "I don't think I slept at all," she began. "I—"

"Oh, but of course you did," he murmured, drawing her down to sit beside him and nestling his cheek against her hair. His warmth and gentle strength almost made her forget her anxiety, and the familiar voice gave her a sweet comfort.

"You did sleep, I assure you. I held you close, and listened to the soft sound of your breathing, and placed my hand over your heart to feel its life and warmth. You slept beautifully, dear Shannon."

Her own hand moved to touch her chest. "Did you now," she whispered.

"And now you look as fresh and beautiful as a new *samhaircin*, the first rose of spring, covered with dew after spending the night in the woods and the meadow with one who loves you."

Such lovely words she had never heard. If only they had just met—if only they had not—last night—

Lips parted, she could only stare up at him as her intense attraction for him warred with shame and embarrassment.

"Did it really happen?" she said at last. "Did I dream it?"

"You did not," he answered, "though a lovelier dream I would never have had."

She was crimson with embarrassment, but tried her best to regain what little dignity she had left. "Then we—you and I—we—"

Shannon stopped, and closed her eyes. "I'm sorry, Ian. I'm not in the habit of sleeping with men the first night I meet them. I don't know what happened. But I'm sorry." She looked away, but he reached out to her and gently raised her face.

"I can see that you are frightened—or ashamed," he said, and shook his head. "Allow me to tell you what I know. We came together last night out of a love for life, out of a desire born from the heart of the Goddess herself, who loves nothing more than to see her children reveling in the pleasures she has granted them. For us to come together on her night, the night of Beltane eve, is no cause for fear—much less for shame.

"Besides," he said, smiling now and drawing her close, "should a wife be ashamed to lie with her husband?"

She looked up at him, blinking. "Husband?"

"Surely you have not forgotten so soon. Last night, at the fires—the ceremony—you agreed to a marriage with me. Do you not remember?"

Shannon thought back to the wild ritual of the night before. It was a confusing series of riotous images now, and she remembered how difficult it had been for her to follow. She'd had a hard enough time trying to decipher everyone's Gaelic, let alone fathom what was going on around her.

But Lasairian was right. There had been a ceremony, although a very brief one. They had stood before the druids, draped in greenery and blossoms, and had their wrists bound together by a green vine fresh from the forest. "A marriage based on affection alone . . . not on price or contracts," she whispered, remembering how sweet those words had sounded.

"Then we are married?" she asked him. "We are truly, legally married?"

"Married, beautiful Shannon," he answered, and kissed her forehead.

She looked away, momentarily bemused. "I'm not sure which is worse," she murmured. "Sleeping with a man I hardly know, or marrying him."

He smiled, the bright and engaging smile that she was already growing so accustomed to. "I am beginning a journey this morning. Please tell me that it will be our journey. Tell me that you will come with me."

"A journey?" She could only gaze at him, puzzled now. "Where are you going?"

"To begin a new life. A new life with you. We will return at the end of the season, but for now we can live together in the beauty of the hills with only the trees and the birds and the placid cows and their herders for company."

"Oh . . . I see. A honeymoon, in the country! It sounds lovely."

He leaned close to her, his voice low and intense. "Tell me that you will come with me, Shannon Rose."

Shannon looked up at him, at Lasairian, who was the image of the Ian who had come so close to capturing her heart back in the old world. But this man was hers, and hers alone, in a place of enchantment and escape. The old gray world of pain and loss and loneliness was now far behind. In its place was a world which contained all she had ever dreamed of—though a small voice at the back of her mind warned that some dreams could, indeed, be too good to be true.

But she only looked up into his beautiful dark eyes, and smiled. "I will come with you, Lasairian. I will come with you wherever you are going."

He got to his feet, smiling down at her, and picked up both her woolen *brat* and his own before reaching for her hand to help her up. Shannon expected that they would walk together down the hill to the bank of the lake and wait with the others for a boat. But to her surprise he led her the other way, walking quickly across the top of the hill toward the thick woods beyond the meadow.

For a moment she was confused—and concerned. Why was he taking her away from the others, into the dense woods? There was no one around. Did he think they would continue their liaison of last night? Is that what he thought of her?

Then she stopped. What was she thinking? They were *married*. This man was her husband—this handsome, broad-shouldered, sweet-natured man with the voice of a poet was all hers. She was free to approach him in any way she wished. She could offer herself to him anytime, anywhere, it was all right, they were married, *married*. . . . She had fallen into a world where magic was real, and nothing could be more magical than waking up and finding herself married to a man like this.

They walked into the forest. Shannon turned to him, gathering her courage. He seemed to draw her to him with no effort, just by his presence. . . . She could not resist, and she began to reach for him.

Lasairian stopped as they reached the shelter of the trees and politely reached for her outstretched hands. "Ah, the ground is rough up here, and you are not accustomed to it,

I can see. Here, sit up here, on this smooth stone."

He guided her to a large boulder, threw her woolen cloak on top of it and, with both hands on her waist, lifted her up to it. She held tight to his arms, wanting nothing more than to pull him close—it had been so easy, so natural, last night in the glare of the Beltane fires—

But it seemed that here, in the ordinary light of day, she was uncertain of approaching him. Her natural reserve took over once again and she could only look at him as he patted her hands.

"Wait here for me. I will go and gather what we need. I am sorry to leave you, but there is little time. They will be leaving. I'll come back to you and we'll catch up to them."

"Catch up to who? Where are we going?" Shannon was curious, and confused, but at the same time barely interested in anything beyond this very moment. She was amazed at her own feelings and almost unable to resist them. *Oh, why don't you take me in your arms, right now, in the quiet of the forest. There's no one to see us, come here, oh, come here!*

But she simply could not. What would he think of her? Even if she was his wife, and even if he did seem very much like the Ian she had known before, he was still for the most part a stranger to her. She did not want him thinking she would seduce him simply out of lust—though she'd never been closer to it than she was right now.

Lasairian kissed her gently on the forehead. "Wait here for me, lady. You will be safe, here in this quiet house which the trees have made for you. I will be back so soon that you will hardly know that I was gone." And with a final kiss on her cheek he turned and left the forest, half running across the sunlit meadow and disappearing down the hill.

Shannon sighed and slid down from the rock. The ritual of last night resonated within her, though she still found it difficult to think about. It was almost as if it had all happened to someone else. Such things never happened to Shannon Grey. No doubt the wild feelings within her would subside as the memory of the bonfires faded.

She stood up tall, and stretched, and breathed in the purest air it had ever been her pleasure to enjoy. It was almost intoxicating in its cool freshness. She walked a few more steps into the forest, to the edge of the small stream, the water dark and clear beneath the trees, and drank down handfuls of the cold sweet water.

Now she felt refreshed, and even hungry. She hoped Lasairian would bring some food back with him. She tried to think of something ordinary, like breakfast, but found her thoughts drawn instead to Lasairian . . . his smooth hot skin, his soft black hair falling over her face and throat as he embraced her, the shine in his dark eyes, the irresistible strength of his body as he pulled her so very close. . . .

Finally she climbed back up on the rock once again, on top of the rough woolen cloaks. Settling herself, she began picking out her long fine hair several strands at a time with her fingers, carefully separating each and every tangle. Perhaps by forcing herself to concentrate on such a small and tedious task, she could once again gain some control over her own feelings, before such control was lost to her for good.

Lasairian walked briskly down the hill, passing the last of the straggling men and women making their groggy way back to the boats. He felt as though a weight had lifted. After a single night, so much had changed!

He no longer cared that he had been thrown out to live with the cowherds. Shannon knew nothing of what he had been before. Gone was the dismal prospect of a summer spent with herdboys and cattle; of being hardly more than a slave when he had been born into the privileged nobility of living the dusty life of a herder instead of relaxing in comfort as a bard with no harder work to do than playing his harp.

Now, stepping into the boat with a few others and starting it across the water, he saw a stretch of pleasant months with a new and mysterious young woman, a woman who seemed quite content, indeed relieved, to find that she was his wife. How much care could a herd of cows require, anyway? He and Shannon would have long warm days, endless days, to spend together with nothing to do but enjoy each other's company.

And perhaps most gratifying of all, neither his father nor the king would have any idea that he was doing anything out in those hills but following cattle. They certainly would not know that he was spending a leisurely summer with a wife stolen out from under the king!

If he was lucky, he would not even break a nail.

He hopped out of the boat, leaving it to the slow-moving passengers, and hurried across Abhainn Aille toward his house. Lasairian was practically whistling as he strode across the island, but then he caught sight of his father watching from the doorway of the King's Hall.

Quickly Lasairian slowed his steps and looked downward. Anyone seeing him would have thought he had the weight of the world on his shoulders—or that he was, at the very least, quite dejected at the prospect of leaving home for a summer spent following cows.

In the cool dimness of the house, he found, to his relief, that his wife and his mother-in-law were gone. Rummaging through the shelves and wooden chests, he found a couple of large leather drawstring bags and began quickly packing up anything he thought might be useful out in the hills.

Here were Clodagh's gowns. Surely she would not miss two of the woolen overgowns and two or three linen undergowns—and if she did, she and her mother had plenty of time to weave and sew more. Here was some food, enough at least for the day's journey: oatbread baked just this morning, hard white cheese, dried yellow-green apples, a piece or two of dried smoked fish. No doubt it was intended for Bevin and Clodagh's breakfast, but there was plenty more where this had come from. Never was there a shortage of food at Abhainn Aille—and he was in a hurry.

He worked faster, catching up whatever objects caught his eye. The smallest of the cauldrons, which just fit into the leather bag. A long iron fork to use when cooking meat and fish. A few of his own tunics and trews, the plainest he could find. And there—

In the corner, safe in its leather cover, rested his harp.

Lasairian paused. His mouth tightened. *You can play your harp for the cows*, his father had said. He ought to leave it here, where his father would see it each time he entered Clodagh's house and remember how he had ordered his son away. And in any case, how could he think of taking his beautiful harp out into a hilltop campsite, where the rain could drench it and the sun could bake it and the cattle could trample it?

Yet he found it equally impossible to leave it behind. The thought of several long months without ever touching the metal strings and hearing their ringing response, without being able to compose any music, was harder to bear than the idea of risking the instrument in the wilderness. Lasairian picked up the leather-wrapped harp, worked it into one of the bags, and then slung both bulging bags over his shoulders.

Struggling to get out of the crowded little house with his burdens, he turned sideways to get through the doorway— and nearly bumped into his father and the king.

Quickly he remembered to mind his demeanor. When he gazed up at his father, his own face was serious and subdued. His father, though, appeared to have the same expression, to Lasairian's surprise. He would have expected his father to be scowling and annoyed, demanding to know why his son had not yet left; but the older man's eyes held only concern.

The king, however, stared down at him with a look as cold as winter rain.

Lasairian ignored them both and merely stood with his burdens, gazing down at the dirt path. After a long moment of very uncomfortable silence, his father spoke.

"I see you have decided to do as you have been ordered, without argument," he said quietly. "You have all you need?"

"I have," Lasairian answered, concentrating on keeping the gleam out of his eyes as he spoke with them. Even now, Shannon waited for him at the edge of the meadow. . . . Shannon whom the king had wanted last night at the Beltane fires. . . . Shannon who had held him so tightly at the foot of the great tree. . . .

"You have your sword?"

Lasairian looked up, blinking. He had not thought of looking for his sword. He had been concerned only with his harp, not with a weapon. "What use will I have for a sword? Are the cattle such a danger?"

In an instant his father's face turned as dark as a thundercloud. "It is part of your job to protect them! The cattle and the herdboys both! How do you expect to do that with a harp and long curling nails? You will find that your laziness will not be tolerated in the hills the way it was in Abhainn Aille!"

Lasairian felt his temper flaring, in spite of his recent good humor. "I am no longer a bard, or a warrior, or a noble of any kind. You have made that very clear to me! I have no intention of being a bodyguard for cattle. I am nothing but a cowherd, and the trappings of a cowherd are a stick to prod them with—not a sword."

King Irial stepped forward, and fastened his cold glare on Lasairian. It was clear that he had not forgotten the events of the previous night. Lasairian swallowed, but met the king's hard gaze nonetheless.

"You have the duties of a cowherd from Beltane to Samhain, and you will perform them or you will answer to me," growled the king. "But you do not cease to be who you are. You will take your sword with you, and you will use your training, and you will protect the cattle and the herdboys as any nobleman would, should any threat arise while he is present."

Lasairian's only response was a stony silence. Though he had no interest in fighting and dying to protect a cow, what he feared most was revealing to Shannon that he was, indeed, a nobleman in disgrace, and not the simple herdsman she had seen.

But she was so strange—she seemed to know so little of their ways—that perhaps she would not realize what the fine sword meant. He could tell her some story about how at least one of the herdsmen was always provided with a warrior's sword while the herds were in the high pastures.

No doubt she would believe anything he chose to tell her.

Snapping back to the present, he gave the pair of them a most formal and courteous smile. "Of course. I must have simply forgotten my sword, I was so anxious to be off." He set down the heavy leather bags and turned to go back into the house, but was stopped by his father's powerful hand on his shoulder.

Lasairian froze. "And where," came that deep, ominous voice behind him, "is that woman?"

Lasairian carefully assumed a casual expression before turning around. "I don't know," he said with a shrug. "When I woke this morning she was gone. No one else had seen her. I searched, but found no sign of her. I could only assume she had run away again, as she had when she found us the first time." He looked down, dejected and sad, his disappointment threatening to overwhelm him.

Out of the corner of his eye he could see their glowering expressions. "If you should find her," he murmured, ". . . please. Please see that she is cared for. Please search for her. Please find her."

His father frowned. The king's mouth twitched. "I suppose it's just as well," said the king, with a hard look at Lasairian. "But we will continue to watch for her."

Lasairian's face brightened considerably in relief. "Of course. I will get my sword, but I must go quickly. I have to catch up to the others out at the fields. I will see you at Samhain."

His father stood in silence, gazing at his son, and seemed

about to say something. But he only nodded. ''At Samhain, then.''

Lasairian nodded in return, and then hurried back inside to get the sword.

Chapter Ten

An hour passed, by Shannon's estimation, a quiet, dreamy hour spent in the shelter of the loveliest forest she had ever seen. Here at the edge of the wood, the sun found its way down into the widely spaced trees, creating pools of light and gentle, dappled shade. It was the perfect place to catch her breath and try to collect her thoughts.

She took her time untangling and smoothing out her hair, finding that the slow and careful activity helped to calm her and let her think . . . though it was difficult to think of much of anything aside from the sunlit forest, the sweet smell of the fresh green grass in the meadow, the birdsong floating high among the trees, or the tiny bright yellow flowers growing in little clusters in the sheltered light where the forest met the field.

It was all so sweet, so hypnotic, that it seemed she could sit there all day—if not forever—basking in the lovely surroundings and in the feelings of complete contentment which resonated through her from last night. But soon she was finished with her hair. And as the sun warmed the forest, and the morning stretched on, Shannon began to feel her sense of time return.

It was as if she had just awakened. How long had Lasairian been gone? What time was it? And where was he now?

He'd said he was going to the island—back to the island to get what they would need for wherever it was they were going. But she didn't care where they might be going. She wanted to know where he was *right now*.

She slid down from the rock and walked out from under the high canopy of trees into the meadow. Looking out at the island in the distance, she could just make out a small black speck moving across the lake in her direction. No one else waited on the shore—it could only be that someone was returning here.

The smallest feeling of relief washed over her. Had she really believed that he might leave her out here alone? Would he abandon her here, she, a stranger, alone in this very strange world?

It was not possible that he would ever do that, not Ian, not Lasairian . . . not after what had passed between them last night. She knew that he was not that sort of man. Surely she would never have stayed with him last night, surrendered to him out there in the twilight forest, if she'd sensed for a moment that he would simply vanish in the morning.

Surely she was a better judge of men than that.

When she saw him climb briskly up the hill, Shannon grabbed her woolen cloak—her only possession in this world—and hurried over to him, anxious to be close to him once more and feel his reassuring embrace. But he kept up his fast pace and simply brushed by her as he went past, dropping a heavy leather bag into her arms and hurrying her along with him.

"Come, Shannon," he said, "we'll be late. We've got to hurry."

"Late?" she asked, breathless, though not only from the jog through the meadow. "Late for what?"

"They will wait, but not for long. Come on, this way!" And he led her across the lush grass to the other side of the meadow and took her once more into the woods, now deep into the forest where all was shadowed and dim.

"Where are we *going*?" she demanded, but he only glanced over his shoulder and smiled at her. Shannon saved her breath for the struggle to keep up, while carrying the heavy bag he had thrust upon her.

At last, out of breath, unwilling to go a single step farther in the unfamiliar terrain, she simply stopped. "Ian!" she shouted. When there was no response, only the sound of his urgent trek through the thick wood, she cried out again. *"Ian!"*

After a moment, the sound of his footsteps ceased. Then he turned and walked back to her, his face serious. "What are you doing? We must keep moving. We can't let them see us."

She frowned. "Let who see us? What are you talking about?"

In an instant his expression changed. Once again he turned his brilliant smile and shining eyes directly on her. "Why, the cows, of course! I meant to say, we have to catch up to the cows. The cows and the herdboys."

"Oh," she said, relief washing over her. "I'm sorry. I probably just didn't hear you correctly. I'm still working on my Gaelic. After years of studying it in school, it's just not the same as carrying on a conversation in it.''

Lasairian shook his head, and again came the wonderful smile. "You speak more perfectly than any woman I know, no matter where you are from, dear Shannon. I am sure the fault was mine. It is just that—they are all on their way now, on this morning after Beltane, this most lovely of mornings.

"I fear they may already have left without us, you slept so long in the sun on the hillside this morning, there beside the brook, lulled no doubt by the song it sang to you. So we must hurry, for I would not want you to miss the sight of the cows in their meadow as they approach the river, in the meadow with the bright yellow *samhaircin*. It is how we know that summer is truly here, now that the Beltane ritual is over and all can relax and enjoy the beauty of the season ... enjoy the long bright days and warm starry nights ... enjoy them with one you love, dear Shannon. ...''

She had never in her life heard anyone whose voice, whose words, affected her the way that this man's did. Every speech was a poem, every word an endearment. It was casting a spell over her, leaving her wanting to hear more, and more, waiting breathless just to see what he might say next.

Long bright days and warm starry nights ...

He caught her hand, and drew her after him, helping her to lift the heavy bag. "Come with me," he murmured softly, his lips just brushing her ear, and she moved after him, floating almost, the forest floor soft as clouds, the leather bag hardly noticed on her arm. Shannon saw nothing but the beauty of this new world she had come to, felt nothing but the warmth and strength of the man beside her, heard nothing but the sweet, caressing words he spoke only for her.

She had wanted nothing more than to escape the dead-end trap which her old life had become—a trap of sadness and loss and grinding monotony. She'd thought to escape it all by leaving for Ireland and starting anew, and so she had, in a way she'd never dreamed possible.

She had found beauty and magic as she had always hoped to find, had never given up on finding . . . and most of all she had found Lasairian, a man like none she had ever seen, or even scarcely dared imagine . . . Lasairian, whose hold on her heart increased with each passing hour.

Here was a man entirely different from those of her own time, most especially from the one who had wounded her so deeply. Lasairian, it was plain to her, cared nothing for wealth or status or position or privilege. He did not look at her and see dollar signs, as others had. Here was a man who valued other things, who knew what was really important in life—the land, and poetry, and even the cows and the flowers. She had the feeling that even if he thought she had a million dollars, he would only smile at her and talk of how the rain had taken its color from her eyes.

Shannon smiled to herself and breathed deep of the morning-scented air, feeling certain that she had found, at last, what she had searched for for so long—a world made of magic and a man who might love her for herself alone.

They left the forest before long, starting across the grass-covered hills and traveling in silence for a time. Any sense of fatigue Shannon might have felt at the long overland hike was lost in her exhilaration at being here at all with Lasairian. Yet as they came over yet another rise, she was glad enough for a chance to set down the enormous leather bag and catch her breath.

Lasairian went a little ahead of her, to the very top of the rise, and quickly beckoned to her. "They're here! We've found them. Look there."

Leaving the bag in the grass, Shannon took his hand and allowed him to lead her to the top. "There," he said again.

Just below them at the foot of the hill ran a curving river, shining like a wide ribbon of silver in the sunlight. Scattered across the lush green grass between the river and the hill was a herd of perhaps twenty small red-and-white cattle.

They looked somewhat familiar. "Are these—are these the same ones I saw last night at the bonfires?"

"Of course. These are the cattle of Abhainn Aille, the best to be found anywhere in Eire. Sweet butter, good leather, and the very best beef, right there in front of us."

The slow-moving creatures grazed calmly on the lush green grass, seemingly oblivious to the herdsmen who surrounded them. A few of the cows lay resting, placidly chewing their cud, their short, wide-spread horns almost brushing the tall grass and tiny white and yellow wildflowers.

"It is a lovely sight, isn't it?" said Lasairian, half to himself.

"You sound like you're seeing it for the first time," Shannon said, with a little laugh. "Surely this is an old scene to you by now."

He glanced at her, and then gave her a quick smile. "Why, only because I am seeing it through your eyes, and it is a sight new to you."

She turned back to the herd. "So—we're going to be

staying with the herdsmen?'' she said. ''Helping them to care for the cattle?''

Lasairian cleared his throat. ''That is right, beautiful lady. I am one of those who helps to guard and care for the cattle while they are at the high pastures for the summer. We will be staying with the other herders at the booley camp, and a fine place it is. But I am just very, very grateful that I will be able to share this summer with you.''

She smiled back at him, and together they shouldered their leather bags and made their way down the steep slope to the water's edge. With the cattle resting and grazing calmly, the ten herdsmen had gathered together on the rocks near the bank of the river to eat their own supper.

Or herd*boys*, thought Shannon, noticing how young they all appeared—there wasn't one who could have been over twenty. The only exception was the man who walked toward them now, an old grizzled man who she supposed was in charge of all the boys.

''So it is true,'' said the man, ignoring Shannon and eyeing Lasairian without offering any sort of greeting. ''I was not sure that you—''

''Aed, I must apologize for being late,'' Lasairian said smoothly. ''Beltane made time stand still for us all. We followed you as quickly as we could.'' He settled himself on a comfortable stone and drew Shannon close beside him, rummaging in his bag and pulling out oatbread and dried apples for them both.

Shannon started to accept the food—she was very hungry after their long walk—but then froze as complete silence fell around them. Aed and all the herdboys stopped eating, and stopped talking, and stopped moving, and sat and stared at her.

She could not bring herself to move. Once again she was

the object of curiosity, stared at, whispered about.

Lasairian spoke up, looking at all of them. "This is Shannon, in whose eyes shines the light of the Beltane fires, and in whose heart resides my love. I can see that you are as struck by her beauty as I. But you will grow accustomed to her in time."

Aed shifted. "She is staying?"

"She is my wife."

Shannon's heart warmed at the words. She began to relax just a little. Now, there were words she'd all but given up on ever hearing. . . .

"My wife stays at Abhainn Aille while I am away—as I thought yours did," said Aed, staring straight and cold at Lasairian.

Lasairian stared right back at him. "But as you can see, this time, my wife stays with me." After a long, cold moment, Aed turned away, and sat down, and went back to eating as if nothing at all had happened.

Lasairian held very still. When he turned back to Shannon he looked quite happy and unconcerned. But just as the two of them began to eat their bread and dried fruit, Aed stood up, cried out to the herdboys, and started the cows across the river.

At Aed's shouted command, the ten herdboys surrounded the grazing cows and began helping him drive them toward the river. But the cows, it seemed, were not so keen on getting wet. They stopped and balked and rolled their eyes at the sparkling waters, stubbornly swinging back to the lush grass along the bank each time the boys tried to drive them across the water.

Shannon, sitting beside Lasairian on the rocks, suddenly found herself surrounded by cows. Up close the beasts were enormous, as big as horses; she had ridden for several summers and had never been afraid of horses, but these animals were wandering about completely uncontrolled and it was plain that they were not happy with the prospect of being told where to go and what to do.

"Stay here!" Lasairian turned around, slid down the other side of the rock, and splashed through the edge of the river until he reached the other herdboys.

Of course, it was his job to help get the cattle moving. But the cows crowded close to the rock where Shannon perched alone, the whites of their eyes showing and their horns clacking together. She shrank back from them, pulling her feet up underneath her, not knowing what the agitated creatures might do. Why, she'd never so much as touched a cow in her life!

He feet slipped on the rock. She caught herself, but fear suddenly hit her hard. If she slipped, she would fall right under those trampling hooves. "Shoo, cow," she said hesitantly, waving her hand at them. "Shoo!"

The only response was a bellowing *"Mooo!"* from the nearest cow. Shannon shrank back even more, and in desperation looked around for help. "Lasairian!" she cried. "What do I do?"

He was well on the other side of the milling herd, watching Shannon over the backs of the cows. Why did he hesitate to come back to her? "Help me, would you please?"

He started toward her, hesitated again, then steeled himself and walked with great determination toward the herd. "Go!" he shouted at the nearest cow. "Go!"

Immediately the cow lowered its head and turned toward him, swinging her heavy horns right at him.

Shannon's heart nearly stopped. "Lasairian!" she tried to shout, but she could only watch. Eyes wide, Lasairian leaped back, and the cow turned away to join the herd once more. As he stood helplessly, Shannon could have sworn she heard muffled laughter coming from the herdboys—and there was Aed, standing by the river with his arms crossed, a malicious grin on his weather-beaten face.

Now a few of the herdboys began returning from the scattered trees at the foot of the hill, carrying long leafy switches. Shouting and insisting this time, they used the switches to whip the ground at the reluctant cows' feet, sometimes swatting an especially balky cow across the rump to send her toward the river. Finally the first cow plodded into the water, and then a second, and a third, and then the whole herd was splashing and lunging its way through the cold rushing waters.

Shannon breathed a sigh of relief and slid down from the rock. Hurrying to Lasairian, she caught him by the arm, not sure whether she was more frightened or annoyed. "Are you all right?" she said.

"Of course," he said easily. "Let's go now—they're almost across."

"And they almost killed us both!" She trembled now with fear at what had seemed like such a benign and lovely part of the scene. "I would never have thought a milk cow could be deadly. Why did you leave me sitting out there like that? You know all about handling cows. I don't know anything about them! Didn't you realize that?"

His eyes grew wide and serious for a fleeting moment—but just as quickly the old brightness returned. "Of course. I should have known that. Look at your hands, so smooth, so fair, untouched by any trace of work less noble than fine embroidery. Yours are the hands of a highborn lady, not of a milking woman."

She relaxed, with a small sigh. Of course he had no way of knowing what she had done before she had come here. "But, you know all about herding cattle. Why didn't you—"

"Look there! We can follow them across right here, upstream—look!" He caught her by the hand and led her to the edge of the bank, a few yards up from where the animals had crossed. "Here—"

As she watched, he stripped off his tunic, soft boots, and leather pants, and she could only stand and stare as he flashed her a quick smile, ran a few splashing steps into the river, and dove headfirst into the sunlit water.

Shannon's heart pounded. The last thing she'd expected was to have him strip off his clothes in front of her, right here, right now! She'd not had a clear look at him last night in the darkness of the forest. In many ways he was still very much a stranger to her, his body new and unexplored . . .

"Come in!" he called to her. "It's a fine opportunity for a swim! Come in!"

Only his head and shoulders showed above the surface, silhouetted against the glitter of the sun on the water. Perhaps she would be able to think clearly so long as she did not see the rest of him.

But go into the water? Dive into a river as though it were a pool? Surely he didn't expect her to pull off her gown and jump in naked!

"Shannon! Just pull off your gown and jump in! It's wonderful, but we haven't much time. Don't you want to swim?"

She struggled for words, for breath. "I—I can't go in without anything on! I just can't. How can you ask me to do such a thing?"

Lasairian stood up and began to walk toward her, rising

up out of the water like some beautiful ancient god come to life.

She wanted to look away. She did not want to stand there staring like a woman who had never seen a naked man before—but he made her feel exactly as if she never had, or certainly never one who looked like this.

Tall and graceful he was, with long legs and long arms and fine strong muscles like a racehorse or a deer. Young and fair, with smooth and perfect skin, a glorious male body delighting in the open sky and bright light of the sun, with the breeze playing over him and the water running off his back and legs.

She had never imagined any man like him. And had never hoped to stand in front of such a man and look into his dark and shining eyes as he reached for her.

He drew her close, and she could feel the cool water which still ran down his body begin to soak through her gown. After that came the slow heat of his skin. He began to pull her after him, and she moved as though she no longer had control, or thought, or care, as though all that mattered was to follow his lead, to let him draw her close, and move with him wherever he was going. . . .

A sudden movement forced her to look up. To her horror, Aed stood on the side of the hill above the river with two of the herdboys beside him, looking down at her and Lasairian.

"I can't," she said, forcing herself to step back from him. "I can't! Look! Up there. They're watching us!"

Lasairian looked up at the hill and stared for a long moment—until Aed and the two boys turned around and left. "There. You see? They're gone. Come, now." He reached for the sides of her gown and made as if to lift it off over her head.

136

But she took hold of his wrists and stopped him—trying not to notice how smooth his skin was, and how warm, and how fine were the dark hairs that covered it, still cool and wet from the river. . . .

"How can you ask me to do that? They can see us from up there! What are you thinking?"

He placed his fingers beneath her chin and raised her face to look at him. "I am thinking that you would enjoy a cooling swim, and feel refreshed by the water, but that is not the only reason."

Taking her by the hand, he began to lead her toward the river. "Last night, you and I lay together beside the bonfires. The smoke of the Beltane fires rolled over us both, and we took from it the strength and protection of the flames. The cattle were driven between the fires for the same reason—to protect and renew them for the season to come.

"Now the herd receives the second half of its renewal— first fire, and then water. Their swim through the water leaves them refreshed and renewed for the summer season, and it will do the same for us. Come with me now, into the water, as clear and cool as the smoke was hot and murky. Come with me now . . ."

And she did follow him, still dressed in her lime-green gown and yellow sash and plastic sandals. The cold water bit her feet, instantly sending a charge through her whole body. Following Lasairian's firm lead, holding tight to his arm, she stepped in, ankle-deep, then knee-deep, the sharp cold awakening her like an electrical charge, and then together she and Lasairian dove forward into the river.

Chapter Eleven

She lost hold of his hand as the water closed over her head. Instantly her whole body was seized by the sharp cool water. Shannon broke through to the surface with a gasp and then quickly dove under again, reveling in the crisp cold and caressing currents as they flowed over her body and pulled at her long skirts.

A part of her realized that there was nothing she needed more than a bath. She had spent the night with a man, and slept out in the open with smoke drifting over her, and today had hiked for miles in the warm sun. Just feeling clean again would do wonders for her state of mind.

Yet the cold rushing waters cleared away more than just the sweat and dust and fatigue of the long night and morning. It was as if her past, too, was being washed away— the despair which had held her down, the grief which had chained her to a life of uncertainty and loss, were dissolved in the cold pure currents of the river.

Now, as her head broke through the surface again, she took a breath of the sweet pure air and felt reborn, renewed, in a world which she had so longed to find and somehow, miraculously, had entered.

Her sandaled feet found the rocky riverbed. Taking hold of Lasairian's outstretched hand, she clambered out of the water and onto the far side of the bank. With cold water streaming from her hair and sodden gown, she saw the new world she had found as if for the very first time; and most of all she saw the face of Lasairian, her husband, the man she was growing to love more and more with each passing hour.

Lasairian returned to the other side of the bank, walking through the shallows to retrieve his clothes and get their leather bags. While she waited for him, Shannon wrung out the lightweight fabric of her gown and combed out her hair with her fingers; neither clothes nor hair would take long to dry in the warm sun and gentle breeze.

As soon as he was dressed, the two of them started after the herd on the last part of its journey to the high pastures. She walked with renewed energy beside Lasairian, feeling as though she could walk forever through the lush green grass beneath blue skies studded with puffy white clouds. As the last of the clear river water evaporated from her hair and clothes, the last of her fatigue and care left her too, and she walked happily beside Lasairian to wherever they might be going.

The shadows began to lengthen as the herd reached its summer pasture, a series of hills, gently rolling almost as far as the eye could see. It seemed to Shannon that the cows knew where they were. As soon as they reached the top of their hill, they dropped their heads to graze on the thick grass and began to spread out across the field, their dark red-and-cream coats a bright contrast to the emerald-green grass. A few lay down with a sigh, all four legs propped under them, and sat chewing with the utmost contentment.

The cattle taken care of, it was now time for the people to settle in. At a small depression between this hilltop and the next ran a single stand of trees, almost certainly tracing a stream. And as she followed Lasairian, Shannon saw a row of small stone huts in front of the trees.

She smiled in relief, very glad to see that there was some kind of permanent shelter up here. Much as she loved the beauty of this place, she was not exactly looking forward to camping out beneath the trees all summer.

There were four huts, and quickly Shannon did the figuring in her head. Surely she and Lasairian would be allowed to take one of the shelters for themselves, and the remaining eleven herdsmen could divide up among the other three.

But as Lasairian led her to the hut that seemed the largest, Shannon's heart sank. Through the filtered sunlight which found its way in through the small doorway, she could see just how small it really was—perhaps seven or eight feet square, with a bare earthen floor scattered with rocks and what looked like a couple of bones. The walls, which appeared to be made simply of piles of stone, were cobwebbed and damp. And it looked as if there were barely enough room for her to stand up, let alone someone like Lasairian.

She turned back to Lasairian and tried her best to smile up at him. "Well, it seems a bit small to me, but I'm sure you must be used to it,'' she said, trying to put on a brave face. She wanted desperately not to lose the fine sharp glow she had felt ever since emerging from the cold waters in the bright sunshine of the afternoon.

But he seemed not to have heard. He simply stood and stared at the little huts as though he'd never seen them before, his expression showing dismay and disbelief.

Then he realized that she was looking at him, and his expression quickly changed to a dazzling smile. ''Why— of course I'm used to it, but I just never thought of two of us staying here together. I'd, ah, forgotten just how small the booley huts are.''

Shannon could not help smiling. So, he had not brought any other woman up here with him, it seemed clear. She was reminded again of how much a stranger he still was to her—but she was very glad to know this much.

Aed came walking up to them. ''So, Lasairian, what will it be? We'll have to have three folk in three of the booleys, and four in the one remaining. Which two of us do you want to share with?''

''Two?'' Shannon glanced again at the tiny stone hut, and then up at Lasairian again. ''You mean there will be two of them living in here—with us?'' There would barely be enough room for four people to lie down and sleep, much less to store any of their belongings—or have any space for living.

''Of course,'' said Aed, also looking at Lasairian. ''It'll be me and Crevan in with you. Crevan's been up here before too, just like you and I. You wouldn't want us to take the first-year boys, who are still trying to adjust to all of this, and make it that much harder for them—now, would you?''

Lasairian stared back at him, his expression grim. No

doubt, Shannon thought to herself, he was simply upset at the prospect of the two of them having so little privacy. Well, she certainly felt the same way herself!

"Of course I would not want to inconvenience anyone," Lasairian answered, and she could not miss the rising irritation in his voice. "My wife and I will make ourselves a camp beneath the trees, along the stream. Shannon—this way."

With an increasing feeling of dismay, Shannon picked up the heavy leather sack once more and followed Lasairian to the scant shelter of the narrow line of trees. Well, she supposed they'd be all right there—at least until the first time it rained.

Lasairian turned to her and gave her a smile that even she could see was forced. "I am sorry, Shannon. Your husband does not offer you the house you deserve. But if we can only stay here tonight, I will return to Abhainn Aille tomorrow and bring back more of what we need—wool *brats* to keep off the rain, leather sheets to build a roof."

"Oh . . . of course." She could scarcely imagine living out here for the summer beneath cowhides and blankets, but at the moment she did not see that they had much choice.

She tried, as her husband did, to put her best face on it all. Shannon offered him a wan smile, and as she looked into that face, framed now by the lowering sun and towering white clouds, it was almost enough to make her forget the bare circumstances they found themselves in.

Yet she was having to struggle to keep at bay a growing feeling of despair, much as she tried to ignore it. Is this what a magical world was really like? She could have believed that Abhainn Aille, and Lasairian, were indeed what she had been searching for—but the prospect of a summer spent with only trees for shelter and eleven strange men for company, even with Lasairian at her side, was beginning to unnerve her just a bit.

The damp chill of the evening, rising from the ground, was beginning to make itself felt. And the exhaustion, now, of the long wild night and she-knew-not-how-many miles of walking was beginning to set in.

She wanted a warm bath and a hot meal and a clean bed to lie in. The scant shelter of tree limbs and blankets was not at all reassuring.

But it seemed there was little choice. Even if she could get back to Abhainn Aille, she would not go alone—she would not go without Lasairian.

There were heavy footsteps behind them. "There is another choice for you, Lasairian, if you wish," said Aed.

"And what is that?"

Aed pointed down the hill, toward the deep woods where the river ran. "You must have forgotten, I'm sure," he said. "The *crannog*, down there at the river."

"*Crannog*," answered Lasairian. Then he suddenly brightened. "*Crannog*! Ah, of course! The *crannog*! At the base of the hill!"

"At the base of the hill. In the river. Your memory is flawless. One would think you were a bard."

Lasairian suddenly shot him a fierce glare, startling Shannon. She'd never seen such an expression on his face. But Aed only scowled at him and then turned and walked away, back to the herdboys and the tiny stone huts.

But Lasairian paid him no attention. Quickly he gathered up their belongings. "Shannon! You shall have your home after all. There is a *crannog*, and we will stay there, just the two of us."

Shannon had no idea what the word meant. "What is a—*crannog*?"

Lasairian paused, then looked at her and smiled. "You must not have lived on the water, in the place where you are from."

"You're right. I didn't. I lived in a small house, in a town surrounded by fields as far as you could see. There was no river within miles. It was nowhere near the water." She paused, her sprits beginning to rise again. "This *crannog*. Is it a place like Abhainn Aille?"

"Why, it is not like Abhainn Aille at all, dear Shannon, it is far more beautiful, a place suited to a new wife, and I have no doubt that you will love it and we will be very happy there. I had nearly forgotten all about it, since, of course, as one of the cowherds I have always stayed in the huts." He came close, and kissed her soft and gentle on the skin beneath her hair. "I must have been distracted by you, for I can think of little else."

She closed her eyes, and found that she could think of little else herself except the touch of his lips on the side of her neck. But as she turned to him, she faced the sun, and could not help but notice how low it had gone in the sky. The shadows were long, the light a dusky gold.

"Shouldn't we go? The sun is setting. How far is the *crannog*?"

Even as tired as she was, Shannon was surprised at how anxious she was to be alone with him again. Thoughts of last night came stealing into her mind. She had hardly allowed herself to think of it all day, so powerful and frightening had it been; but now, with the day ending and the night approaching, bringing with it the prospect of another night spent with Lasairian—her husband—it was almost as if she could hear the drums once again, and smell the smoke of the bonfires.

He smiled down at her. "Not far, not far. But you are right, we should be going now. Gather your things, and wait for me here."

He walked back to talk to Aed, who only stood and scowled. Finally the older man pointed toward the woods and appeared to say a few words, and Lasairian turned and came striding quickly back to Shannon. "This way," he said, and she hurried to catch up to him, hefting the heavy leather bag as she went.

The world vanished as they walked into the woods. The dense canopy of low trees, thick with dark green leaves, closed out the last of the lowering sun and left them in a dark and murky twilight. Together they started down a damp and slippery slope, ever deeper into the forest, following the stream just a few feet off to the side.

Shannon kept her eyes fixed firmly on Lasairian's feet and concentrated on making her way down the rocky slope, slick with clay, brushing the damp overhanging leaves out of her face with one hand and struggling with the leather bag with the other. They seemed to be descending into darkness, silence, and isolation; she could easily imagine wild creatures watching them from the damp shadows . . . wild creatures and strangers and heaven only knew what else. . . .

As they made their slow way down, Shannon became aware of the sound of rushing water from somewhere far below them. There had to be a waterfall at the bottom of the hill. No doubt it was beautiful, but at this point she was almost too tired to care. Her arms and legs trembled from fatigue, from the ever-increasing weight of the leather bag, from the strain of struggling on the wet clay slope.

She was greatly tempted to brace against Lasairian's broad shoulders and let him ease her way down, but resisted the temptation with the last of her strength. If they were going to be out here alone, they would have to depend entirely upon one another. She did not want him to start out thinking she would turn helpless as soon as the going got a little rough.

At last, slipping and stumbling, Shannon reached the bottom of the slope. She stood up, shifting the heavy pack from her shoulder, and tried to straighten her dress. It was bunched and wrinkled, the pale green hem soaked and gray-brown from the mud and dampness. With a sigh she looked up and tried to see just where they were—and momentarily forgot her exhaustion as, once again, a strange and magical sight awaited her.

There was indeed a waterfall beside them. The stream tumbled down the steep hill, over a small ledge of rocks and into a little lake, a still and quiet lake that was not much bigger than a pond. Out in the center of the water, lit by the glow of the rapidly fading sunlight where it filtered through the heavy forest, was Lasairian's *crannog*.

It was a round platform perhaps thirty feet across, surrounded by a high solid fence of what appeared to be sapling poles standing side by side and lashed together. It was impossible to see what, if anything, was inside.

"It looks like a perfectly round little island," marveled Shannon. "Or is it floating? And how did it get here?"

"This place was built many years ago, as a shelter for the herdsmen," said Lasairian. "It is, as you said, an island, a constructed island as solid as any made by nature."

Then she began to wonder: *Why is it fenced? Why is it enclosed? What is there that must be shut out?* But before she could ask any more questions, he had caught her by the hand and was leading her toward the shore.

"Here," he said, "I've found the boat. Let us go, so that we might get comfortable before darkness falls."

"There's nothing I would like more, right now, than to be comfortable," murmured Shannon, but managed to smile up at him as she said it. "After the booley huts, this place looks like the Ritz Hotel." She dropped her bag into the tiny, narrow boat—it appeared to be nothing but a roughly hollowed-out log—and cautiously stepped in.

Lasairian picked up the long pole which lay in the boat and pushed them off. The two of them quickly crouched down so that the narrow little craft would not capsize.

They started across the dark water, and she realized why the light had so quickly turned to heavy gray. It was not just the trees that were closing out the last of the sun— raindrops were beginning to fall, leaving circles traced on the water. A fog began to rise from the damp ground beneath the trees.

Shannon kept her eyes fixed firmly on the outline of the *crannog*. She told herself that in a just a few more moments they would be safely within their own private shelter, and tried to ignore the ominous surrounding forest with its massive tall trees and enormous overhanging branches.

It was not far to the *crannog*—perhaps forty yards, Shannon guessed—but the water was quite deep. The pole Lasairian was using, much taller than he was, sank to within a foot of the water's surface. Again she wondered why such protection would be needed—high walls, water deep as a moat? There did not seem to be any immediate threats here, save for cold and wet and hunger and fatigue.

She told herself that Abhainn Aille had been much the

same. This place would be just a smaller version, with safe solid houses in a quaint fairy-tale setting.

The light all but vanished as the boat bumped gently against the edge of the *crannog*. Lasairian tied it with the heavy braided rope which hung from one of the poles. He stood up gingerly, bracing against the walls, and pushed hard against the saplings. A piece of the wall moved, opening inward like a gate, and scraped across the dirt floor of the *crannog*.

He stepped up to the ledge and reached down for the leather bags. Shannon felt the stillness and isolation of this place all but swallow her when he took the bags and disappeared behind the walls. It was only for a few seconds, but it was long enough to make her realize just how alone she really was here—alone on this small deep lake in the very heart of the forest, with night falling heavy and the misting rain coming down.

She was very glad to see him appear once again and reach down for her. Shannon grasped his strong hand and climbed up to the ledge, pleased at how absolutely solid the *crannog* felt beneath her feet. At least they would be safe here. They could tie up the boat and lock this gate and no one and nothing would disturb them.

Shannon walked one slow step at a time toward the center of the *crannog*. In the damp, fog-shrouded darkness, the place was as creepy as any old deserted house.

The floor was solid, mostly just packed dirt under her plastic sandals, but it was also strewn with rocks and litter. There seemed to be bones, broken tools, rags, and other assorted trash scattered all over. She picked her way across it as carefully as she could, afraid of stumbling and falling on heaven-only-knew-what in the darkness; but there was a single shadowy building near the rear of the *crannog* and she was determined to get to it.

The little building wasn't much. Even in the dark she could tell that it was made of rough wood, just small saplings and branches woven and lashed together. There was no door to open or close, merely an opening left in the wall with an old scrap of leather hanging down over it.

She hesitated. As much as she wanted to go inside, it certainly did not look very inviting. But it was all they had tonight. Shannon reached out for the ragged leather hanging, and just as her fingers brushed it, a bright orange glow lit up the night.

She turned quickly. Lasairian knelt beside a ring of stones near the center of the *crannog*, blowing gently on the small flame which now burned within it. "There are a few bits of wood lying about, but we'll have to get more soon. Though this will get us through the evening, I am sure," he said to her.

"The house," she said, taking a step toward him. "Is it usable? Do you know what's inside?"

His glance shifted to the building. In the flickering light, she could see that it was little more than a shack. "Why, I will show it to you," he said, smiling, and getting quickly to his feet. He picked up a length of wood with a small glowing flame at the end of it.

He went straight to the house and cautiously pulled back the leather. Slowly he eased his way inside, holding the little torch ahead of him. Shannon followed closely, wanting to see what was there—

Her heart sank. She took a step backward, toward the door, and hugged herself with her arms.

The walls looked even more rickety from the inside. The gaps between the saplings showed clearly in the light of the flame. Up above was a roof made of old dried rushes tied together, blackened with dampness and age, apparently held together by the thick grey cobwebs which stretched from corner to corner. A couple of spiders went scuttling along the rushes, startled by the sudden murky light.

But as awful as the roof looked, the floor was far worse. It was just a solid mass of reeking mud with a pool of water standing in one corner. Like the ground outside, it was littered with bones and trash and rags, with a few half-buried wooden plates and cups stuck fast in the mud.

She could only look at Lasairian, speechless. He, too, seemed to be stunned, for once in his life at a loss for words.

Chapter Twelve

"What happened here?" Shannon said at last. "Didn't you live here last year? Was it always like this?"

"Ah," Lasairian began, and shook his head. He raised the torch again. "I suppose—I suppose the herdboys—the other herdboys—neglected to repair the roof before leaving last season."

There were gaps and holes in the rotting stacks of rushes. Even now the slow rain was beginning to drop through, adding to the mass of mud on the floor. "I suppose they did," whispered Shannon.

The place was a horror. She had not been expecting the Hyatt-on-Capitol-Square, but she had at least hoped for some place to offer shelter and warmth for the night. This old shack was worse than any fraternity house on campus— and then she realized that that was just what this place reminded her of.

She'd actually gone into a frat house once, when her fiancé had taken her to a party. That house, too, had been falling apart and full of junk and trash, yet was still considered livable by the rowdy young men who inhabited it. And that, she realized, thinking of the young herdboys who'd come with them, was exactly what must have happened to this place.

Shannon turned away and walked back to the fire. The cold rain fell steadily now.

Lasairian followed her and crouched beside the sputtering fire, stirring the feeble embers in an attempt to revive it. "We will need some more wood for our fire, a little sooner than I thought," he said. "I'll go and—"

"You won't have to go anywhere for wood," she said, her voice trembling. "You can start with that!"

She thrust her pointing finger at the house. Lasairian's mouth tightened, but then he tried to smile up at her. "Why, Shannon," he began, "if we burn our house, what will we do for shelter?"

"That isn't shelter! It's a pit of mud with a leaky stack of branches over it! Did you really live here all last year? Surely it didn't look like this! What could have happened to it?"

"Why—ah—of course not. Last year it was very fine, as fine as any home on Abhainn Aille. It's just that—I suppose the storms must have been unusually severe over last winter—"

"This is not anything like Abhainn Aille! Abhainn Aille is beautiful and clean. The houses are no worse than the cottages that any number of modern Irish live in. But this— this! I wasn't expecting room service and hot showers, but how could I have been so wrong? How did I end up trapped here, in mud and filth and cold and wet—"

She stared down at him, tears burning her eyes, almost overwhelmed with bewilderment and despair. "Here I am, through some miracle of magic that I will never fully understand, with the most kind and beautiful man I have ever known—a man who is, incredibly, my husband. Unfortunately, we're together in a pit of mud and trash.

"I can stand hard work, and plain food, and killer cows, and even bedsheets for clothes—but I cannot stand not having anything resembling a home."

He stood up and began to approach her, but she only gave a nervous little laugh. "Technically, I suppose, I am now on my honeymoon; but this is not the way I ever expected my honeymoon to be."

"A honeymoon? Tell me what that is, Shannon Rose. What can I get for you that would provide you with a honeymoon?"

She laughed again, but there was no happiness in it. "Oh—a bridal suite in a fine hotel, with a king-sized bed and smooth sheets and soft pillows and a great warm comforter. There would have to be a luxurious bath, and an enormous breakfast delivered up by room service. But here—here—oh, how did I manage to end up married to the man of my dreams and trapped in a place like this?"

She could not say anything more. She could only look around her, blinking, hoping that perhaps she would wake up and find that this place was just a bad dream.

But she did not wake up. Her world now consisted of a bare dirt-and-gravel floor, with patches of mud for variety. A forbidding wall of branches and saplings lashed together, shutting out the sight of the rest of the world. A smoldering fire in a rough ring of blackened stones. The smell of lake water permeating everything. And the house—that house—

Shannon walked straight past Lasairian and made for the

sagging gate, struggling to pull it open. "I thought my old life had been dull and gray! At least it was dull and gray with modern plumbing!"

He caught her arm, and for the first time she felt the real strength in him. "What do you mean to do?"

"I don't know," she said, her teeth clenched. Again she wrestled with the half-broken gate. "But I won't stay here. I cannot stay here! I want you to take me back to Abhainn Aille. There simply is no place for either of us here."

The shock was evident in his voice. "I—I cannot go back. The king—I am required to stay here, as are Aed and all the other herdboys. I have no choice in the matter."

She took a deep breath. "Then I'll go back to Abhainn Aille myself. I'll see if your family will let me stay with them, at least until you come back at the end of the summer. If I am gone, then you can stay in one of the booley huts with two of the other boys. Those are grand accommodations compared to this!"

"Shannon, surely you would not leave me this way— we've only just arrived, there is much that can be done to make you comfortable here—"

"That's what I'm afraid of. There's *too* much that has to be done. Maybe you and the rest of the boys could work together to repair this place over the summer, but no one should have to stay in it the way it is now! Not you, and certainly not me!"

Lasairian pulled her firmly away from the gate and slammed it shut. "You cannot go, Shannon. Even in daylight, how could you hope to find your way back? And you cannot think that I would let you walk alone into the darkness."

She glared up at him, still trembling with anger and despair. He was right. The very thought of trying to find her way back those many miles to the island terrified her, whether it was darkness or day. But she clenched her fists and continued to meet his gaze. "Maybe Abhainn Aille is not the only place I could go."

He frowned at her. "What do you mean? Where else would you go?" He paused, and his eyes widened. "Have you remembered where you are from? Do you know, now, how you got to the hill above Abhainn Aille? How you came to find me?"

"I know how I got there. It was just as I told you—a combination of music, and magic, and a powerful longing to escape to a new life. I am not from Eire. I am from a place very much farther away."

Lasairian stood very still, and nodded slowly. "It is possible. I knew, from the moment I saw you, so strange, so beautiful, so lost, that you were not from this world."

He relaxed a bit, and took a step toward her. "There are many stories, dear Shannon, of those who come to us from a place that is not Eire—from a place very much farther away, as you said. It is known to us as the Otherworld, a place of great beauty and comfort and magic. And if nothing else convinced me that you have crossed the veil between the worlds and gone from yours to mine, your insistence on comfort would leave me no doubt."

But the tension did not leave her. "I was able to find my way in once. Perhaps I can find my way back out again."

He froze. "Find your way back out again? Do you mean—do you mean to leave Eire and return to the Otherworld?"

She raised her chin, but swallowed hard and did not look at him. "If I cannot find any place here where I can belong, then I can only go back to the life I knew before."

155

"Do you have this power, Shannon? Do you have the power to walk at will between this world and the Other-world?"

"Well—it's only happened once—but if it happened once, it can happen again."

He shook his head. "It is not so simple as that. No mortal man or woman can simply walk in and out as they wish . . . and though you are as lovely and mystical as any goddess might be, I do not doubt, after our first night together at the fires, that you are a mortal woman after all."

She looked away from him, but he caught her cheek with gentle fingers and turned her to face him once again. "Even if a door can be found, there is a great danger of being lost in the Otherworld forever. Dear Shannon, if you are to find your way back, you would have to find the same door through which you walked to get here."

"At Beltane."

He nodded. "It could only be at Beltane, a time of great power . . . power enough to bring you here across the worlds."

Shannon was still for a long moment. "Then I only have to stay here for a year. After that . . ."

He touched her cheek, and his voice dropped to a whisper. "Is there nothing I can do to make you stay? Are you running away from me, Shannon?"

She stopped.

Are you running?

"I . . . I don't . . ."

"It is easy to run, when things go badly." He paused. "I will admit to you that I have done it myself, in my own way. Simply turning away from difficult or uncomfortable things . . . things I had no wish to do. But—"

He placed his hands on her shoulders, and looked down

into her eyes. "Please say that you will not run away from me, Shannon Rose. I vow to you that I will get whatever you require to let you live in comfort, as any noble lady ought. But please say to me that you will not run away this time."

She stared back at him, her mind spinning.

Are you running? Are you running?

"I don't know," Shannon whispered, brushing past him and walking back toward the little fire. *I don't know, I don't know, I don't know. . . .*

The sun must have been up for some time when Shannon finally awoke, for the world was suffused with a dull gray light. She could see nothing but the seamless gray sky and a few overhanging branches; the high walls of the *crannog* shut out the rest of the world.

She threw back the green-and-yellow wool cloak and got to her feet, taking care not to disturb Lasairian. He had to be very tired after the long trek. It occurred to her that as a herdsman he should be well used to such a life; but still he slept soundly on the ground, securely wrapped in his own dark brown cloak.

She walked across the *crannog*, carefully avoiding the trash as she went. With a determined effort, she managed to unbar the gate and drag it partly open.

A fresh breeze blew through, and the sight of the world was open to her once more. She almost forgot her dismay at the dreadful *crannog* upon taking in the beauty which surrounded it.

The shoreline lay shaded and cool beneath the shadows of enormous trees, trees which continued up the surrounding hills as far as she could see. The water of the lake rippled gently as it flowed around the little island that had been built in its path. Dragonflies flitted across the water, dipping down to the surface and then flying off again.

And directly across from her, splashing into the lake, was the waterfall she remembered from last evening. Even from here she could see that it fell into a pool among the rocks, and from there tumbled a second time into the lake.

Footsteps behind her, and then a gentle hand on her shoulder. "You would not leave before having a morning meal, would you, Shannon?"

She smiled, and lay her hand over his.

"Or a bath. Look, there, at the waterfall! Think of what a lovely bath you could have there, in the cool clear water. Here is what we will do: I will get out some food for us, and as soon as we have eaten we will spend a lovely morning in the waters of the pool. I cannot believe that even the Otherworld has a finer pool than this one."

"I could not think of leaving before breakfast and a bath," she said softly. "Of course I will stay."

"Good. Wait here, and admire the beauty of the forest and the waters for as long as you like. In no time we'll have a feast that would be the envy of the king and queen."

He turned to go, and she sighed, embarrassed by the thought of her behavior the night before. It was not his fault if the *crannog* shelter was in such poor condition. He would have had no way of knowing. And she did feel better now after some sleep, with the prospect of food and bathing before her.

Bathing. She was quite certain that she'd never been so dirty in her life—not even yesterday morning when she had awakened in the meadow beside Lasairian. Today she was covered with dirt and sweat from the long hike through the hills, the hem of her dress was dragging with mud, and her skin and clothes and hair all reeked of smoke from the long damp night spent beside the fire.

That waterfall was looking better and better.

But as she gazed at it, another sound began to emerge from the steady song of the rushing waters.

Footsteps. They grew louder, occasionally punctuated by the cracking of a fallen branch and the rustling of leaves and brush.

Someone was coming through the heavy forest. Someone was coming right at them.

"Lasairian!" Tension suddenly held Shannon fast. "Someone's coming!"

In an instant he was at her side. "Where? Who is it?"

"I didn't see anyone. I just heard them. Listen!"

The sounds of cracking and rustling grew louder. "Whoever they are, they're bold, and making no effort to hide."

"Who would be coming down here?" she asked. "The herdboys?"

"Perhaps. But they would be busy with the cattle, they'd have no reason to come here." He caught her arm. "Look—"

Their visitor emerged from the trees, reaching the foot of the slippery clay slope. It was a man, but they could not see his face; his plain brown cloak was pulled up over his head as protection from the wet and dripping forest.

Lasairian pulled her behind him. She could see nothing but the tall trees over his shoulder, but did not protest; they had no way of knowing who was approaching so boldly. They certainly could not pick up a phone and call an emergency number for assistance.

There was no one to rely on but themselves.

Shannon tried to relax, tried to breathe. "It's probably just one of the herdboys," she said, trying to reassure them both. She ducked down to peer beneath his arm. "And no matter who it is, they can't get over here anyway. Not unless they can walk on water."

The hooded man continued moving toward them, stepping out onto the water and continuing on his way to the *crannog* as if he walked on a paved road.

Shannon froze. She clutched at Lasairian as his arm tightened around her. "What—what is that?" she gasped. "How is he doing that?"

Lasairian stayed silent and perfectly still. The two of them could only stand and watch as the man approached them, making a wide turn out on the surface of the lake. His soft leather boots sank down a little in the water, Shannon noticed, and he stepped very carefully—two short steps, one long one, a short step left, a long step right.

She could feel Lasairian relax slightly. "It's Aed, come to see us," he said, and stepped back a pace from the gate.

Now Shannon could see him too; it was indeed Aed, the old man in charge of the herdboys. She let her breath out in a long sigh. "There's something under the water," she said, marveling now. "There are stones—or a bridge of some kind—just beneath the water!"

But before either of them could wonder why he was here, Aed had stepped up onto the *crannog* and pushed past them through the gate. He seemed not to notice the condition of the place at all, but only looked sharply at Lasairian.

"It's past dawn. We looked for you. Why did you not come up to the pastures?"

"Ah—why, of course, my wife was very tired after the long journey. She is not accustomed to traveling so far in one day, you see, and when we arrived here, and saw that the house was damaged, of course I planned to work today to repair it. I will be up at the pastures just as soon as—"

"There's work to be done with the herds. There's work to be done to maintain the boys."

"I know there is, and I promise I will be there—it is just that I need some time to repair the house and clean up the *crannog* and make it fit for my wife to live in—"

Aed stared at him in complete silence for a long moment. "I can see that there will be no peace for you until the *crannog* is suitable for your wife."

The insult did not fail to reach Shannon, but Lasairian seemed not to notice. He smiled brightly at Aed and told him, "I will work very hard to finish this place in the shortest possible time, and then I will be up at the pastures with all of you and working twice as hard to care for the cows and help the herdboys live in as much comfort as the hilltop can provide."

Again the long glowering silence. "Three days."

"Three days?"

"You have three days to build the *crannog* to your liking. After that, you will be at the booley camp with the other herdboys each and every morning at the first light of dawn. If you are not, I and two of the others will be here at your gate to fetch you."

"Of course. Of course. I understand."

Aed peered at him from beneath the dark brown cloak. "There is perhaps two weeks until calving time. Every hand will be needed."

"Calving time?"

Shannon almost laughed. "Of course, Lasairian, could you have forgotten so soon? It's late spring. Even I know that the cows would be having their calves now. It's certainly the ideal time for them, with all the beautiful green grass waiting for them on the hilltop."

"That is exactly right," said Aed, glancing at Shannon.

Then he looked back at Lasairian. "Three days."

"Three days," Lasairian agreed, nodding.

Aed turned to go, but just as he stepped off the *crannog*, Lasairian placed a hand on his arm. "Show me how to use the stones beneath the water. I want to be able to walk out here without the boat, if need be. Please—show me."

Shannon frowned slightly. "I thought you lived here last year," she began. "Didn't you—"

But he kept his attention solely on Aed. "Show me how to use the stones."

The older man turned away and stepped out onto the water. It looked as if he would simply ignore the question and go on his way, but then Shannon realized that he was speaking as he walked.

"You can see the stones only a little in daylight, and not at all at night," Aed said, as Lasairian followed him closely, "but you can remember where they are. Finding your way is like memorizing a poem. Anyone who knows anything about how the bards learn will have no trouble."

Shannon watched, tense, as Lasairian awkwardly followed the other man across the water. There was a pattern to it, as she had seen when Aed first came across. She just hoped Lasairian would be able to find his way safely back. Well, she supposed she could always take the boat and go and fetch him. . . .

Yet the question nagged at the back of her mind. If he had been herding cattle up here for years, and living here on the *crannog*, how was it that he did not know about the underwater stepping stones?

But she had no time to wonder, as Aed disappeared back into the forest and Lasairian started his return across the stones. Step after cautious step—two short, one long, a short step left, a long step right—she held her breath as he made his careful way and then stood with her once more on the littered floor of the *crannog*.

"Simple! So simple! A fine thing to know, and you can learn it too! I'll teach you!"

She smiled. "But I wonder . . . how is it that you're only learning this today?"

He looked at her, his smile fading as he realized what she had asked. "Why—why, it is a privilege that must be earned, to be sure. It is shown to no one until they have been here for, ah, several seasons at the very least." His smile returned as he finished. "That is why Aed came down here this morning. He wanted to show me this secret!"

"I see." She sighed. "I don't suppose you'd want just anyone to know a way to walk across the water to your doorstep. But he also said—did I understand him correctly?—that we have three days to fix this place up, before you have to join the other herdsmen up on the hill?"

"You did indeed hear correctly, beautiful Shannon. We have plenty of time to make the *crannog* a comfortable home for you. I believe that may even be enough time for, as you said last night, a 'honeymoon.' "

"A honeymoon." She could not help smiling again. "Three days . . . a lot can be done in three days."

"It can, it can," he answered, reaching out and pulling her close. "And we will start just as we intended this morning—out there, at the pool, where the water flows so beautifully."

"I think I would follow anyone, anywhere, right now, if they promised me a bath," Shannon said; but her spirits had indeed begun to rise. In no time at all they had collected a change of clothes and taken the little boat across the lake to the pool.

Chapter Thirteen

The beautiful forest pool seemed to have been designed for bathing. The waters were clear and clean from the waterfall, the bottom was covered with large smooth stones, and it was perhaps eight feet across and four feet deep. Just the kind of thing people in the modern world might pay a great deal to have built—but this one was theirs alone, just for the taking.

Shannon sat down on the rocks at the edge of the rippling pool and eased her feet into the water. She started to untie her yellow sash, but then hesitated.

Their first night together had been fired by the ritual of Beltane. The magic and power had swept them into each other's arms, driving them into the smoky woods with a crowd of other men and women who were equally compelled by the flames and the dancing and the enchantment of a moonlit night.

But now she was alone with this man, alone in a quiet morning in the ordinary gray light of day. Any feelings they had for each other would come not from the forces of magic, but only from within, from the heart.

Lasairian stood quietly on the other side of the pool. For several heartbeats her eyes never left his.

At last she untied the sash and pulled off her mud-stained gown.

He was her husband, her lover, her friend. There was no need to feel any sense of embarrassment at being alone with him in this way. Indeed, at that moment there was nothing she wanted more than the reassurance of his touch, the closeness of his embrace.

She noted the faint look of surprise when he saw the cream-colored, lace-trimmed lingerie she wore, but he quickly forgot about her strange underclothes when she took them off and set them aside. Quickly she slid into the cold clear water and washed away, as best she could, the dirt and fatigue of the long journey and longer night.

In a moment Lasairian was beside her. He drew her into his arms, his skin hot beneath the cold water. She moved gratefully, eagerly, into that strong, sure hold, feeling that, at long last, she had come home.

Again she surrendered to Lasairian, as he did to her . . . but this time the water was as cool and soothing as the flames of the Beltane fires had been hot.

The sun was high behind the clouds when Shannon and Lasairian returned to the *crannog*, and the world was suffused with a silvery light. After finishing the last of the food brought with them on the journey, the two of them stood up and made ready to take on the seemingly monumental task of making the half-demolished place into a home.

Shannon had put on a fresh gown, one of the three long bleached linen undergowns which Lasairian had brought along for her. It was somewhat scratchy, but lightweight and cool, and so she tucked up the end of it into her brown leather belt and got to work.

The first thing she did was rip down the ragged piece of leather which hung over the doorway of the house. It worked very well as a makeshift sack to hold the bones and scraps and other decomposable refuse scattered all over the *crannog*. Three times she and Lasairian filled up the sack and emptied it into the lake, letting the waters and the fish make an end of the garbage.

Next they sorted through the broken tools and implements that were left. There was an old wooden bucket, muddy but still in one piece; strips and scraps of leather which could serve any number of purposes; woolen rags, a few wide, flat pieces of wood, a rusted iron poker, and a couple of large iron rings. She gathered it all up and left it in a heap on top of the piece of leather. There was no telling when any of it might prove to be useful.

The hardest job lay ahead. Using the flat pieces of wood, they began scraping the mud from the floor of the house and carrying it out to the lake. It was clear that this was going to take some time—and they would have to replace the mud with something solid and dry.

"It's going to take a lot of hauling," Shannon said, shaking her head. "But it's got to be done. We'll just have to figure out a way."

"We will find a way. I have no doubt of it. At least—I have no doubt that *you* will find a way."

He laughed, but Shannon was already thinking ahead.

"We'll need to bring in as many rocks as we can, nice flat rocks to build up this floor. And rushes, too, bundles and bundles of them, to cushion the floor and fix the roof. These walls will need patching—clay, or rushes, or branches— something to fill in the cracks and make it a little more solid. We could—"

"Shannon, Shannon!" Lasairian broke in, laughing again. "Were you a builder of houses, a worker in stone, before you came to me? You know so much, and I know so little when it comes to this!"

"All I know is what I've read—what I've heard about," she said. "Don't you know how these houses are made? How are the walls done?"

"Oh—well, of course, I am naught but a cowherd, dear Shannon, I know nothing of building houses. Abhainn Aille is largely built of solid wood pieces, and at any rate was there long before I was born. I think we shall have to learn together how to build our house."

She smiled at him, thinking of how fine and noble he looked even in the clothes of a cowherd, shoveling mud in the warm and muggy confines of a tiny house on a lake in the forest. "I don't suppose I could explain to anyone just how to build houses in my world, either, even though I've seen it done. You're right. We'll learn to do it together."

Late that afternoon, after taking the time to bathe once again and then dressing in a clean linen shift and the finest of the two woolen gowns, Shannon followed Lasairian back up the hill to the booley camp. After the long hours of cleaning and shoveling, she did not think she had ever been so hungry in her life; but in many ways she had never felt better.

She had spent the day with her husband, her handsome

and loving husband, working alongside him to quite literally build a home. And after the sweetness of the morning spent in the pool, it seemed that nothing could spoil the fine glow of happiness which surrounded her—not even a day of shoveling mud and picking up trash.

After several minutes of hiking up the steep and slippery trail, the two of them reached the top of the hill and walked out into the booley camp. Shannon looked around her, and up at Lasairian, and broke into a delighted smile.

The great golden sun hung low over the horizon, casting a glowing light over the grassy hilltops and distant cattle. In front of the four huts, all of which appeared clean and swept, with belongings neatly piled within, was a crackling campfire with an iron spit propped over it. The roasting meat smelled delicious, as did the flat oatbread baking on the stones at the edges of the fire.

The boys greeted them with waves and shouts, and seemed to be happy to have more company. "Sit down! Sit down, we'll bring you food, it's nearly ready. Though next time you may be the ones to do the cooking!"

"That will be fine with me," said Shannon, accepting a wooden plate piled high with steaming food. "I'll do whatever is needed to help out."

Lasairian smiled at her and accepted his own plate. Shannon found that they had been served thick slices of what seemed to be beef, steaming hot and lightly sprinkled with salt, with several chunks of oatbread underneath it. There was something that looked like steamed greens—and so they were, she discovered, identifying peppery watercress and grassy clover and slightly bitter dandelion leaves, all soaked in juices from the beef.

The flavors were very strong, especially of the greens; but she ate eagerly, as if it had been days since her last meal. The hard work had roused her appetite, and she knew enough of nutrition to realize that the heavy, unfamiliar food—which she would have considered far too high-calorie in her old life—actually had everything which her body now craved: protein and fat for strength and energy from the meat, complex carbohydrates from the oatbread, and vitamins A and C from the strong-tasting salad with its rich dressing of beef drippings.

There was no fork or knife or spoon, so she simply followed everyone else's lead and ate by hand. In no time the plate was clean. She sat back with a sigh, suddenly feeling sleepy. Perhaps she could rest her head on Lasairian's shoulder, and . . .

Just then the sound of drumming began. Shannon sat up with a shock. For a moment the flames of the campfire danced before her eyes and she was forcibly reminded of the Beltane ritual. But then she realized that it was only a couple of the herdboys playing on their small hide drums, and the rhythm set the rest of them to jumping and dancing and shouting out loud.

She had to smile at them. They looked like kids let loose for the summer, and indeed they were. They had months of hard work ahead of them, but months of freedom too, living in a wild and beautiful place with good friends and an important job to do. They had a wonderful sense of purpose, a sense of being needed.

Looking up at Lasairian, Shannon knew exactly how they felt.

After two long and hardworking days, and sleeping two more nights wrapped in their warm wool *brats* on the bare ground of the *crannog*, Shannon and Lasairian had managed to haul enough rock and gravel and earth to the little house to patch up the holes, raise the floor, and make a smooth dry surface. At last, after endless backbreaking hours of scraping and shoveling and hauling and leveling, Shannon walked inside the home she now shared with her husband.

It was hardly the place she had dreamed of when she thought of where she might begin married life. Sunlight filtered in through the loosely bound sticks and branches which made up the walls, and so, she knew, would the winds and the rain. The roof still looked ready to fall in. But in the space of just two days, she and Lasairian had managed to turn a wet and muddy pit into a smooth dry surface, solid and clean. It was a small miracle, one which she and her husband had done all on their own, together.

Perhaps it could be done. Perhaps it was possible for her—for the two of them—to carve out a new life in this strange wild place. It seemed impossible; but where yesterday there was a muddy pit, today there was a floor.

Climbing easily up the path to the booley camp, Lasairian felt more relaxed than he had in many days. Shannon followed closely behind him, holding her skirts up out of the damp earth with one hand and balancing against the trees with the other. She actually hummed a little song as she made her way up.

Lasairian smiled as he listened to her. "It seems, Shannon Rose, that all you required to make you happy was a decent place to live."

The humming stopped. So did her footsteps. "Do you think that is too much to ask for?"

He halted his climb and turned to face her. She stood alone in the dripping forest, looking startlingly young and small, staring up at him with surprise and something like guilt on her face. "I am sorry I was so angry that first night we were here," she began. "It was just all so strange—and I was exhausted, even scared, I don't mind telling you—"

"Shannon, Shannon! I am trying to tell you how fortunate I am that you have asked so little of me, for I have so little to offer you."

She started to speak, but he moved to stand in front of her and placed his hand on her cheek. "You did not ask for gold, or stacks of new wool gowns, or cattle, or the moon, as so many women might have done, even when they knew such things were not in my power to give. All you wished for was a place to live that was comfortable and clean—and because you insisted upon it, the two of us now have a fine home for the rest of the season. We have a home that is sheltering and secure, and above all, a home that is only for the two of us alone."

He set down the small leather bag on his shoulder and took her in his arms. "Ah, it is a fine season we have to look forward to. I shall watch the herds in the countryside during the day, and you may come with me if you wish—how difficult can it be to watch cows graze?

"At the day's end we will go back to the camp for a good meal and an evening of laughter and storytelling. And after that—after that, you and I will return to our own private home, the home which you yourself created, there to lose ourselves in each other without a single worry for anything else."

She sighed, and briefly rested her head on his chest in contentment. "Let's go, then," she said. "You make it sound so wonderful, I cannot wait to begin!"

Lasairian smiled at her and lifted the leather bag to his shoulder once again. He sighed, breathing deep of the fresh damp morning air, as they started on their way. It would, indeed, be a fine season for them both. As he had said—just how much trouble could it be to watch a herd of cattle?

At the booley camp, Lasairian kissed Shannon on the cheek as he prepared to leave with the rest of the herders. "I have only a single word for you this morning, dear Shannon," he said.

She grinned. "Only a single word? Now, that would be a surprise."

"Watercress."

"Ah."

"Watercress is my favorite. Since you are to stay and gather food with Tully and Ercan today, then I will ask you to search out all the watercress you can, and think of me as you gather it . . . think of me, and how we will share what you have found when I return this evening, for I will surely be thinking of you all this day, from morning to high sun to the beginning of twilight. . . ."

Laughing, she placed her fingers over his lips to quiet him. "Watercress it is," she said. "Though I've never heard anyone ask for such a simple thing in such a manner!"

He kissed her fingers and smiled at her in farewell. "Until twilight then, Shannon Rose," he said, and turned away to hurry after Aed and the cows and the rest of the herdboys.

Lasairian followed along at a polite distance behind the cattle and their herders, leaving the work of prodding and guiding the balky beasts to the ones who actually knew how to go about it. He was certain that he would only be interfering if he tried to help, so he was careful to do the courteous thing and just stay out of the way.

The day was a fine one, the mist clearing as they walked over the hilltops and through the forest trails. He found his thoughts turning once again to his poetry and music. Surely this would be the finest of places to hear the music, high in the hills among the ever-singing rivers and streams. One day, perhaps, he might even bring his harp along with him.

It did not take long for the herders to get the cattle to the next valley. It seemed that the sun had hardly moved at all before the cows were allowed to scatter over the grass-covered field between the hills, and left alone to graze.

And since he had not brought along his harp this time, but only an iron fishhook and a length of braided linen cord, he would have to settle for merely sitting beneath a tree at the edge of the nearest stream and waiting for his supper to bite.

Lasairian headed straight for the forest at the side of the valley, toward the place where the trees grew the tallest. He stopped to listen once, and then again—and there it was—the sweet singing and rushing of a fine deep stream, just beyond the trees.

Ah, now, this was not such a bad way to spend the summer! He was still helping the others, he told himself, as he took a chunk of beef fat from the supply in his leather bag and worked it onto the iron hook. The others would be glad enough that he'd spent his day this way when he brought in a string of beautiful silver salmon for their supper. He could all but taste them now, cleaned and cut and coated with honey, roasted to perfection over the fire. . . .

He tossed the baited hook into a pool among the jumbled rocks and settled back against the tree. And just at that moment he heard the sound of footsteps, a single set of footsteps, coming over the grass behind him.

Quickly he turned, startled, but then relaxed again. "Ah, Crevan!" he called, settling back against the tree once more. "Come to join me, have you?"

Crevan knelt down at the edge of the pool and began to fill the first of several waterskins he had brought with him. "I don't think so," he said, eyeing Lasairian and his comfortable spot beneath the trees. "The others will want their water."

Lasairian waved his hand. "Of course they will. But they do not need it at this very moment, do they? Now, here is what I believe has happened, and you can tell me if I am wrong. The other herdboys just drained the last of their water in the last few moments, since they arrived, and sent you to get more—which they will not have need of until some time later in the day. Is that wrong?"

Crevan finished filling the waterskin as a slow grin spread over his face. "You would not be wrong, Lasairian."

"Then, come on over here and join me! I have another hook and cord. Think of how many more salmon we'll have for tonight!"

"I can taste it already," Crevan said, gathering up the empty waterskins and coming over to take his own place beside the stream. "You say you have another hook?"

Lasairian handed him the end of the cord he had been holding and began to search in his bag for the second hook and cord. And then both he and Crevan looked at each other as a sudden rumbling sound came toward them.

The two of them grabbed their waterskins and fishing lines and rolled out of the way just as the entire herd of red-and-white cattle came trotting over to the banks of the stream. The animals waded into the shallows to drink, churning the formerly clear waters and frightening off every fish within a day's ride.

Lasairian and Crevan stood with their backs against the tree, surrounded by the milling herd, and could only stand and wait until the cows had had their fill of water and begun to move off once again.

"Lasairian," called Aed, as the cows ambled off, "you are here to help Crevan fill the waterskins?"

"I—"

"Good. I know he will be grateful for the help. And I know that you, an older man, will be a good influence on a young one like Crevan, who would simply sit under a tree and spend the day fishing if he thought he could get by with it. But you would not let him do that, would you, Lasairian?"

Lasairian could only look at the old man. He knew when he'd been caught. "Of course I would not," he said easily, and reached for the waterskins. "Come with me, Crevan. We'll finish this task upstream—where the water is a bit clearer."

Much to his dismay, Lasairian quickly discovered that filling waterskins was only the beginning. While the cattle grazed, and rested, and relaxed, the herdboys did no such thing. All nine of them, Lasairian included, took up stations around the herd to prevent them from straying into the forest or going off into the wrong field or valley. And the one to be watched the closest was the wily old lead cow, the red one with the white streak down her back, the one who bossed all the other cows and decided where the herd would go. If she could be made to head in the right direction, the others would follow—but first she had to be persuaded.

"What difference does it make where they graze?" La-

175

sairian said to Crevan, as the two of them stood guard in the sun beside the woods and watched as three of the others drove the lead cow away from a path she seemed determined to take.

Crevan cocked his head and looked sideways at him. "There are any number of reasons," he said. "Some grass must be saved, rotated you could say, for later in the season. We don't want them to trample every field at once."

"There is an endless supply of grass in Eire. I cannot believe that even this herd could eat it all."

The younger man shrugged. "It is not only the grass. They could easily stray onto another tribe's land. Or they could be seen by raiders. Aed is very careful of where they go, and when, and has a plan that would be the envy of any warrior king for never letting them graze the same place twice."

"Raiders."

"Oh, and there are wolves, usually at night, so we do not want to let them get too far from the camp—"

"I understand, Crevan." Lasairian smiled, though he shook his head. "And I thought I would only be watching cattle graze."

Chapter Fourteen

It seemed to Lasairian that somehow, on this day, the sun had simply decided to stop in its course across the sky, for he was certain it would never end. He walked, and walked, and walked, and chased the stubborn cows, and watched for signs of raiders, and hoped he would not see a wolf.

At long last Aed gave the signal to turn the lead cow and start her on her way home, and he followed along to keep any stragglers from stopping to graze on the tempting grass beneath their feet as they headed for the camp.

Again Lasairian wondered at the strangeness of this day, for not only did it seem endless, the distance back to the booley camp seemed at least twice as far as the distance out to the pasture. But finally, just as a star or two began to appear in the dark blue twilight, they came over the last hill and into sight of the little fire at the camp.

Here the cattle were allowed to graze or rest as they

wished, and only two of the boys were set to watch them through the night. The rest walked happily into camp, looking forward to a good evening meal and a bit of fun and laughter. Lasairian walked slowly after them, the last to arrive, every muscle aching. He sat down in front of the nearest hut so that he could lean against the stone wall.

"Lasairian!" He opened one eye to see Shannon hurrying over to him. "I am so glad you are back! You'll be glad to know that I collected an entire bagful of watercress. There's plenty for all of us." She crouched down beside him and kissed him, gentle as a drop of spring rain on his mouth. "And that's not all I did today. I've got a surprise for you. Come over here, to the fire!"

He was quite certain he could not move at all, ever again, but she reached for his hand to pull him to his feet. Making his way to the campfire, his attention was caught by the delicious aroma floating over to him.

"Look! I caught them myself! Tully showed me how it's done, and I did the rest!"

Cooking on flat stones at the edge of the fire were lovely small slabs of what could only be silver salmon, their honey coating already forming a glaze. "Practically leaped into her net, they did," said Tully with a grin.

"Leaped into her net," muttered Lasairian. Then, seeing the pride on Shannon's face at yet another new thing she had accomplished, he smiled at her.

"I thank you, Shannon, for what you have provided for us all. And I shall remember, from this day on, that while I may be the king of the cows, you are truly the mistress of the waters."

And with that he sank down beside the campfire and stretched out on the soft thick grass. In a moment he was blissfully asleep.

* * *

"Lasairian . . . Lasairian!"

He stirred in the soft grass. How long had he been asleep? Such a long and exhausting day it had been. "I'm coming, Shannon," he murmured. "I'll be right there."

Just as soon as he had strength enough to open his eyes, he would rouse himself from the grass beside the booley hut and go with her back to the *crannog*. Only one last journey and then he could collapse onto their lovely bed with Shannon and sleep until the dawn.

He did not even want to think that he might be facing yet another long, long day of hauling water and traipsing after stubborn cattle and never having a single moment to stop and relax and simply catch his breath, never mind sit down in the forest to hear whatever song it happened to be singing that day.

"Coming, Shannon," he whispered again, opening his eyes just a bit and blinking in the light. The boys must have built up quite a good fire this evening, though they were very quiet; he heard no voices, no laughter, no drumming. Ah, well, no doubt they were as tired as he was, whether they were willing to admit it or not.

"Lasairian! It's *breakfast*—remember *breakfast?* Oats and dried apples and honey. It will be ready soon up at the camp, if it isn't already. If we don't go soon there won't be any left!"

He began to remember. *Breakfast* was one of the *English* words she was teaching him, and never had he heard stranger words. But he did find it quite a marvelous thing to learn a whole new way of speaking, and was fired by the thought of someday composing a poem in *English*. For now, though, it was time to get back down to the *crannog*—

Then he paused, as at last a single thought became clear in his mind. If this was night, why was Shannon talking about *breakfast*?

He reached his hand back against the stone hut to push himself up off the ground—but instead of encountering stone, his fingers found heavy wood and wicker.

Lasairian opened his eyes and sat up. He was back inside the house he shared with Shannon on the *crannog*, and the light which made him squint came from the sunrise, and not from a campfire.

He fell back to the soft rushes with a groan. Morning. It was already morning, already time to start battling the cows once again.

Never had he thought to feel so much dismay at the thought of *breakfast*.

Lasairian had feared that his second day with the herds would be as bad as the first one, but he quickly found that he was wrong.

This one was turning out to be far worse.

It had started off well enough. He and Shannon made the trek up the hill to the booley camp, a climb that was getting a little easier each time he tried it. They'd had a fine *breakfast* with the herdboys, and then Lasairian had gotten to his feet and picked up his waterskins.

"I will see you at sunset, Shannon," he said, giving her a kiss on her forehead. "And I hope to be a bit more lively company for you this evening than I was last night."

But she only shook her head. "I want to go with you today," she said, gazing up at him with solemn blue eyes.

He blinked. "You want to go with me? Out with the cows? Why?"

"I want to know everything that must be done out here.

If you do it, I think I should know how to do it, too." She smiled. "Besides—it would mean that we could spend the day together."

"That it would, Well—if you are certain, if you are sure you will not find it too tiring—"

"I'm certain. Give me just long enough to gather up some food, and I'll be ready!"

And so the two of them had walked together after the cows, over the gently rolling hills lush with grass and dotted with forest, until at last they reached the grazing for the day. Now that he'd been through it once, Lasairian thought he knew what to expect, and was almost beginning to relax.

Then had come Aed's shouted command from out of the forest.

"Lasairian! Here! Now!"

He and Shannon looked at each other. "You'd best stay here," he said quickly. "Perhaps you could get some water while I am gone."

She nodded. "Just call, if there's anything I can do. I didn't come all the way out here with you just to stand around and watch."

"Of course not. And I am glad you came, though I would have been happy to simply tell you—"

"Lasairian!"

His heart sinking, Lasairian followed Aed's gruff voice into the shadows at the edge of the forest. They had just stopped at that day's pasture, and the cows had only just put their heads down to graze, and already Aed was shouting at him. What could possibly be so urgent that he had to—

"Oh . . ." he said, stopping beneath the trees, unable to take another step.

In the dimness of the heavy shade, Aed stood beside the

lead cow, the old red cow with the white mark down her back. She was on her feet, but it was clear even to Lasairian that something was wrong with her. The animal stood with her legs braced and her sides bulging, and as she turned to look at him, he was startled to see that her eyes were huge and glittering.

"What's wrong with her?" he asked, watching in fascination as the animal's sides seemed to ripple and move. "Is she sick?"

The cow let out an agonized bellow as Aed peered closely at Lasairian. "Calving," he said, and grabbed the old cow by her horns as she tried to walk away. She stopped, her head twisted upward by Aed's firm grip, and bellowed again.

"Ah, I see," said Lasairian, nodding. Of course—it was early summer, and even Shannon had known that it was time for the cows to give birth to their calves. "But—why do you need me? Shouldn't I go and get one of the other herdboys? Surely they would know much more about this than I—"

"The others will make sure the cows learn the boundaries of this day's grazing. It takes experience to teach them that. I require only a strong pair of hands." Suddenly he shot Lasairian a fierce look. "Those fingernails—do you still have them?"

Lasairian clenched his fists for a moment, his face grim; and then he spread his fingers wide to display them for Aed. Each nail, formerly long and thick and perfect for strumming and plucking the bronze strings of his harp, had long since broken off during the endless hours of work to restore the *crannog*. Lasairian had finished the job by cutting off the jagged remains with a small iron knife. "Gone," he said.

"Good. Now, come here and take this cord."

"Cord?" In answer, Aed tossed him a slender line made of braided linen strips. "What's this for?"

Just then the cow bellowed again. Aed twisted her horns hard and pulled her head up to keep her standing where she was.

"There," he said, nodding toward the animal's rump. "Tie it to the feet."

As Lasairian stared, he realized that he was indeed seeing two small hooves projecting from the beneath the cow's tail. "Tie it—?"

"Quickly!"

Swallowing, Lasairian stepped up to the cow and gingerly reached out for the hooves. How small and slippery they were! Surely Aed could not be serious. But the thought of asking him any more questions was even less inviting than carrying out the task as ordered, so he gripped the feet as best he could and managed to get the linen tied around them.

"Done!"

Clear fluid poured from the cow as she strained, but the hooves stayed right where they were. "Take up that cord," ordered Aed, "and pull when I tell you to."

"Pull—?"

Aed looked at him as though he were an idiot child, and Lasairian vowed that he would never ask the man another question as long as he lived. Just then the cow's flanks locked in another great strong contraction, and she began another terrible bellow.

"Pull!" shouted Aed, still holding the horns. "Pull down, toward the ground!"

Cautiously Lasairian pulled downward on the cord. Rewarded by a small but definite sliding of the hooves—he could see now see the legs almost up to the knees—he pulled harder.

There! A nose, definitely a nose, resting against the legs. He pulled again—and was horrified to see a great rush of bright red blood.

"Aed!"

The older man shook his head. "Nothing for it now. Be ready to pull again, quick."

Lasairian tried to brace himself, but got only a sick and sinking feeling when he looked at the suffering, laboring animal who was losing her lifeblood even as he watched. He barely had a chance to take a breath before the cow's sides went rigid and she groaned, not even able to bellow this time.

"Pull!"

He pulled with all his strength, amazed at the enormous power of the animal to resist, gasping as he pitted his mere muscles against a force of nature. And he could only close his eyes against the river of blood which gushed from the cow and poured down onto the ground.

The cord twisted in his hands, and suddenly gave, and he fell hard to the ground. Had the cord broken? He raised himself up on one elbow and saw the red cow lying on the earth. Aed still gripped one horn as though trying to hold her head up—but there, lying right in front of Lasairian, its white coat wet and stained with blood, lay a calf. A big white calf with flopping red ears.

"It's alive!" he cried, watching as the calf raised its shaky head and flung out one trembling foreleg. "But what about her?"

As if in answer, the cow groaned and flung her head back to the ground, jerking her horn out of Aed's hand. She lay still, flat on her side, her breath coming hard with exhaustion and her eyes still bulging with fear and shock.

Aed could not look away from her. "Cannot say," he muttered. "Cannot say."

He glanced back once at the calf. "Get it out of the blood. Take a cloth from over there and dry it off."

Lasairian got up and walked to the trees, where Aed had left a couple of waterskins and a bundle of coarse wool scraps. Shaking out one of the large scraps, he went back to the calf, and with all his strength lifted the awkward creature out of the pool of blood and onto a clean patch of grass a short distance away.

As the calf flopped and struggled, opening its eyes and blinking, Lasairian rubbed it briskly with the wool and was glad enough to have something to keep him occupied— something that would keep him from having to witness the terrible sight behind him.

He heard a gasping snort, followed by the sound of a big animal trying frantically to get to its feet. Lasairian closed his eyes. He had no love for cows, but had no wish to witness this one in its death throes. He went on rubbing down the calf, which was now becoming dry and clean; and as he worked, it raised its wavering head and let out a small bleat.

From behind him there was a low *moo*. Lasairian turned around—and was amazed to see the old red cow on her feet, legs braced and head down, taking one shaking step after another toward her calf.

Quickly he moved out of the way. "She's all right?" he asked, as the cow dropped her head to lick the calf.

"It would seem so," Aed whispered, and Lasairian was surprised to see the whiteness of the old man's face, the relief in his eyes. "But there will be no more for her. Not after this." Aed turned away and walked back to the place where the cow had fallen. In a few moments he had covered over the blood with handfuls of clean earth, and the forest glade was as it had been before.

Lasairian smiled, both in relief and in understanding. No doubt the old man and the old red cow had made many of these yearly journeys together. He was happy to know that their partnership wasn't over yet.

"Lasairian!"

He turned at the sound of the sweet high voice, and saw Shannon hurrying into the dappled shade. "Lasairian, are you—oh!" She grinned in delight at the charming scene before her, watching as the red cow continued to lick and nuzzle her milk-white calf. "You are very lucky, you know. Your work is special! You get to help with wonderful things like this, while I only search for rocks and pull up rushes."

She laughed, and slipped her arm through his. "It is a lovely sight, isn't it?"

Lasairian drew a deep breath, and his eyes met Aed's even as he smiled. "More than you know, dear Shannon. More than you know."

Chapter Fifteen

Lasairian was called upon to help with one more calving that day, but it was a younger cow and all went well. There was no need to use the linen cord. And after that was over, and the wobbly red calf was on its feet, he realized that the shadows were indeed lengthening, and it was time for them to start the herd walking back to the camp.

He fell into step beside Shannon and the two of them trailed the slow-moving herd. "This life seems to go well with you, Shannon Rose," he said, shifting the newly refilled waterskins on his shoulder. "You look as fresh and beautiful now as you did when we left this morning."

She smiled, and as always a faint blush crept over her fair skin. "In some ways, this is very easy," she said.

"Easy?" He nearly stopped in his tracks, but went on. "I am—that is, I am not ashamed to tell you that I find it hard work, even though I am of course well accustomed to it as one of the cowherds.''

"Of course." She looked down at the grass as they walked along, seemingly lost in thought. "But I wasn't talking about the work itself. It's just that out here, there's no time to worry about what you're going to do each day, or how, or why. It's all clear-cut and right in front of you, and there's nothing to make a decision about.''

"Ah . . . I think I understand. You are saying that life is simple when you don't have to make choices.''

"It is. And this is a good life, Lasairian. Someone like Aed, he's found what he wants to do. He's found the place where he fits in, the place where he matters.''

"And you, Shannon?''

She shook her head, and started to speak, but then paused. "I thought I knew what I wanted to do before— before I came here. I was absolutely certain of it, in fact. But now—'' She looked up at him, and there was a look of pain and uncertainty on her delicate features. "Now, I have choices again.''

Quickly he pulled her close and hugged her shoulders as they walked along, trying hard not to think about his own choices. "But you do not have to worry about any of those things today, Shannon Rose. You need only walk with me back to the camp, and then back to our home, and make no decisions more difficult than which gown you might wear tomorrow—or how many times you might wish to make love.''

She glanced up at him as redness crept across her face and neck, but then she grinned. "It would be so easy," she said, almost to herself, as she continued on her way. "So easy . . .''

"I will always do my best to make it easy for you," he

said gently, walking with her. "That I promise."

But she was not listening. She had slowed, and stopped, and now stood watching something far out in the distance.

"What is it?" Lasairian asked. But then he saw it, too. Riding across a far-off hilltop were two, no, three riders, trotting along at a casual pace.

"Who are they?" asked Shannon. "Do you think they were looking for us?" She raised herself up on her toes, straining to see. "They're riding away. Maybe they don't know we're here."

"And I am sure that is for the best. If anyone does not know we're here, it is because they are not supposed to know."

They watched in silence as the riders moved up over the hill, and vanished.

The days began to settle into a routine, a series of long, hardworking days filled with soft gray clouds and fleeting sun and gentle soaking rains. Shannon and Lasairian rose at dawn each morning, as soon as the light found its way down past the mist-covered mountains and dense green trees and the high wooden wall around the *crannog*. Lasairian would step out of the house to stir the fire while Shannon prepared their breakfast of oats with dried apples and honey, boiling it all together in the small black cauldron. And with calving season beginning, there was fresh milk to add to their breakfast as well.

Aed had allowed them to take a ration of food and a few tools and implements with them to the *crannog*. They had their own stores of oats and dried fruit, starchy dried peas, and hard white cheese, along with a small stone bowl of sweet honey and a leather bag containing a handful of salt.

She was filled with a real sense of accomplishment

whenever she looked at the house and saw how the awful little wreck was beginning to improve. They had found a couple of large flat stones and flat slabs of wood; these served quite well as shelves, set into the floor, and on them she could place their stores of food and their two wooden buckets of fresh water. The clothes she kept folded and secure in one of the large leather bags, hanging from a corner rafter. And in a far corner of the house, sitting on a stone with a slab of wood covering it, was the old wooden bucket which now served as a chamber pot.

What luxury! Looking at the battered bucket, Shannon could only shake her head and wonder at how far she had come. Never, before this, would she have imagined being willing to live under such circumstances. But it was not just the beauty or the strangeness, or even the miracle and mystery of how she had come here which had begun to change how she felt. There was only one thing which drew her to this place and made her willing to stay in it, if only for a while.

Lasairian.

After breakfast they would get in their little boat and paddle across the quiet water to the other side, tie the boat near the base of the waterfall, and rinse out the linen clothes and rags with the clean clear water from the fall. Then began Shannon's favorite part of the day—bathing in the pool with her husband, safe and sheltered in the forest.

She had little fear that they would be spied upon. Aed and the herdboys were, Lasairian assured her, quite well occupied with tending the cattle and caring for themselves. And Aed had certainly not been pleased about having to come all the way down here to speak to Lasairian; he'd done nothing but grumble about it.

Here in the lovely pool they were safe; here the time

they spent together was all their own. With nothing but trees and water and sky to look at, she could even imagine that she was back in her own modern time, at a private resort, perhaps, with this wonderful man who was her husband. When he cast his strange clothes aside and wore only his own smooth skin, glistening wet, he could have been a man of her own time and place.

It all seemed so confusing sometimes. She could almost forget that she had traveled to some alternate, magical world, that she had gone through a door she would never have believed existed if she had not stumbled through it herself . . . and on the other side of that door had found a man who looked exactly like Ian.

But surely this *was* Ian, and they had just gone camping in the forests of southern Ohio. She had married him and they were on their honeymoon, at a mountain resort with a natural pool and a waterfall, and there was a guest lodge just up the hill with a telephone and a warm bed and a coffeemaker and a quietly humming refrigerator stocked with orange juice and strawberries and champagne.

And then Lasairian would draw her close to him and they would begin to make love . . . and she would close her eyes and be lost somewhere in time, somewhere in a strange land, lost in the arms of the man who was her husband and whom she was coming to love with all her heart.

Yet even at such moments, there was one piece of reality which Shannon did not forget. She was not ignorant of the usual outcome of lovemaking, and had tried to think it through. The idea of having a family with Lasairian was one which touched a special place deep within her; he had been her husband and lover for many weeks now, and she had accepted the chance of having a child as part of having a husband in a world such as this one.

But she had been quite relieved to learn that there would be no child coming from their night beside the Beltane fires. And now, since she could not exactly walk to the corner drugstore or make an appointment with her doctor, she would have to make do as best she could, keeping track of her cycle and finding different ways to make love on the days which she judged risky.

So far she had been successful. Lasairian had agreed to her precautions; this was no place for her to become pregnant. With any luck she would make it through the rest of this year, at least until next Beltane . . . when she could, if she chose, find her way back to her own world.

Eventually they would climb out of the pool, dress quickly, and take their buckets of fresh water and newly rinsed linen back to the *crannog*. Shannon would lay out the rags and gowns and tunics on the roof to dry, and hang the woolen things from the rafters outside the house for a good airing.

Then it was time for Lasairian to cross the water again and begin the long climb to the hilltop pastures, and although it was not required of her, Shannon always went with him. There was much to be done back at the *crannog*, but she was not yet ready to stay there alone. Besides, what they needed most of all right now was vast quantities of materials—fresh rushes to be bound up in thick bundles for the roof and strewn to make a thick soft carpet on the floor; good flat rocks and pieces of wood for placing in the rushes to keep their belongings clean and dry; and wood, wood, wood.

Wood for burning in the firepit. Wood for patching up and filling in the walls of the little house. Wood for making tools and shelves.

But for this crossing of the lake, they did not take the

boat. Lasairian insisted that both of them learn to make their way back and forth on the underwater stones, explaining that, if nothing else, they did not want to leave the boat ashore for anyone to take to the *crannog*. Though Shannon had to steel herself for each journey across the water's surface, she knew that he was right. It was safer to leave the boat tied up at the gate—and, she had to admit, it was quite handy to be able to walk on water to one's home.

Once at the booley camp, Shannon would occasionally go with Lasairian to help keep watch on the cattle; but most often she remained near the camp with two or three of the herdboys who stayed behind each day to clean the camp, gather watercress and clover, and spend time fishing in the stream. Here she searched the edges of the forest and the banks of the stream for her rushes and wood and stones. She would help the boys prepare food for the midday and evening meals, learning more and more about just exactly what was considered good to eat around here and how one might find it and prepare it.

About once every eight or nine days, a couple of men from Abhainn Aille arrived with pack ponies, carrying a few supplies—necessary staples such as oats and dried apples and salt. But the majority of their food was gathered and cleaned and cooked right there on the hilltop.

By late afternoon, as the sun began to approach the horizon, Lasairian would return with the cattle and the rest of the herdboys. Shannon and all the rest of them would sit together to eat, taking shelter in the small stone huts if the rain got too strong. But most evenings found them all gathered around the fire, singing, drumming, dancing, occasionally breaking into the precious stores of honey wine and making their nightly gathering into a genuine revel.

At last Shannon and Lasairian would make their way

back down the hill, carrying as much of their store of rushes and branches and stones as they could manage, slung over their shoulders in leather bags or tied together in bundles on their backs. There was food to be carried each night, too: slices of roasted beef or cooked fish, oatbread thick with butter, a bucket of milk which could be kept cool in the water of the lake. If the darkness had set in, Lasairian would hold a torch to light their way.

Already the *crannog* was beginning to seem like home. It was their own private little haven, where they could talk, and make love, and work together, and sit and watch the night sky, safe and protected by its high walls and natural water moat.

It is only for the summer, Shannon would tell herself, *only for this one summer. All of us will return to Abhainn Aille in the fall and stay there for the winter.*

And after that, in the spring, would come Beltane. Ever since that first miserable night on the *crannog*, she had insisted that she would make the attempt to return to her own world when the door opened once again at Beltane . . . but now, surrounded by beauty and challenge and purpose, kept warm and safe and protected by the love of the man who was now her husband, Shannon began to wonder.

What would she do when Beltane arrived?

Chapter Sixteen

One evening, at what Shannon judged to be near midsummer—for the days were very long—she and Lasairian made their careful way back to the *crannog* after dinner with Aed and the herdboys. It had been a long and exhilarating visit filled with music and dance and fabulous stories, stories which Shannon could follow better and better now that she was immersed in a Gaelic-speaking world. They had left only reluctantly, and now Shannon found herself still wide awake, still in a mood to talk.

It seemed that Lasairian was, too. He took a few pieces of wood from the sizable store they kept beside the house and stirred the smoldering fire into a cheerful little blaze. Above them the twilight sky, perfectly clear for once, showed itself deep blue above the dark silhouettes of the trees. A star or two began to appear as they sat down on smooth wooden slabs placed beside the fire, listening to the quiet splash and slap of the water against the little island.

Lasairian placed his arm around her and drew her close. "It is a beautiful evening," he said. "Its beauty nearly matches yours."

Shannon smiled. It was the kind of thing he said so often, it seemed to come natural as breathing to him.

"Yet I believe I see a new beauty in your face tonight," he went on.

She glanced up at him. "Why do you say that?"

"Because . . . you have changed, slowly but surely, since coming here—coming here with me. You have found a home, a place for yourself. Most of all, you have found love. In short, dear Shannon, I believe you are happy."

She sat up. "Happy? Why would you think I was not happy before?"

He shook his head. "You were afraid, and confused, and lost. Yet I saw your courage as you tried to make a place for yourself here in my world, which was clearly so strange to you. And I believe you have done that, even in this rough and simple place."

He paused, and she felt him draw a deep breath. "I am afraid that as your husband, I have little to offer you," he said tightly. "As you can see, I cannot give you gold, or cows, or a fine house, or beautiful gowns, or even a decent ledge to sleep on. I can only offer you this place, bare and lonely as it is, for the rest of the season—and then a house shared with my family at Abhainn Aille after that.

"I can offer you little but love, Shannon, for now, and perhaps for a long time to come."

Shannon sat back so that she could see him, his face soft and clear in the glow of the fire. "I told you that I do not know where I came from," she began, "and I did not lie to you. But I do know that I am not from here—not from this place—and not from this time.''

She waited for his reaction, but he only looked at her, his gaze steady, waiting, holding very still.

''I started to tell you, when I first arrived here, what I thought had happened to me. At the time, I was—as you said—so confused and disoriented that I was almost afraid to think of what might really have happened. But now, since we came here, I *have* thought about it. It seems that hauling water and cutting rushes and picking up stones gives you plenty of time to think.''

Shannon paused, and closed her eyes. ''You know the tradition of the Otherworld.''

His voice was very quiet. ''I know it well.''

She gazed into the fire, trying to gather her thoughts, trying to find the words to explain what she believed had happened to her. ''I feel certain that the place I come from would be known to you as the Otherworld, just as this place seems like the Otherworld to me. It is a different place, a different time, yet one which had a door—a door which somehow I managed to find, and step through . . . and here I am.''

Still Lasairian sat motionless. He scarcely seemed to breathe. She could only imagine what an Otherworldly visitor would seem like to a man of his time. It would be like someone from her own time walking in and claiming to have arrived from another planet.

Shannon reached for his hand, and covered it with her own. ''But none of that matters now. Truly, it doesn't. Strange as all of this is, there's nothing any of us can do to change it now.''

''Except, perhaps, at next Beltane.''

She nodded once. ''Perhaps. But next Beltane is a long

time away. And I've got to live here now—today—tonight.''

Shannon looked up at the stars, now appearing like bright jewels in the blue-black sky. "In the place where I lived, before I came here, I had everything that any young woman could want. My family was wealthy. I had a life of comfort, surrounded by beautiful things. Everything seemed perfect—until one day when all of it vanished. My father lost his wealth and my life turned upside down.''

"That would explain many things,'' Lasairian murmured. "Your unfamiliarity with the customs here . . . your beautiful ring, worked of the finest gold, with a stone I have never seen the like of . . . even your hands, so smooth, so free of blisters, clearly the hands of a noblewoman, not a servant, or even an ordinary freewoman.''

She smiled a little. "Well, my hands *used* to be free of blisters. And you are right when you say that I was never a servant. But I might have been better off if I had been.

"I missed my old life terribly. Though I can only imagine how selfish it sounds to say so, I loved the privilege I had. I loved being free to learn and travel and see and do almost anything I might wish. But that was not the worst of it.''

She closed her eyes again, caught momentarily in a strange sense of *déjà vu*. Hadn't she just told all of this to Ian, not so long ago? And wasn't Ian sitting right here beside her now?

She looked around her again, at the little wooden house, the high *crannog* walls, the brightly burning campfire. Ian was part of another life, another time. Right now she sat beside Lasairian, here in the long-lost past, in the place known to her as Ireland . . . as the Otherworld.

Yet it was important that Lasairian be told the whole

story. He was her husband, wasn't he? He had to be made aware of everything that had happened to her, though it might be nearly incomprehensible to him ... though things might never be the same between them.

Shannon steeled herself. It had been long enough. She should have talked to him long before this.

"You said that the loss of your father's wealth was not the worst of it," Lasairian prompted gently.

"The worst," she said, "was that the man I was to marry—a man I trusted, a man I was certain loved me with all his heart—that man vanished without a word as soon as my family's wealth was gone."

The fire crackled and snapped between them. "I will tell you what is selfish, Shannon Rose," came Lasairian's quiet voice out of the darkness. "It is that my first thought was of how glad I am that this man walked away from your life, because that allowed you to find your way from the Otherworld, and find your way to me."

She turned so that the firelight warmed her face, wanting him to see exactly how she felt. "I did learn something from it all. Though I would always miss the beauty and the freedom of my old life, I vowed that I would never again allow any man to deceive me the way he—the way it happened before. It is why I still wear this ring. It never lets me forget that what happened once can happen again."

Lasairian sat up and took her hand in his. "I am very glad to know this," he said, his voice so soft she could scarcely hear him. Then, to her surprise, he patted her hand and got to his feet. "Wait here, please," he whispered.

Shannon watched him go to the house and disappear into the darkness inside. She could hear him moving around, apparently digging through the leather bags, searching for something. She was intensely curious, but he had asked her to wait; so she gazed up at the sky, admiring the beautiful yellow crescent moon which had just begun rising beyond the trees.

After a few moments, Lasairian emerged from the house. He moved slowly, awkwardly, and seemed to be carrying something rather large beneath his cloak.

He sat down beside her, but turned away, so that she could not see his face. He shifted about, adjusting his position, and finally sat very still for a long moment. Then he turned toward her and drew back his cloak.

"Oh . . ." Resting on his lap was a harp, shining metal strings surrounded by a graceful frame of dark heavy wood. And on the wood were inlaid curving patterns of what could only have been pure gold, beautiful interlaced lines which she knew were called, in her day, by the name of Celtic knotwork.

She could not resist reaching out to touch it. The heavy wood, smooth from long handling, held a gentle warmth from the fire and from his body. The shining gold patterns gleamed beneath her caressing fingers. And the strings, taut and strong, were eager and ready to respond to her lightest touch.

She withdrew her hand and looked up into his eyes. "How did you come to have this beautiful thing? How is it that a cowherd plays the harp?"

He shifted again, and his face disappeared in shadow. "This season is the first that I have been a cowherd."

A great stillness settled over her. "That would explain a great deal," she murmured. "You seemed so different from Aed and all the others. Even I could see that."

"The cows could see it, too."

It was a joke, but Shannon found that she could manage only a small smile. The seriousness of what he had said was beginning to descend on them both. Even his voice had changed, becoming quiet and somber. The flattery and flowery speeches had gone.

Clearly, something very important was being placed before her.

"Why are you telling me this now?"

He was quiet for a long moment. "Because you have done the same for me," Lasairian said at last. "Because it is so important to you to be told the truth, especially from the man who loves you."

She closed her eyes, afraid to look at him, afraid to think, afraid to breathe. The stillness began to turn cold and spread through her.

Was it happening again? Was this man whom she loved, this man she had thought she could trust, about to reveal himself as something entirely different from what she'd thought he was?

Shannon raised her chin and looked directly at him, though his face remained a shadow in the darkness. Only the harp moved, slightly, as he drew breath, its inlaid gold patterns glimmering in the firelight. "What do you want to tell me?"

"I want to say to you first that I am your husband, and I am the man who loves you," he began.

"I am glad to hear that," she answered, carefully keeping her voice steady. "But there must be something more."

He nodded, still keeping hold of her hand. "There is. I am not a cowherd, or a servant, or even an ordinary freeman. My father is a brother to the king."

"The king. . . ."

"I grew up in privilege, even as you did. I suppose that what I have been going through is much the same as what you experienced, back in your own world."

Shannon blinked, staring at him as it began to fall into place. "Then you are a prince, Lasairian. And a bard."

He paused, then ventured to meet her gaze. "You are right. Before, I'd hardly been closer to a cow than the dining boards in the Hall. I was trained as a warrior for a time, at my father's insistence; but my life's work has been as a bard. I play the harp, and sing the poems which my ancestors composed, and someday, I too hope to compose, and be remembered."

"Then you will not just be a bard, Prince Lasairian. You will be—oh, what is the word? I know I saw it while—an *ollamh*. You will be an *ollamh*, and the other bards will sing your words, just as you are singing theirs."

He grinned, and looked quite relieved. "I hope that will happen someday. There—you see? You may be from the Otherworld, but truly, you are not so far removed from this one. You understand more than you will admit, I think. You know this world quite well."

But as she gazed at him, the questions she had hoped never to ask of him forced their way to the front of her mind. "Why didn't you tell me what you are? You are my husband. Why did you let me believe a lie?" Even as she spoke the words, a cold and terrible feeling settled over her heart.

He looked away again. "I can only tell you that I am sorry, Shannon Rose. I can only tell you that I was ashamed, and did not want to tell you—or anyone—what had happened."

"I seem to be the only one who doesn't know what happened. It's obvious that Aed and all the boys know, even though they wouldn't say anything to me."

"They know. I'm sure they thought that you must know

too, and felt it was a private matter between the two of us.''

''I see. Well, then—maybe you can make it a matter for the two of us, instead of just for you alone. Perhaps you can tell me how you went from being a prince and a bard to being a simple cowherd.''

Lasairian set down the harp, placing it carefully on the ground a safe distance from the fire. He got to his feet and began pacing, slowly, restlessly, across the neat dirt floor of the *crannog*.

''My father was displeased with me,'' he began. ''He and I had agreed some time ago that I would be a bard, perhaps one day an *ollamh*, as you said. But we could not agree on how my training would proceed. He insisted that I do it in the traditional way—long hours spent in a dark and smoke-filled house, lying on the floor with the other young men, holding a stone on my belly as I recited and recited and recited for Oran, the chief druid.''

''A stone?''

''To keep you from falling asleep, in the darkness and the paralyzing boredom.''

''Oh.'' Shannon too stood up, and walked slowly across the *crannog*, arms folded tightly to her chest. It really was quite strange, this feeling of detachment. ''The training sounds kind of like some of the college classes I've sat through, although I don't recall being held down by a stone.'' She stood and watched him as the fire flickered and snapped. ''You didn't want to follow the usual training methods. So how did you expect to be recognized as a bard?''

He took a step toward her, and the firelight showed her the earnestness in his face. ''I tried to explain it to my father,'' he began. ''I could not hear the music while trapped in that dark and smoky house. I could only hear it in the waters which flowed past Abhainn Aille, and in the rains which fell in the forest, and in the winds which sang high in the trees.''

She managed a small smile. ''It all sounds lovely, but surely even you cannot learn to be a bard simply by sitting out in the woods and listening to the rain fall. Even the most talented poet, the most natural musician, benefits from discipline and training. In the world I lived in, the finest of them—the classical musicians and dancers and writers—trained and drilled and practiced throughout their lives. For most of them, no sacrifice was too great if it meant accomplishing their goals.''

''Now you sound like my father.''

Shannon looked closely at him, but she saw that he was smiling. He was not angry. He was not petulant. He seemed almost relieved that she was, at least, still talking to him. ''You still have not told me how you came to be a cowherd.''

His mouth twisted. ''My father—and the king—felt much the same way that you did. When my course of study did not meet with their approval, the both of them ordered me to stay out here for a season with herdboys. And here I am, though I never expected to have so lovely a companion. I can only hope that though you did not know everything about my past, that still you trust your heart and realize that you know what is in my own—that I am the man who loves you, riches or no. Do you know this, Shannon Rose?''

''You have taken a great risk tonight,'' she said.

He stood very still, and glanced over at the harp. ''I have. I have heard the way you have spoken about men who care only about wealth and property. I was afraid that, perhaps,

204

one of the things you found in me to love was a cowherd's simple life; a man who has no need, or real desire, for riches.''

She closed her eyes. "I cannot put all the blame on you. I think I knew—I *knew*—that you had to be much more than just a cowherd, but I didn't want to look any further. I saw a wonderful handsome man who loved me. *Me*, a woman with nothing to her name but a gown made out of bedsheets. You saw nothing but what I was, knew nothing about my past.

"It was exactly what I wanted, and I could never have turned away. Not from you . . . never from you.''

"But now you know what I am," Lasairian said. "You know that I am highborn, well accustomed to wealth and a comfortable life, just as you were accustomed to it. And I miss that life in the same way that you miss yours.''

To her surprise, he reached out and took her hand. A trace of warmth began to travel through her.

"I must ask you now, as you must ask yourself—can you still love me, now that you know what sort of man I really am?''

He leaned forward to kiss her softly on her cheek. And almost against her will, her heart began to beat once again.

Shannon stared up at him, at the beautiful dark eyes which gleamed in the starlight. Did she dare to believe him? Did she dare to trust him?

"I do believe I know what kind of man you are," she whispered.

"You do, Shannon Rose?" His voice was soft, but she could hear the faintest tremor in it.

"And most of all, I am glad to find that I can still love you, though your life is not so simple as I thought." Even as she spoke the words, a feeling of relief flooded through her. *It isn't over . . . it isn't over . . . he simply kept it private, even as I did, and he is telling me now, now that I truly need to know . . . it isn't over.*

He took a step toward her. "You can still love me, even though you did not know the truth?"

"I knew the truth, somewhere down deep. I had to know, by the way you dressed, and the way you were baffled by the cows, and the way you have of speaking, and even by those fingernails—the strangest fingernails I've ever seen on any man or woman—that there was no possibility that you were just a cowherd. I simply wanted to go along with you and believe whatever you told me, and trust that you would tell me when the time was right." She gazed up at him. "Was I right to trust you, Lasairian?"

He sighed, long and low beneath his breath. "You will not regret trusting me, dear Shannon Rose. I will make certain that all the rest of your life is as happy, and as beautiful, and as filled with love, as our time in this place has been."

"That would be wonderful . . . though solid walls on the house would be nice, too." She smiled up at him, faintly, but it was a smile nonetheless. "It will be wonderful to hear you play your harp. Perhaps by the time we return to Abhainn Aille, your father and the king will be surprised at how much you have learned about your music. There is nothing but solitude out here in the evenings, nothing at all to distract you from your practice."

She thought he would say *Nothing to distract me but you*, and make a small joke of it, and then draw her into his arms; but to her surprise he turned away and kept silent.

A wall descended between them. Puzzled, Shannon went to him again, and tried to turn him to face her. "You will play your harp for me, won't you, Lasairian?"

"My fingernails are broken from this place," he murmured, his face still averted. "My father told me, when he sent me away, that I could play my harp only for the cows—and so I shall. Without my nails, my playing would scarcely be fit even for them."

She stepped around him, trying to see his face in the shadows. "What are you talking about?"

He sighed deeply, his shoulders rounded and tense. "I will do no more than play for the cows until my father apologizes to me and asks me himself to play for Abhainn Aille once again."

Chapter Seventeen

Surely she had not heard him correctly. "Are you saying that you will never play for your people again?" Shannon asked, in disbelief. "You would refuse to play your music ever again, just to spite your father? How can you be so selfish?"

Finally Lasairian turned to look at her, frowning. "Selfish? I do not understand what you mean."

"You have a gift, a great talent, for words and poetry and music. But you are not willing to put in the work to develop it! You had the time, you had the opportunity—you had nothing *but* opportunity—and you rejected it because you thought it was too demanding! If playing the harp were so simple, so easy, everyone would be doing it. But music is not for everyone. It is for those who find it worth their time, their effort, their days and weeks and years—their lives."

He started to speak, but she cut him off. "In the world where I lived, there were plenty of people who would have given anything for the life you had—a life where you were free to pursue your art with no other demands on your time. I had such a life, for a while, and what I would not give to have it back again! But you threw it all away. You threw it all away!"

Lasairian turned away from her and walked back to the harp. He picked it up without stopping and Shannon thought he would take it back inside the house to hide it away again. But before he entered the doorway, he paused, cradling the beautiful harp in his arms. For many moments he did not move.

Then, to Shannon's amazement, she heard the beautiful liquid notes of the harp.

The notes came slowly at first, carefully, tentatively. She was so surprised that she could only stand and listen. Then the playing became more confident and sure, and a melody began, a sweet song, and it was magic, pure and simple.

Again it seemed that the music was distilled from the sweet singing of falling water, drawn down into notes on the harp. It was the first sound she had heard when taking her first frightened steps in the Otherworld.

But now she knew that the music had not been her imagination. Then, as now, it was Lasairian playing the harp, a harp she had not even known he had.

And in a moment she realized that she recognized the song. It was the same one she herself had played on the piano in her home. It was the same music she had found on the old leather sheet hidden away in the copper cylinder . . . the gleaming copper cylinder which Ian had given her.

But the song was not complete. He was playing only the

first few bars of it, and then it would trail away and he would begin again.

Shannon got up and went to his side. As he began to play again, she added her voice to his music, a wordless song which carried the melody. When he came to the end, she continued to sing, looking up into his beautiful dark eyes and singing the ending for him.

He stopped, placing one hand across the strings to stop their sound, and looked at her with amazement. "How do you know the ending to this song? Can you compose so quickly? This song is my own creation, you could not have heard it anywhere before! How can you do this?"

"I didn't do it," she answered, reaching out to touch the harp with her fingertips. "This song was given to me as a gift, back in the place and the time where I lived. It is part of the reason why I am here now. Though I still don't know how, I believe that you somehow sent it to me . . . and if I know the ending, that is why."

Lasairian started to speak, but it seemed that he could not. He walked back to the fireside and sat down on the ground again, slowly and deliberately, settling the harp on his lap. Shannon followed him and sat down close at his side. Gazing directly into her eyes, he began playing the song again.

This time, as she picked up the melody with her voice, he followed along with the music, and together they completed the lovely song.

When at last the notes stilled and faded into the night, Shannon got to her feet. She reached down her hand to Lasairian, and he rose and stood facing her, pulling her into a close embrace and briefly resting his cheek on the top of her head.

Shannon smiled, thinking she had never felt so secure,

so at peace. She turned and led him inside the little house, the house that was now their home.

Inside, all was darkness and shadow, for the roof was tightly thatched and the walls solid with wood; but Shannon knew the place so well that the darkness did not matter at all. The hard clean floor was cushioned now by a thick pile of rushes. Near the center of the single small room the rushes were covered by a large cowhide, its slick red-and-white hair still intact.

Lasairian placed the harp safely in a corner of the house and reached out for Shannon, but she stopped him with gentle hands on his shoulders. As he waited, she took hold of the gold-and-emerald ring on the third finger of her right hand. With some difficulty she worked the ring off her finger, placed it in Lasairian's hand, and folded his own fingers around it.

"I need it no longer," she whispered.

There was a small sound as the priceless ring fell into the thick rushes. Lasairian pulled her close and kissed her in the darkness, and her only thought was that his mouth tasted sweet as spring water.

In a moment he allowed Shannon to draw him down to the smooth surface of the hide.

As it had gone with the song, so went their lovemaking. He would begin, and she would continue what he had started; they would sing as one for a time, their voices blending together in the most ancient of harmonies, and then at last reach an ending in a sweet crescendo . . . and later, as they rested together and held each other close, the music they had created resonated on, just as the strings of the harp still held their music long after the hands which had played them were stilled.

*   *   *

The next morning, Shannon awakened with the beautiful melody still running through her mind. To hold on to it, she continued singing it, humming it to herself as the two of them prepared for the day.

"Why do you still sing the song? You must like it very much."

"Oh, I do," she said, with a smile. "I don't want to forget it. I must find a way to write it down, or else I'll have to go the rest of the year humming it to myself so that I don't forget it!"

Lasairian looked closely at her. "You said—write it down?"

"Of course . . ." Now it was her turn to stare at him. "You don't use writing here. There's no paper, no ink, nothing like that. I'll bet you've never seen anything written down at all."

"I am afraid, dear lady, that I have not; or if I have, I did not know it, for I do not know what you mean by 'write.'" He smiled. "Will you show me?"

"There is nothing I would like better." She glanced sidelong at him, and grinned. "Well, almost nothing."

"Why, Shannon Rose! How bold you are becoming. I shall have to play my harp for you more often, I think."

Shannon raised her chin and looked at him. It was not the kind of remark that she ever would have responded to before—but as her gaze locked with his, she gave him a slow smile, and then she turned back to tying the long leather belt around her linen gown.

"As I was saying—I'd have to have something to write *with*, and something to write *on*." She stepped outside the house, trying to recall her many history classes, trying to think of what primitive people might have used for making marks.

Then she saw the smoldering coals in the firepit.

"There. Charcoal! Bits of charcoal, maybe with a sharpened stick rubbed in it. That should do for something to write with. But to write *on*—"

Now, that would be the difficult part. There was nothing resembling paper here, and she seemed to recall that paper was terribly difficult to make by hand. What else—what else?

"Oh! The ancients used something else for scrolls—for their most valuable work—it was vellum, it was calfskin!"

She turned to Lasairian. "I wonder—is there a piece of good leather that I could use? I wouldn't need much, just, oh, a piece about as big as my two hands side by side. Do you think it's possible? Could I bargain with someone for it?"

"If a bit of fine leather is what you wish for, dear Shannon, I shall see that you have it. And then you can show me this writing of yours."

He smiled again, but his eyes were serious, and he reached out for her hands. "You talked about keeping the song in your mind 'for the rest of the season.' Do you still intend to leave when next the Beltane fires are lit? Do you still plan to make the attempt?"

She hesitated, gazing at him, searching for words. But before she could respond, he placed his other hand on top of hers, and drew her close.

"You will not leave me, will you, Shannon?"

Now the pain began to grow in her. Now he was forcing her to think of things she had been avoiding. "Leave you," she whispered.

To walk once again through the door to the Otherworld . . . if she dared try such a thing again. It had worked once, though it now seemed like a dream; she could hardly believe she'd done it even once. How could she think of making another attempt? How dare she play with magic and power once again, when she had no way of knowing where it might send her this time?

But one thing was certain. If that door sent her anywhere, it would be somewhere far away from Lasairian . . . and she would be alone, without him, for the rest of her days.

"Come with me," she said.

His eyes widened. "The door was opened for you alone," he answered, shaking his head. He attempted a little smile. "I do not know if it would allow a guest to follow along."

Her hand tightened on his. "I could not go . . . I could never go through that door again without you."

He smiled gently at her. "Then do not go, Shannon Rose. Stay here with me, with your husband, and I will take you home to the rest of my family. They will welcome you and you will find your place among them."

Lasairian drew her close, so that her head rested on his chest, and she could hear the slow and comforting beat of his heart. "Family," she murmured. She closed her eyes. What she would not give to introduce him to her own family, to be home and safe with Lasairian at her side, where she could show him the magic and miracles of the twentieth century.

"I met your mother," she went on, "and your sister, Clodagh. Who else makes up your family?"

He tensed. Perhaps he was not comfortable talking about his parents, or his other relatives, as so many people were not. It was yet another reminder of how little she really knew about him.

"You met . . . my mother?"

"Well—I thought that's what she said. The older woman

in your house, the one who was so kind to me—she told me she was a mother to you. She said that the other woman was her daughter, so I just supposed that Clodagh was your sister."

He exhaled in a long sigh. "I see. And I must apologize, for I suppose I never told you," he said. "My mother died when I was quite young. I was fostered for a time, of course, with the other highborn children; but still I missed her, and my father and I were quite close, especially when I was very young."

"Oh . . . I am sorry to hear that. I didn't realize that your mother was gone." Shannon paused, looking carefully at him. "Then—who were the women in your house?"

"Why—" Suddenly he smiled at her, his eyes as bright as the shining of the sun on the water. She nearly forgot what she had asked. "Bevin is, of course, one of the servants, and she has indeed been something of a mother to me, helping to care for my house. Her daughter—her daughter's husband was killed some months ago. The two of them have lived under my father's protection ever since."

She nodded slowly, looking away. "Of course . . . of course." Quickly she glanced up at him. "Who else?"

Again, the tension. He seemed almost startled. "Who else?"

She almost laughed. "Sisters? Brothers? Cousins? I'm your wife, and I'm not even sure!"

She could feel him relax slightly. "I am the only son of my parents. I have no sisters, no brothers." His voice lightened. "That is why I never spoke to you of brothers or sisters—I have none to speak of!"

Shannon smiled up at him, her heart lifting as one more

mystery was cleared away. "How could I ever think of leaving you," she whispered.

"Then do not leave me," he said. "Stay here, stay here . . . stay here with me forever."

She closed her eyes. "Forever is a very long time. How wonderful it would be if you could return with me! Oh, the things I could show you, the life we could have!"

He tensed again. She pulled back and looked up at him. "What is it?"

She thought he would speak again; she expected him to speak of his misgivings about attempting such a journey as the one she had taken. But she realized that his attention was held by something in the distance, outside the walls of the *crannog*, something in the forest across the water.

Then she heard it too.

A sound of someone, or something, crashing down the hill, breaking through bushes and branches and making no effort to hide itself.

Lasairian rushed to the gate, unbarred it, and pulled it open just enough to peer outside. Shannon crowded against him, holding the gate so that she could see too.

"Open the gate! Open the gate!"

Scrambling out of the woods came the herdboys—six, seven, eight of them. They slipped and stumbled on the muddy banks at the edge of the forest and then began their careful race across the water, hopping and stepping from stone to hidden stone just beneath the surface.

"Open the gate!" Shannon stepped back as Lasairian dragged the heavy gate wider. The boys made it to the edge of the *crannog* and clambered up, falling inside one over the other.

"Close it! Close it!" Without a word, Lasairian pushed

the gate closed, helped by a couple of the boys; two more of them dropped the bar into place.

"What is it? What's happened?" Shannon said, as the boys stood gasping for breath. "Why have you come here?"

"A raid," said Crevan, red-faced and breathing hard. "The Liath tribe—Dowan's men—fifteen, twenty of them, all armed men on horseback."

Lasairian walked to him and caught him by the shoulder. "Where is Aed? And Tully, and Ercan?"

Crevan shook his head. "They stayed with the herd. Aed ordered us to come down here, where it would be safe."

Cold fear began to creep over Shannon, rooting her to the spot. Now she understood why the *crannog*, why the walls, why the moat. Wild beasts could be driven off with fire; wind and rain could be kept out with a decent roof and warm woolen clothes. But the greatest danger of all came from the same source as back in her world—men.

Lasairian frowned. "What can Aed and Tully and Ercan hope to do against twenty men of Dowan? Aed is a brave man, but he is not trained as a fighter. And Tully and Ercan certainly are not."

Crevan shrugged. "Aed will never leave the cows and calves. He will do what he must to protect them—hide them if he can, place his body between the cows and the raiders if he cannot."

"Surely the king does not require him to do that," Lasairian said.

The young man looked closely at him. "He does not. That is why this *crannog* is here—for the herdsmen to take shelter in during times of great danger. Fortunately for us, such times are rare. But when they come, Aed is always the last man to leave the herd."

Lasairian stared at Crevan for a long moment. Then he turned and walked inside the little house.

Shannon followed, leaving the herdboys to keep watch through the tiny gaps in the tightly bound walls of the *crannog*. Inside the house, Lasairian stood with his back to her, closing up one of the leather bags which hung from the rafters of the ceiling.

"Lasairian, what—" He turned to face her, and she stopped, silent. In his hand was a sword, a beautiful sword, short and wide and gleaming.

"I wonder what else you've got that I don't know about," she whispered.

"Nothing else in that bag, I can assure you." As she watched, he placed the sword in a fine leather scabbard and began threading his belt through the end of it. "What are you going to do?" she asked, though she feared she already knew the answer.

"I am going to find Aed and help him."

"Crevan said that he would never leave the cows."

"Aed can take care of the cows. I will take care of Aed."

Shannon felt torn between great pride at his bravery and cold terror at the thought of what he might be walking into. "Stay here," he said, and took the time to kiss her gently before striding out through the door. "You'll be safe with the boys. You can look after each other. I will be back just as soon as I can."

Quickly Shannon grabbed her woolen cloak. She caught up to Lasairian just as he reached the gate and dragged it open.

"Wait!"

He and Crevan took the first step out onto the underwater stones; then, as Crevan went on ahead, Lasairian stopped and turned to look at Shannon. She stood before the open

218

gate, poised on the edge of the *crannog*. "What are you doing?" he asked.

"I'm coming with you," she said, fastening the brooch of her cloak.

He stood very still. The waters of the lake lapped gently at his feet. He looked eerily as though he were standing on the surface of the water. "Shannon, you cannot. You must stay here where you can be safe. I do not know what I will find. I have to know that you are safe."

"And I have to know that *you* are safe."

"Shannon Rose—"

She gathered up her skirts and stepped down onto the stone, her face barely an inch from his. "I cannot stay here, cowering, hour after hour, wondering what is happening to you. I cannot imagine anything worse."

He shook his head. "Please—"

"I won't wait here. You'll have to force me to stay, and I don't think you're willing to do that." She turned and began the tedious, slippery trek over the submerged stones. "I'll go with you, and we'll both find out what happened."

She heard him sigh, and then came the small splashing steps as he followed her across. Whatever they were about to face, at least they would be facing it together.

She always hated this. No matter how many times she did it, Shannon was always certain that this time she would slip off the slimy, mossy invisible stones and go crashing into the water. Lasairian still insisted that they walk across the rocks instead of taking the boat each morning when they left for the campsite; she knew it was for the best, but that did not make her like it any better.

At last they reached the opposite shore. She'd made it

once again—but right now all of them had more pressing things to think about.

They began the long climb up the slope beside the stream, a climb which seemed even longer this morning, with fear making each second seem like an hour. Aed, and all of the herdboys, had come to be like an extended family to her and Lasairian both. It was unthinkable that anything should happen to them—surely not to them, a group of unarmed herdsmen, a bunch of teenage boys just beginning their lives and an old man concerned only with caring for cows!

Her heart began to pound, but not from climbing up the hill. She'd begun to grow accustomed to the life here at the *crannog*, and on the hilltop at the booley camp. She had made a life here with Lasairian and felt she knew what to expect from day to day. But now a frightening danger had intruded, and upset the balance.

The tension began to take hold of her, making her tremble even as she climbed. Though she hated to admit it, maybe Lasairian had been right—maybe she should have stayed behind and left this business to him. He had been trained for it and she certainly had not. All she knew right now was that she wanted nothing more than to turn back and take shelter behind the high walls and deep moat of the *crannog*.

Oh, whatever was she doing out here—she, Miss Grey, sheltered rich girl turned college student—tracking down barbarian thieves? It seemed unbelievable, it seemed unreal. But as she looked up at Lasairian and Crevan leading the way, and felt her leather boots slipping and sliding on the damp rocky path, she knew, truly, that it was all much too real.

Chapter Eighteen

The climb to the top of the hill was only the beginning. Pausing only long enough in the deserted booley camp to catch up a few skins of water and whatever food was at hand, Shannon and Lasairian and Crevan began the search for the cattle and their herders. The three of them moved quietly and steadily through every place the herds had ever been—the lower fields, the forest clearing, the high river pasture.

But there was nothing.

At last, tired from the long trek but growing ever more worried and tense, the little group returned to the camp.

"Where are they?"

Lasairian stood at the top of the hill, near the booley huts. Crevan and Shannon sat down in the grass, but he continued to scan the horizon. "Where are they?" he repeated. "We've been to every place that these cattle have ever been, but there's no sign that they were even in any of those fields today. Where could they be?''

A terrible thought had been following Shannon all during the search, and now she could no longer keep it to herself. "Do you think—do you think that the raiders did take the cows—and took Aed and the boys, too?''

Lasairian paused. "It does not seem likely,'' he said. He looked at Crevan, whose face was pale and still. "They would not care about Aed, or anyone else. They'd only want to take the cows.''

"Unless Aed tried to protect the herd.'' Crevan's voice was cold. "Unless he got in the way.''

Lasairian stared him down. Though neither one said a word, Shannon could feel the chill in the air between them.

Something else was going on here—some other part of life in this place that she, ever the outsider, did not understand. *What are you talking about?* she wanted to shout. But before she could speak, Crevan got up and started off toward the stream. "There is one more place to look,'' he said, as he crossed the water and vanished into the woods.

In her endless search for rushes and wood and nice flat stones, Shannon had become quite familiar with the hills and valleys surrounding the booley camp—but she had never traveled down the trail which Crevan had taken. She'd been sternly warned never to try that path: steep drop-offs, nothing of value, *do not go that way!* But now there was nothing to do but stay with Lasairian as they followed Crevan into the dimness of the thick brush.

Almost immediately the trail made a sharp turn. Lasairian reached back to grip her hand—and she saw the first of the drop-offs she had heard about. A rock ledge, surrounded by trees, appeared to be the start of another path—

but vanished into thin air after just a few feet. She braced herself against the rough damp wall of rock at her back and began edging her way down, trying to look only at the path and not at the sheer drop only a foot or two away.

Surely Aed had not tried to drive the cows down this narrow, treacherous trail!

And then she heard it. Far below was the familiar sound of bawling cattle.

After an eternity of creeping down the winding, crumbling, terrifying trail, they came to a steep narrow ravine where the entire herd of Abhainn Aille cattle were held. The cows were milling and bawling and stumbling about on the sharp rocks and steep walls, plainly longing for their comfortable pastures and frustrated that they were being forced to stay in this awful place.

But she nearly forgot about the cows when she spotted three figures at the far end of the ravine. There, keeping the animals safely inside, were Aed and Tully and Ercan.

Following Crevan's lead through the agitated herd, Shannon and Lasairian made their way up to Aed. The older man's glance went immediately to Lasairian's sword.

"So," he said, "come to join the raid, have you?" His words were light, but his voice was cold and sarcastic.

Lasairian remained cautious, formal. "I've come to help you, if I can."

"We need no help. As you can see."

"Then they're all safe? The raiders didn't get any of them?"

"The raiders got none. But the trail—the trail claimed one." He pointed to a small heap of white and red lying at the base of the rocks. "It is a treacherous trail. Easy for a young calf to be forced over the side by the rest."

Shannon's heart sank at the sight of the dead calf, but

she turned her attention back to Aed. "At least none of you was hurt." She glanced back at the impossible-looking trail, trying to imagine driving some forty stubborn, half-wild cows and calves down that trail and into this ravine. "But—why would you take such a risk? You could all have been killed, just like the poor calf! The whole herd could have gone tumbling down the rocks!"

"Or Dowan's men could have made off with the lot of them."

Shannon shook her head. The tension of the day was beginning to catch up with her, and her voice rose. "Either way, you'd have no cows! What was the point of bringing them here?"

Aed gave her a long look. "Perhaps your husband will be so kind as to explain it to you." Then he turned and walked away, back to where Crevan and Tully and Ercan worked to calm and contain the nervous herd.

Shannon turned to Lasairian. "What did he mean? I don't understand. I love animals too, but—why risk someone's life for a cow? Even a whole herd of cows?"

Lasairian started to speak, then paused. He looked away, and seemed to be deep in thought. "It is not that simple. More is at stake here than just the cows themselves."

"I don't understand." Shannon started to go to him, but he quickly pushed her back. Aed must have decided that it was safe to allow the cattle to return to their pastures, for suddenly the restless herd turned all at once and began a lunge for the narrow opening of the ravine. Shannon and Lasairian edged up the side of the sheer wall as far as they could, until the last of the red-and-white cows and calves crowded past in a last frantic rush, eyes rolling and short horns clacking together.

Shannon breathed a sigh of relief. Peace surrounded them

once more—but still the question remained. "Wouldn't it be easier just to hunt for what you need? For meat and leather? Why are the cows worth risking your lives?"

He jumped down from the rocks and reached up a hand to help her down. "Walk with me. I will try to explain it as best I can."

The only sound, now that the bawling cattle had gone, was the splashing of a waterfall somewhere around the bend. "Could we go that way?" Shannon asked. "There's water there. I drank all I was carrying hours ago, and I'm sure you did too." She sighed. "And after all we've been through today, it would be lovely to just sit and look at something beautiful and not have to worry about anything else."

"Of course," he answered, "though I am the fortunate one; I am never without something beautiful to gaze upon, so long as you are with me."

She smiled up at him, once again drinking in the sight of the young and noble face . . . the skin smooth and fair, eyebrows soft and black, eyes dark and shining as he looked back at her. "I can only tell you, my handsome husband, that it is a good thing there are no mirrors here— even you would be surprised by how beautiful you are."

He said nothing, though she could have sworn that that a faint blush crept over the skin of his face and neck, all the way to the line of his soft hair. "Walk with me," he said again, and together they started toward the sound of the water, toward the opening of the ravine where the herd had gone.

It was a fine place for a talk, with the walls towering above them like a cathedral. "I still do not understand how it is done in the place where you lived," Lasairian began, "but here, hunting is uncertain. Even I know that the men sometimes come back empty-handed—even the most skilled men with the best of equipment.

"There are many people who live at Abhainn Aille and on the small farm homes and *crannogs* surrounding it. It might be possible for all to survive on the hunt alone, but life would be far more uncertain and difficult than it is now. Things would be very different without the fine herds, which—as we have both learned—have been carefully bred and protected for many, many generations."

She nodded. No doubt, hunting was more difficult than she thought—especially in this time, where there were no guns and the hunters did not even use bows and arrows; they had only slings and spears and various sorts of traps. The herds of cattle allowed a steady, dependable supply of meat and hides, with fresh milk and butter in the spring and summer.

"But don't all the kingdoms, all the tribes, have their own herds? It didn't sound like those men were outlaws. I thought you said they were from another tribe. Why would they have to steal someone else's cattle?"

His mouth tightened. "They don't have to steal them. They do it because they want to—because it's the best way to start a full-fledged battle."

"Battle?"

He sighed. "Perhaps the men want to prove their strength. Perhaps they are testing us, to see if we will fight back, to see if maybe one day they could take our lands and people for themselves. Perhaps one of them wants to be the next king of his tribe, and knows he must prove himself in a real fight first.

"If the raiders are not stopped, if they do make off with the herd, then the king and the warriors of Abhainn Aille will immediately retaliate to get the animals back. Soon no one will even remember what they are fighting for. Only the fight will be the important thing. Many will be hurt . . . and some might die.''

''So it isn't just the cows you're defending. It's all the people, too.''

He nodded, slowly, thoughtfully. ''I suppose you could say so.''

She smiled. ''It seems that even you have not thought of it that way.''

''I am ashamed to say that I have not. Not until now. And it seems that you were the one who forced me to think of it.''

Lasairian stopped and turned to Shannon, resting his arms on her shoulders as he gazed up at the towering rock walls. ''Here is something else I had never considered before. You told me that the gentle arts, things such as poetry and music, must be carefully nurtured, and so they must. Yet it occurs to me that such arts might be at the height of life, up with the winds and the clouds and the rain; but humbler things, like the cattle and the crops, and even the rushes and the stones, form the base, and are like the fire and the earth.

''The lofty arts could not exist without the basics of life . . . and both must be endlessly worked, and cultured, and tended, and even loved.''

She smiled up at him. ''That is as fine a thought as any I ever heard from any poet or philosopher. And I agree with you entirely.'' They turned and walked hand in hand over the rocks, reaching the mouth of the ravine and rounding the tight corner which led out of it.

The path opened out into a wider section, and off to the side was the waterfall—nearly thirty feet high, Shannon guessed, and crashing noisily into the stream below it.

"Lovely," she murmured. Even with as many beautiful sights as she had encountered there, she never grew tired of seeing new ones.

After drinking deep of the cold clean water, Lasairian pulled off his soft folded boots to rest his feet in the rushing stream. Shannon, though, felt drawn to the spectacular falls. They were higher than any she had seen here, a lovely and powerful force of nature. It was likely that she would not travel down here again—at least, not with any sort of luck—and she did not want to miss the chance to visit such a place.

"I want to see the waterfall up close," she called. "I'll be right back."

He nodded. "I could hear it singing your name," he answered. "But we should be leaving soon, before the light begins to fade."

Shannon nodded and then started down the rock ledge which ran along the stream, following it around the wide pool which the thundering falls had created. She stood right beside the crashing waters, delighting in the fine spray which misted her face and hair.

Then something caught her eye.

Near the edge of the pool, at the point where it narrowed into the stream, rested something bright and gleaming. It was almost dazzling with the splashing water flowing over it; she was certain that it could not be any sort of natural formation. Perhaps someone had lost something, something of great value. Cautiously she moved to the edge of the pool and reached for the shining object.

It was bright copper and almost as long as her arm. Wet and shining, it seemed like new, but it wasn't new . . . she had seen something like this before. . . . She had seen this very object before, a slender copper cylinder covered with primitive patterns, Celtic patterns, birds and trees and rippling lines like water.

She nearly dropped the shining cylinder. Instead, she sat down hard on the rock ledge, staring at the wet and dripping object in her hand, unable to believe what she was seeing.

"Lasairian," she whispered. "*Lasairian!*"

In a moment he was there, boots in hand. "What is it? Are you all right?" Then he paused, looking at the bright copper piece she held. "What is that?"

She held it out to him—and then, to her even greater amazement, she realized that he was having the same reaction to it that she had had. He stared down at it, eyes wide, hardly breathing, mouth slightly open as though he wanted to speak but could not.

"Where did you find this?" he whispered at last. "How is it that you have this thing?"

"I had it once before," she said, very carefully, making certain that she heard herself correctly. "There could only be one such object as this. I had it once before, back in the world where I lived before I came here. And I am sure— I am positive—that *this* played a part in sending me here." Her hand tightened around the cylinder, fearing she would drop it.

"How can we both know what this is?" Lasairian said, reaching out to stroke the shining surface. "How can we both have had it in our possession? Like you, I am certain that it is exactly the same copper piece. There is only one, now and always; there has always been only one." He paused, taking a deep breath. "Tell me, Shannon, how did you come to have this thing back in the world where you lived?"

"I got it from—I got it from a friend, who gave it to me

as a gift, though he told me—I remember now—he told me that it was a family heirloom. That it had always been in my family and now it belonged to me.'' She shook her head. ''I didn't see how that could be possible, but I accepted the gift anyway.''

''And I . . . I was given this thing by my father, who, long before that, gave it as a bride-gift to my mother.'' Lasairian closed his eyes, and his voice became very soft. ''My father wanted me to give this to the woman I loved above all others, the woman I wished to marry. And I did not want to tell him that—on that day—I believed, with all my heart, that I would never find the woman who could make me forget all of the others.

''It seemed wrong for me to keep such a gift when I felt so certain that I could never make use of it. I did not want to hide my mother's treasure away . . . and so I gave it to the waters, to the Mistress of the Waters, asking her to keep it safe for me.

''She did keep it safe . . . and now she has given it to you. I do not know how you came to have this thing in your other life; I only know that the waters have brought it to you now, to you, Shannon Rose, the woman I love above all others.''

With the gleaming copper cylinder cradled in her arms, Shannon walked with Lasairian back into the rocky ravine and soon reached the foot of the steep and narrow trail. There, forgotten, lay the body of the calf which had lost its life in the mad dash to safety.

Shannon walked over to it and crouched down. Most of the cows here were a kind of marbled red-and-white, but this calf was nearly solid white. Only its ears were red. ''It looks like—this looks like the calf that you helped deliver, on that day that I went with you to the pastures. It seems so long ago now.''

The little creature, so recently alive and well, looked as if it were only resting, and she found that she was not afraid to touch the smooth white coat. ''This one was lost, so that all the others could be saved,'' she said. ''And perhaps the folk of Abhainn Aille with them.''

Lasairian nodded. ''That is how Aed and all the others would perceive it.'' He paused, and then touched her shoulder. ''You asked me for a piece of leather. Here is your small piece of leather, Shannon, if you wish it. The calf no longer has need of it, and if you do not take it, the wolves and crows surely will.''

She looked down at the small body again. ''Such an unusual color . . . this one certainly would have stood out in the fields.'' She sighed. It pained her to think of skinning the poor little calf, but where did she think leather came from? ''Should I ask Aed first? It seems that I should, since he is in charge of all the cattle.''

Lasairian shook his head. ''Aed might be able to get the herd down that trail, but even he could not drive them back up. He will have to take them far around the hills to get them back to their fields. I would not expect to see him until tomorrow when the sun is high, at the soonest.

''But I can tell you—I do not believe he would object. If you have more use for the calf than the scavengers, I think he would be pleased.''

''All right, then. I would like to do that. I would like to use the leather from this calf who just might have saved everyone at Abhainn Aille.''

He patted her shoulder, and then leaned down to hoist the limp body of the white calf up to his shoulders. Together he and Shannon started back up the trail.

*   *   *

Halfway up the long and treacherous trail, Shannon wished fervently that they had taken the same route back as the cows. At this moment she did not care how long it would have taken! But neither of them knew the way for certain, and Shannon was in no mood to sleep outside unprotected in yet another strange place. She just wanted to get back to the booley camp, for this trail was certainly no place to be after dark.

At last, after what seemed like hours of tedious, terrifying climbing, they arrived back at the camp. After crossing the last few steps over the stream, Lasairian let the body of the calf slide to the grass and sat down beside it, his head hanging down, too exhausted after the long, long day even to speak.

Shannon too sank down on the cool soft grass, the copper cylinder resting on her lap. She reached up and rubbed Lasairian's tight shoulders for a moment, and then rested her head against his arm. "It's good to be home," she murmured.

"So it is," he said with a sigh. "And it will be even better to be back at our own home. Though I must admit, even the thought of yet another journey is too much. Would you care to just stay here tonight?"

"I was hoping you'd say that," she answered, lying back on the grass and closing her eyes. "I don't think I could go one step farther tonight."

"I do not think I could either. Besides, this place is ours; Aed will surely not be back with the herd until tomorrow. And there are eight rowdy herdboys staying at our *crannog* tonight, no doubt making an end to our every bite of food and last twig of firewood."

"Oh, so there are," she said with a groan. "I'd almost

forgotten. I just hope they don't do any damage, after all the work we put into the place!''

"I am certain they will not," Lasairian said. "They realize now that they would have to answer to you." He lay back beside her and together they looked up at the deep blue twilight sky. A few stars were just beginning to appear among the high wispy clouds.

It was a beautifully romantic setting, Shannon thought. Just the two of them out here alone beneath the twilight and the stars . . . her husband beside her, reaching for her hand. Though he was certainly very tired, as she was, perhaps he would forget his fatigue and turn to her and . . .

"Hungry?" he asked, still looking up at the sky.

Shannon grinned. Well, maybe some things did take precedence. "I believe I am, now that you mention it." She roused herself, groaning a little, and got to her feet. "Wait here—I'll see what I can find."

She took her copper cylinder and placed it for safekeeping in the first of the booley huts, and then searched for whatever food was at hand. In a few moments she had collected some rather stale oatbread, a small wooden dish of butter with a little honey mixed in, and some dry smoked fish.

It wasn't much, but as hungry as they both were, Shannon knew that even this would be a feast. She and Lasairian sat together on the grass, eating in peaceful solitude and watching the final moments of the sunset.

And then they heard it. A distant rumbling, low but growing closer, from somewhere just beyond the nearest hill.

Chapter Nineteen

The sound, like distant thunder, came not from the twilight sky but from the darkness of the valley down below. Shannon and Lasairian sat very still and looked at each other as the rumbling grew closer. "I thought you said the herd wouldn't be back until morning," said Shannon.

"Aed is quite resourceful. Perhaps he knew another way." Lasairian smiled. "He does enjoy keeping me from knowing all about him—he likes to keep a few secrets. And surely they are all anxious to get back, though I suppose we will have to either go back to the *crannog* tonight or else pass this evening in the company of several others."

"And a whole lot of cows," laughed Shannon. "Ah, well—so long as you are here, I am happy. I am happy wherever you are."

She smiled up at him, searching out his gaze. But suddenly he was looking far past her, as though she were not there.

He set aside his wooden plate. Slowly, eyes wide, he stood up, placing one hand on Shannon's shoulder as if to push her behind him.

"What is it? What's happened?" And then she saw it too, just as Lasairian pulled her inside one of the huts. Quickly they both peered out through the tiny window at the back.

Riding into the valley just beyond the hilltop, headed straight toward the booley camp, was a group of men on horseback. They galloped over the grass on their small but powerful horses, the swords at their belts bouncing carelessly as they rode.

At first, her only thought was of how very startling it was to see a group of strangers. She had grown so accustomed to the faces of Aed and Crevan and Tully and the rest of the herdboys that she'd all but forgotten what it was like to see someone else. Even the cows were more familiar than any outsiders.

"It's the Liath tribe," said Lasairian. "Led by Dowan. They couldn't find the cattle and now they've come full circle."

The men drew closer. There were perhaps twenty of them, rough and coarse and hard, as shaggy and unkempt as their horses. Their clothes were stained and worn and their faces grim and cold.

Shannon froze. She clutched Lasairian's arm. "What will they do when they get up here and find only two people all alone?"

He made no answer. She felt him go rigid, almost trembling. He started to move, slowly, unable to look away from the raiders, slowly pushing her out of the hut and back toward the trail to the *crannog*.

Then he stopped, and took a deep breath, and she felt a change come over him. He looked at her with calmness in his eyes and quiet confidence in his voice. "Shannon—go back to the *crannog*. Go now, before they get here, before they find us here alone. They'll be angry enough at not finding the herd."

"I can't leave you here!" She didn't know what she could do to defend her husband against a horde of armed barbarians, but she knew she had to try!

"You must go. You must!" His voice was low and urgent. "There is nothing you can do here. But if you go, you can warn the boys, and make sure they don't try to come back."

"But—"

"Do you want them to walk headlong into that?"

Shannon looked again at the rapidly approaching raiders. "All right," she said, her voice a dry whisper. "All right."

"Good. I'll be there just as—just as soon as this is over."

A cold fear engulfed her. As the rumbling of the hoofbeats grew louder, she found herself rooted to the spot. She reached for Lasairian but he had already gone striding ahead to stand at the very top of the hill, sword drawn, feet braced wide apart, his dark hair floating out behind him on the wind.

A great change had come over him. No longer was he the spoiled young prince, disdainful of hard work lest it break a fingernail. He had made the choice to leave his easy life behind. He had found the courage to take up the sword when it was demanded of him. Now he was a warrior, a fighter, a protector of his people, a defender of his own.

She knew that he felt fear, just as she did. But now she saw what courage really meant. Courage was what happened when you knew fear, but faced it down anyway.

She could not leave him. If he could face such a danger, she simply could not leave him. She would stay at his back even if she had to hide herself to do so. Quickly Shannon ducked back into the booley hut and stationed herself at the window.

The raiders swept up over the hill and dragged their snorting horses to a stop. The biggest of them stared at Lasairian for a moment, and then—much to Shannon's surprise—burst out laughing.

"Surely this is not Lasairian!" he shouted, and he and the rest of them practically roared with laughter. "But it is! It is Lasairian, the bard, now the defender of the cattle!"

"I am neither, Dowan," he said, still unmoving. "I am the defender of the people."

"People!" The huge black-haired man threw a leg over his horse's neck and slid to the ground. "I think you have been up here far too long! You can no longer tell cows from men—or women, either, I would bet!"

Lasairian simply stared him down as the men on horseback slapped each other and shouted out loud at Dowan's insult. "At least all of my cattle—and all of my men and women—are still alive."

Instantly the mood changed. A glowering silence fell over the crowd. "If any are dead, it is because the men of Abhainn Aille killed him," said Dowan. "And because one is dead, we are here to take our revenge for him."

"So, you have come all the way out here to take revenge upon yourself? Only a fool tries to avenge a death that he

237

himself is responsible for. Shall I step back out of the way while you fall upon your sword?''

Dowan fairly growled with anger. "I killed no one! The only man who died was killed by one of yours!"

"So he was—killed by men defending their own lives and property. Your man died a thief, led by a coward." Lasairian cocked his head as if to study Dowan. "Do you not care that every bard in Eire tells your story, and tells it true? That you are sung for a liar and a criminal at every encampment and great hall and hearthfire in the land?"

"I care nothing for bards! Weak and whining boys! Soft and spoiled princelings, just like you!"

"Well, then," said Lasairian with a shrug, "since you have no pride, no care for what anyone thinks of you, I suppose there is only one thing left for you to do."

"And what is that?" said Dowan, his hand on the sword at his belt.

"You will have to fight me."

A moment of cold silence, and then suddenly the raucous laughter came again. "That will be a very short fight, Lasairian! It will take us no time at all to kill you! We hoped you could provide us with more amusement than that!"

Shannon thought her heart would stop. He could not be serious! Even the most experienced, highly trained warrior could not hope to stand against Dowan and a dozen of his men. What was he thinking?

She went to the door of the hut and peered cautiously around the corner. She hoped that the falling night would conceal her, but even her faint shadow instantly grabbed the attention of the men.

A couple of them shouted and pointed. Lasairian glanced quickly over his shoulder to see where they were looking, and she saw his eyes widen with anger and fear. "Shannon! Go from here! Go *now!*"

After only the slightest hesitation, she went. She turned around and dashed into the woods, flying down the treacherous but now familiar path.

Even in her panic, it distressed her to think that Lasairian must surely think she was running away either out of fear or because he had ordered her to run—and she was most certainly not doing either one. She intended to get back to the *crannog* and bring back the herdboys. There was nothing she could do to help him alone, but with the rest of the boys he might have a fighting chance.

She forced herself to think not of Lasairian but of the ground beneath her feet. Never before had she raced down the hill like this; always she and Lasairian had taken their careful time, especially when—as now—night had begun to fall.

Deep beneath the trees, the world was lost in almost total darkness. She had to slow down, had to feel her way along the trees, had to pick her way down the damp and slippery path as best she could.

Shivering with tension, she paused at a steep and rocky drop to turn sideways and edge her way along—and behind her came the sound of footsteps.

For an instant she stopped in her tracks. Could it be Lasairian, escaped from the raiders and following hard on her heels? She wanted to cry out to him, but stopped. If it was Lasairian, he would surely have been calling to her. But all she heard was the crashing of brush and the heavy, determined tread of someone pushing his way down an unfamiliar trail—and not caring who heard.

Terror flashed through her. She leaped over the drop and set her feet to racing down the path. In her mind she called up a picture of the trail and forced herself to follow it, twisting, turning, dodging the big rock there, ducking under the hanging branch here. But though she hurried as fast as she dared, as fast as her trembling legs would carry her, the footsteps still closed in. The sounds, the crashing, the breaking of bush, grew louder and closer by the second.

She was nearly at the water's edge. She could hear the soft rushing sound of the falls, feel the faint spray on her face, smell the heavy dampness of the lake.

And there, glowing like a mystical forge out in the center of the water, was the *crannog*, the orange-red light of the campfire suffusing its wooden walls.

Now—the smooth slick clay at the very edge of the lake. The sloshing of the water itself as it lapped at the banks. Her heart pounded so loudly that she could scarcely hear anything else, but she forced herself to stop for an instant and listen.

Still there. Her pursuer still came, moving faster, growing closer.

Shannon drew a deep breath. There was nothing to do but run for it across the stones, across the dark and glistening water toward the great glowing cinder that was the *crannog*.

The first step. The first smooth and slippery stone. Ordinarily she would take her cautious, careful time and only try it in the bright light of day—but now she had to hurry in the dark, further dismayed to find that the firelight cast a glare across the dark water and concealed the stones even further.

Step quick, leap one, jump left—with every move she was sure she would slip and fall and find the cold waters closing over her head. But she kept on, pushing faster, stepping quicker, her feet skittering over the slippery stones, for now the footsteps behind her were splashing—he was following her, he was on the rocks and crossing the water—

"Open the gate! Covey! Open the gate!" She dared not look up—she could not see the stones, but still kept her eyes fixed on the black and glittering water. *"Open the gate!"*

After a heart-stopping moment of no response, she heard the sound of the heavy gate being dragged open. Gasping, she made one last desperate leap and threw herself across the ledge of the *crannog*, across the open doorway.

"Close it! Close—" Strong arms caught hold of her, and before she could finish her shouted order to the boys, there was a tremendous splash out in the darkness.

They lifted her through and pushed the gate shut. The footsteps came no more.

"Where is he? Where is he?"

Shannon pushed herself up off the dirt floor and scrambled to her feet. "He's out there somewhere! He was right behind me! Did he fall? Where is he now?"

Together they stood in the open doorway and peered out into the darkness. One of the herdboys raised a torch. And out there, just a few yards from the *crannog*, the body of Dowan lay on its back, half-submerged, across one of the stepping stones. On his forehead was a great gash, dark and wet in the flickering light of the torch.

"You were brave to do that," said Covey. "You knew he would try to follow, even in the dark."

Shannon leaned against the gate. "I did nothing," she whispered, staring into the darkness. Then her grip tightened on the rough wood. "But I'm going to do something now. We all are."

They turned to look at her, and all began talking at once.

"What do you mean?"

"What can we do? We are just herdboys!"

"Dowan is dead. You killed him! The others will leave, I'm sure, now that their leader is gone!"

"All we have to do is wait for Lasairian to come back!"

"We are safe, thanks to you!"

"I caught some fish earlier today. Come on, I'll build up the fire and start them cooking!"

They began to move toward the flickering warmth of the campfire, the tension broken, grinning and even laughing in relief.

Shannon grabbed Covey by the arm and turned him around hard. "What do you mean? Lasairian is still up there, up there alone with Dowan's men! We're not going to leave him!"

All of them stopped and stared at her. "Think about this!" she cried. "How long do you think it will be before those men come down here looking for their leader?"

Covey blinked at her. His expression was one of confusion, but she heard the slight shake in his voice. "There is nothing we can do to help Lasairian," he whispered, "We are only cowherds. What could—"

"What could I do, Covey? I am not even so much as a cowherd, and there lies Dowan, dead! I tell you, we will not sit here and have a nice supper while Lasairian faces those killers alone! I am going—and if you will not go with me, just remember one thing. You will have to face *me* when I come *back!*"

They all stood very still. No one said a word. Finally a few of them glanced at one another, and they all looked sideways at Shannon.

"We will go with you," said Covey. "If you are not afraid—then we are not afraid either."

She looked at Covey with a wry smile. "I didn't say I wasn't afraid. I just said I was going."

Two of the herdboys remained behind, to close the gate and guard the fire. The rest of them stepped cautiously out onto the stones in the lake. The first two boys dislodged Dowan's body from the rock where it lay and pulled the body through the water until they reached the shore. The others followed with Shannon at the rear.

She picked her way across the stones once more, able to use caution this time. Yet in some ways this trip was even more terrifying than the one only a few moments ago, running for her life with Dowan coming closer by the second. At that time it had only been her own life at stake. Now it was Lasairian's, and nothing had ever frightened her so much as the thought of what she might find at the top of that hill.

As quietly as they could—as quietly as any group of people could while hauling a dead man on their shoulders—Shannon and her group of herdboys made their way up the hill. The sounds of strangers, of invaders, the raucous drunken shouting of a large group of men, reached her first. And then she saw them.

They'd built a campfire and were grouped around it, some sitting, some standing, all laughing; but two of them had their swords drawn and pointed at the tall, proud man who was held in the firm grip of two more.

She could see his face clearly by the light of the fire. Lasairian stood his ground, refusing to step back as the men goaded him with the points of their swords and shouted at him in an effort to get some kind of fight out of him. But he would say nothing, only gazing at them with a cold, still expression as though feeling himself to be far above the drunken louts who had nothing better to do than toy with him.

"We want you to tell us where the cattle are, and we don't care if you sing it or spit it! We've come to take them and take them we will!"

Lasairian only shook his head. "Again, I will tell you nothing. You may certainly kill me if you wish; I cannot stop you, and there is no one else to stop you either. But then you would be known far and wide as the ones who murdered the nephew of King Irial. Are you sure it is worth it to you?"

The first man actually grinned, a slow and malicious expression. "Perhaps it is worth it," he said. "The stories do travel, as you say. And we know that your king is not so fond of you right now, is he, Lasairian the cowherd?"

"It's too bad we can't just kill you now!" the other man raged, furious and frustrated at Lasairian's lack of response. "But Dowan wants you as a hostage! You'll have more to say when he gets back!"

At that moment, Lasairian looked toward the forest. His eyes widened and his lips parted as though he were about to speak—but he kept silent.

Finally, his tormentors noticed that something else had caught his attention. They, too, turned around to look, and grinned at each other. "Dowan! We've been waiting for you!" they cried. "And so has your hostage!"

The man who had held Lasairian at swordpoint went striding toward the forest, followed by a few of the others. He kept on calling out to Dowan, whom he saw standing at the edge of the woods.

"We've been saving your prize for you! Though I'm surprised you've finished with the other one so quickly.

Have you brought her back with you, perhaps? Now, *that* would be—''

He stopped in his tracks as Dowan fell forward with a heavy crash and lay unmoving, facedown in the long grass.

For a long, stunned moment, the whole group stood still, blinking, as they slowly began to realize what had happened.

Shannon stepped out from the darkness of the woods and stood beside the body. Behind her came the silent herdboys.

''Drowned,'' she said, dismissing Dowan with a wave of her hand. ''He tried to follow me. The water claimed him.''

The Liath man took a step toward her, but she could see the hesitation in it. ''You've killed him! How could you have done this?'' He raised his sword and shook it at her. ''Where are your warriors? Why are they hiding behind you? Send them out! Give us men to face, not women and boys!''

''There are no warriors.'' Shannon walked slowly toward him, amazed at her own calm, but well aware that at this point she had nothing to lose. She had to do this thing if she was to help Lasairian, and was far more frightened by the thought of him being dragged away by these men. ''You have only us to face.''

She continued to stare coldly at the invader, her courage buoyed by the sight of his widening eyes and uncertain stance. ''We have come to return what is left of Dowan to you. The Mistress of the Waters took his life for herself.''

This time the man steeled himself, putting away his sword and striding forward to the place where Dowan lay. Quickly Shannon moved to block him.

''A trade,'' she said, staring directly into his uncertain eyes. ''Leave Lasairian for us and you may have Dowan.'' When he did not respond, she looked past him to the men

245

who still held Lasairian. "Or do you wish to follow us back? The Mistress may not be sated. She may yet welcome any number of you."

He stared back at her, fear and anger both showing on his face. Then he glanced back at his men and waved at them to bring Lasairian forward.

Bring him they did, and gave him a great shove intended to send him sprawling at Shannon's feet. But he kept his balance and caught himself, slowly straightening up and adding his own cold stare to Shannon's as he gave his captors a last hard look.

"The Mistress of the Waters does indeed reside in this place," Lasairian said. "Are you sure you are welcome here?"

Without a word, two of the men lifted the body of Dowan by the arms and dragged it away. In a moment they were all on their horses and galloping back into the darkness.

Chapter Twenty

Instantly Shannon turned to Lasairian and caught him by the shoulders. "You're all right?" she said, looking him up and down. "They didn't hurt you?"

"They did not. But what about you? What happened down there? What happened to Dowan?"

She closed her eyes. Now that the danger had passed, she began trembling. "He tried to follow me across the stones. But he never had you nagging at him to practice them each morning. He fell in straightaway." She shook her head. "Why would he try to follow me over the stones? It's hard enough for us to do."

Lasairian shrugged. "He probably thought it was a land bridge beneath shallow water. The fool didn't realize what his enemies had."

"Deep water and slippery stones . . . now I understand." She reached for his hand, not caring if he felt her shaking.

"Will they come back, do you think?" she whispered. "Should we all stay at the *crannog*, at least for a while? They could come back any time, there could be more of them—"

He placed a gentle hand on her head and began to stroke her hair. "They will not come back. Not for a few seasons, at least. Sword and battle they can understand, but not this—not the strange and mysterious ways of the Mistress of the Waters. It will take them some time to forget their fear. We will be safe, at least for the rest of the season."

"I killed him," she whispered.

"He killed himself. He should never have followed you, should never have been here at all. It was his choice. And I will tell you, he should count himself fortunate that he merely slipped into the cool embrace of the water. He is lucky that his men grabbed me. If I had gotten hold of him, he would have begged for such a death."

"That may be true, but even so—a man is dead because of me. I never thought to kill anyone. Now I have, and even though he did deserve it—it's a terrible thing to think about."

"Shannon Rose, because of your courage, there may yet be peace for Abhainn Aille, and the herdboys may sleep at bit more quietly at night." He reached for her hand, and by the light of the fire she could see his serious face. "Come with me. There is something you should hear."

He led her back to the camp, a little ways from the fire where the boys talked and boasted, to a place in the soft grass where they could sit in the quiet darkness outside the stone huts. "Last season, before you came here, Dowan led his foolish, vicious men on another cattle raid. Their hope was to provoke an all-out battle by taking someone else's herd. He chose to steal Abhainn Aille's cattle, and steal them he did.

"But there was a price. A man of his own tribe was killed and a woman left a widow, a widow filled with sorrow and bitterness and hatred for every man who ever lifted a sword. She—was forced to marry a man from Abhainn Aille, since no one else in her own tribe would have her, and it was hoped that such a marriage would bring peace between the two tribes. But it did not.

"His success at taking the cows, and his rage at the loss of one of his best men, led Dowan to believe he had a right to continue taking Abhainn Aille's cattle and to avenge the death of his man any way he could. That is why they came here. Long years of raids and endless battles for revenge might have followed, but your courage has stopped all of that. Now, at last, it can be ended."

"Ended." Shannon looked up at him. "And this woman at Abhainn Aille? Did it end for her? Did she find peace at last?"

He was silent and still, and looked off into the darkness for a time. "I cannot say. But she remains at Abhainn Aille, and I can assure you that she is well cared for. Sometimes . . . sometimes that is all that can be done."

Before she could say anything else, Lasairian drew her close. What a great solace it was to close her eyes and rest her head on his chest and let him comfort her. "You did not have to come back for me," he said. "I only wanted you to get away and stay safely at the *crannog*. I never meant for you to come back here."

She drew back, and looked up into his eyes. "You took up the sword," she said, "and in my own way, I could do no less."

"But you risked your life! You should never have come

back! I can tell you, Shannon Rose, that we have many bold and brave women at Abhainn Aille, and throughout the land—but I did not know any woman would have such courage."

She smiled, and then laid her head against his broad chest once again. "You needed me," she said softly. "You needed me."

The days and nights drifted past, flowing one into the other, and ever so gradually the seasons began their timeless change. The evening had a definite chill to it now and the coolness was not just from the water. The air was growing colder, the days becoming shorter. Even Shannon had to admit that now, at long last, the summer was ending.

And with the turn of the year came a growing sense of urgency. Shannon began to feel an increasing need to finish all the preparations for the journey back to Abhainn Aille, to tie up any loose ends before she and Lasairian had to leave this place for what might be the final time.

At first Shannon concentrated on the small things which nagged at her. The white calfskin must be tanned and finished and prepared for her to use. She must take the time to learn to work with crude charcoal pieces, the only writing tools available to her, in order to draw the notes of the music on the skin. But once these things were done, and the calfskin was carefully rolled up and placed inside the copper cylinder for safekeeping, the sense of pressing need and unfinished business still remained.

At last she had to admit to herself that her worry was caused not by a few small tasks, but by one large piece of uncertainty: She and Lasairian had still not arrived at a definite answer as to exactly what their future would be.

Oh, he had no end of lovely words and flowery speeches

about how beautiful and perfect their life together would be—but she had begun to realize that never did he mention specifics. She had no idea where they would live or what either of them would be doing after the cattle were returned to Abhainn Aille.

But perhaps she was expecting too much. In this place and time, life was lived as it came, and definite long-term plans could not always be made. Surely she had learned that much during the months that she had spent here! It was not Lasairian's fault that she was having difficulty adjusting to a very strange and totally different world.

Yet one morning, as she arranged the bed of rushes in their house so that it would be ready and waiting when they returned that evening, she found a small and shining object which had been dropped and forgotten some time before.

Her emerald ring.

For an endless moment, she gazed at it. She remembered why she had worn it all that time, remembered why she had, at last, slipped it from her finger and let it fall.

There was no longer any reason to keep this ring. She ought to take it outside, open the gate of the *crannog*, and drop it into the lake. There was no need to worry anymore that any man would ever deceive her, no need to fear that she might once again be taken in by a man whose love was false.

She stood up and started for the door of the house. But there in the corner, gleaming even in the dimness, was the copper cylinder she had found beneath the waterfall.

Shannon took one more step toward the door—and then, in a swift move, she picked up the cylinder, pulled off the disk at one end, and dropped the ring inside with the calf-skin. After resealing the cylinder and placing it back in the

251

corner, she left the little house and vowed never to think about the emerald ring ever again.

On a cool damp morning a few days later, Shannon sat near the front of their little boat with fresh new rushes heaped up all around her. She was happy to have the insulating warmth they provided, for she could not remember a day in this place with the chill that this one held. Lasairian knelt behind her, slowly poling the boat as it headed upstream back to the *crannog*.

All around them were the signs of autumn. The leaves were fading to pale green and yellow, falling in a slow rain onto the water and lining the banks in thick mounds. Acorns fell among them, too, and hazelnuts, and occasionally a bold little animal could be seen gathering the bounty: a quick-moving otter, a thickly furred mouse, a nervous hare. Shannon had herself spent many days at the booley camp gathering sackfuls of hazelnuts, blackberries, and wild green apples, along with small plum-like fruits from the blackthorn trees.

"It won't be long now, will it?" she said.

He did not reply at first. Shannon continued gazing at the leaves drifting on the river, searching idly for the bright and darting dragonflies . . . and then realized that it was now too late in the year for them.

Lasairian carefully guided the boat over to yet another stand of tall green rushes, which stood rustling in the cool breeze. But he made no move to cut them; instead, he sat down close behind Shannon, and drew her back to lean against him.

"You are right, it will not be long now before we go home," he said quietly. "The moon was full last night.

The day before it reaches full again, we will take the herd back to Abhainn Aille.''

"One month," she said. "Only one month more. And it will pass by quickly." She glanced up over her shoulder, but all she could see was the towering canopy of brown and yellow and pale green leaves. "Lasairian—I have to know. I have to know what we will do when we return. Will your father—and the king, too, I suppose—let you go back to your old life? Or will they insist that you stay with the cows?"

His broad chest lifted as he sighed. "Nature prepares for winter with no doubts as to what she should do. She looks forward to yet another year. It is not so simple for the rest of us.

"I cannot say what my father, or the king, might require me to do. But I must admit—if I am made to stay with the cattle and the farmers, it may not be such a bad thing after all. I find that I am really quite attracted to the quiet, simple life of the herdsman. Think of the gentle cows, so easily led; the friendly neighbors who come round to visit; the warmth and comfort of the accommodations. Now tell me, dear Shannon, who would not long for such a life?"

She grinned, and leaned her head back against his shoulder. "Is that all you find attractive about this place? Wild cows, criminal men, and leaky roofs?"

"Why, of course not! The real attraction is the serving women who are sometimes found traveling along with the herds. They are so sweet, so docile, so easily—*ohh*!"

An elbow in the ribs stopped him. Shannon started to twist around in an effort to see him, but then squealed and quickly grabbed the sides of the boat as it began to rock. Lasairian pulled her close and held her tight until the rocking subsided and the boat rested once again among the rushes.

"I never want it to end," she whispered, clinging to his hands as he continued to hold her. "Never, never. . . ."

Gently his head rested against her shoulder. "We will make certain that it will not end," he said. "We will be back at home soon."

"But—where is home? Where can we be together? If you are ordered to go on serving the king as a cowherd, does that mean we can live together only in the summer? Would I have to live apart from you at Abhainn Aille all the rest of the time?"

"I've thought about it for some time now," he said, "and I believe I have found a way."

She sat up and twisted around as much as she dared. "How?"

"Do you know what a *rath* is? Ah. A *rath* is like a *crannog*, only on land," he explained, seeing her puzzled expression. "There are many small *raths* scattered about the winter fields. The farmers and herdsmen live in them when they are not at the hilltop pastures. If you are willing, Shannon, we can live in one of the *raths*. I will build one for you myself, if need be, and it will be the finest *rath* in the kingdom. You would be safe there no matter where I was."

She smiled faintly. "It is a possibility," she said, "as long as you are there to share it with me."

"I would be there at least part of the time," he said, "though of course I would be expected to stay with the herds, and keep them close, much as I do now. And I would have to go away to Abhainn Aille from time to time, to see my family and inquire as to whether they need anything of me."

"Oh," she breathed, with a sigh of relief, "that would make life on the *rath* a bit easier, if I knew that we would be visiting Abhainn Aille from time to time. Such a beautiful place! I look forward to seeing it again."

After the briefest hesitation, Lasairian responded, "Of course!" he said brightly. "Of course, you could go with me to Abhainn Aille to visit."

"Lasairian—" Shannon glanced back at him, and hesitated. "If there is no *rath* where we could live—or if you have to be away for days at a time—I am not sure I could stay alone at such a place. Could I wait for you at Abhainn Aille, instead of living alone on an isolated little farm?

He stared at her for several heartbeats. "Shannon Rose, even if I am to stay with the herders and watch the cattle in their winter fields, you would not have to stay alone. Of course you can be a guest of my family. You could go back to Abhainn Aille, and stay in a fine house, and be warm and safe when the gales of winter arrive."

She shook her head as doubt continued to assail her. "I would love to stay there—but are you sure I would be welcome? How could I stay at Abhainn Aille, if you are not there?" Shannon well remembered the strangeness of the people there—the wild and terrifying ritual of Beltane— the king approaching her in the moonlight.

But Lasairian only smiled. "You will be most welcome there. I can assure you of that. They are my family, and now you are my family, too. You are a part of them and you belong there just as much as any of them."

"I belong with you," she said firmly.

His arms tightened around her. "You do," he said. "You do. We belong together, now and always."

She sighed. "But I must tell you . . . I am surprised that you would be willing to stay in the hills and just be a cowherd for the rest of your life. How could you—a prince, a bard, a man who so loves the music of the harp—how could you be content to do that?''

''Ah, Shannon, Shannon . . . let me explain something to you. In many ways, I am not the same man I was at the beginning of the season.''

She had to smile. ''So, you believe your father was right to send you out here?''

''Well, I would never say such a thing directly to him.'' She could hear the laughter in his voice. ''But I have learned any number of things while following the cattle.

''I watched Aed, a simple and uneducated man—he knows no poems, can play no music. Yet he has the greatest knowledge and wisdom when it comes to his own profession of caring for the cattle. I watched the herdboys who, young as they are, know the importance of what they do. I learned something of what the fighting man must face, of how he must train day after day, year after year, for the one moment when his training may be needed to save his life—or someone else's.

''The herdsmen and the warrior share one thing: They have respect for their professions, no matter how great or how humble. And I will tell you this, Shannon Rose, though I may never say it aloud to any other: I too have learned that my profession is worthy of respect.''

Her heart lifted. ''Then—you will play again? Even if it's only for the cows?''

''Even if it's only for the cows.'' He pressed his cheek against hers. ''But in my heart, it will be you that I am playing for, wherever you are, with me or not, always and forever.''

Chapter Twenty-one

And then the final day came, lovely as all the others had been; and then the day was over. The sun faded away and in its place rose the great yellow moon, just one night away from being full.

Shannon knelt beside the familiar flickering light of the central campfire. From it she lit her lamp, made from a small stone with a shallow curve in it like a bowl, and carried it into the house.

Lasairian was already there, packing up the last of their belongings. As she watched, he wrapped the gold-trimmed harp in a sheet of linen and then began tying it up within its leather case. "Oh," she said, as the harp disappeared beneath the leather. "I hope that will not be hidden away for long. I would miss it terribly."

"Not for long. Only for the journey back."

"But after that? We still don't know if you will be out

in the fields with the herdboys, or if I will be with you there, or at Abhainn Aille, or what we will do. . . ."

He took her in his arms. "It is true, I will almost certainly remain with the herds for a time, while you stay safe and warm at a fine *rath*. But it will not be for long. I promise you, Shannon Rose, that just as soon as we can, we will stay together at Abhainn Aille. And I also promise that until that time, every night, as the moon rises, I will play my harp for you; and as you watch the moon come up, you will hear the music and know that it is for you."

She leaned her forehead against his shoulder, and sighed. "I used to think my life was uncertain back in the old world—until I came here. Now it's more uncertain than ever."

"It is uncertain, at present, but not for long. Only across the winter will things remain unsorted. Then, in the spring, all will be settled and decided. My debts of service will be paid, and my father content, and the king satisfied, and Shannon Rose will have found her place at Abhainn Aille, just as she found it here."

She looked up, staring at the tiny open flame of the lamp. "We have another choice, you know."

"Another choice?"

Her voice was barely a whisper. "We could go back. Back through the door when it opens at Beltane. Back to my world."

He became very still. "Back . . . to your world?" He drew back, and placed his hands on her shoulders. "Do you remember your world, now? Are you saying—saying that now you remember where you are from?"

She shook her head. "There's nothing to remember. Like I told you before, I'm not an amnesia victim.

"You were right. You had the answer the first time you

spoke to me. My world would, here, be called the Otherworld—the place where spirits from other times dwell. I simply know it as the future.''

"The Otherworld," he whispered. "I did believe you were from that place. I still do." He let go of her shoulders, and sat down on the smooth cowhide which lay on the rushes and served as their bed. "You are proposing that I go with you to—to the Otherworld."

"I am proposing that we both go there together."

His gaze locked with hers, and she could see that for once he was completely, entirely serious. "Go back—with you?"

She reached for his hand and sat down close beside him. "With me. Together. We could return to my world together."

"Do you know this thing, Shannon?" She could hear the awe in his whispered question, hear something almost like fear in his voice. "Do you know that you can walk through the door again?"

She shrugged. "Of course I don't. All I know about the door is that it exists and I found my way through it once. And I believe—somehow, I am certain—that I can find my way through it again."

"When the year ends, and the circle becomes complete, the door must swing back the other way before it closes forever."

"That's it! That's exactly how it seems to me!"

"You seem so certain. But have you thought of where you might emerge, if you do step through again?"

She stared up at him. "Why—back home, of course, at the place where I left—"

He shook his head. "It is not so simple as that. You can

be sure of only one thing: You can be sure of nothing at all, when it comes to the Otherworld.''

Shannon smiled. ''I am sure that the Otherworld gave to me that which I wanted and needed, above all else, even though I did not know it at the time.''

He smiled back at her, and relaxed ever so slightly. ''It gave a gift to me too, Shannon Rose, a gift greater than you will ever know.''

''Then come with me! I can't go back without you! I can't, I can't—''

He pulled her close, and for a moment she hid her face against his shoulder, shaking, trembling, fighting for control. Finally she raised her head, and he placed a gentle hand on her cheek.

''I do believe that the door will be waiting for you next Beltane Eve,'' he whispered. ''You may be able to take that step, that unknown step into the Otherworld, but I cannot take it with you. We have no way to know where it would take us! We could be lost forever in a world of twilight and shadows. How can we risk the life we have now, here, together, on such a terrible uncertainty?''

She looked up at him, and tried to speak, but he reached for her hands and went on. ''Ah, Shannon . . . we have been so happy here. We can be happy for many years longer still. We have a life here. You will always be a part of my life, the best part, the greatest part! We will always be together here and I will always take care of you.

''Think of it,'' he said, almost pleading now when she made no response. ''Think of the long years which wait for us here, think of the beautiful house we will have on Abhainn Aille, think of the children we will someday have together. You found the courage to leave your old life behind so that you could come to me . . . and now we have each other to love. Why should we risk all that on the wild uncertainty, the terrible danger of the Otherworld?''

She could only gaze at him, and open her mouth to speak, and search for words, and then shake her head slightly when she could find none.

He pressed her hand hard. ''You will not leave me, will you, Shannon?''

Again, his words, and the soft glow in his dark eyes, and the sweet warm closeness of him, did their work. As the flame in the tiny lamp flickered and went out, she leaned her head against his shoulder and sighed.

''How could I ever think of leaving you?''

For what Shannon well knew could be the last time, she and Lasairian left their *crannog*. This odd little place, alone on the river in the forest, had become home to her in a way she'd never imagined that even a modern home, with all the conveniences and luxuries her world had to offer, could be. But now she had little choice but to gather the last of her belongings, step down into the boat, and tie the gate behind her as securely as she could.

The boat remained on the shore, resting in the same spot as it had when Shannon first saw it. In silence, she followed Lasairian up the familiar climb to the booley camp, hardly needing to catch her breath even with the pack she carried.

Silence hung over the camp. She was almost startled to look up and see Aed and the herdboys in front of the huts, their belongings packed and ready. Even the cows were quiet and subdued. They were gathered close together on the hilltop, standing and watching the booley camp, their ears flicking back and forth. Not one of them was grazing or lying down as they ordinarily would.

In the cool damp light of the autumn dawn, she found

herself admiring the cows, who did indeed have their own kind of beauty. Great strong creatures they were, with glossy red-and-white coats and large, round, glittering brown eyes. They were placid and motherly one moment, fiercely protective the next. The calves all looked strong and healthy. All of them had survived, all save the one lost over the edge of the cliff . . . the one whose white-coated hide had provided Shannon with the fine leather she'd used to write the notes of the song.

None of the people spoke a word. They were a strangely somber group; somehow Shannon had thought they would all be celebrating their return to Abhainn Aille, their return to family and friends and warm comfortable houses. She'd expected to find them hardly able to contain their excitement. But the boys stood in silence and Aed met no one's eyes. Even the cows made no move at all, as though the last thing they wanted was to leave this spot.

Then Aed walked over to the lead cow, the one who had lost her calf. To Shannon's surprise, the normally wary old cow stood and watched him approach. Aed placed his hand on her head, between her short upcurving horns, horns in the shape of the crescent moon, and held it there for a long moment. At last he withdrew and turned away from the herd, and started down the path which led to Abhainn Aille. The old cow started off behind him, and slowly the herd began to follow, surrounded at the sides and back by the somber herdboys.

At the last, following in a silence of their own, walked Shannon and Lasairian, back to Abhainn Aille and into a river of uncertainty.

They kept to a steady pace, not hurrying, but not dawdling either, and so it was that the afternoon sun still lingered as cows and calves came down the last valley and approached the expansive lake, which lay glittering in the late-day sun.

Tired as she was after the long trek, Shannon's spirits lifted at the sight of Abhainn Aille. She paused at the top of the hill, beside the lone hawthorn tree, to drink in the sight of it. How strange it seemed, how open and big, and how large and luxurious the houses! She'd grown so used to seeing the tiny booley huts, and living in a house that was not much bigger on the *crannog*.

Would it be so bad if this beautiful island was to be her future? It was Lasairian's home. It could be her home too. And though she had learned that she could be happy no matter where she was, so long as she was with Lasairian, she could not deny that Abhainn Aille also held a special place in her heart.

Down below them the herd approached the edge of the lake, walking eagerly toward it to drink. But as Shannon started to follow them, heading for the path which led to the boats, Lasairian placed his hand on her arm and stopped her. "Will you leave without saying goodbye, Shannon?"

"Leave? What do you mean?"

"Why . . . as I said, I am all but sure that I will have to stay with the cattle, out at the *rath*. But I must wait for my father and the king to tell me what I must do. They will be here soon, as soon as they realize that we have arrived, and I must wait here for them.

"But you, dear Shannon," he continued, before she could speak, "can stay here, in my house, with servants to care for you, and find something of the rest and comfort which you have earned tenfold."

"But—"

"Ah, now, let me kiss you, and then I will let you go on to the rest you must be longing for. See, the boats are there, you can easily take one across the water. I must be going, the herdboys are moving the cattle out again, and I cannot be left behind—''

She glanced over her shoulder and saw that the herdboys were, indeed, moving the cows and calves down the plain toward the forest. No doubt they were going toward the small winter fields which, she recalled, were not far from Abhainn Aille.

And then her attention was caught by the herdboys who followed them. They were all carrying long heavy tools over their shoulders—tools which glinted in the setting sun—axes.

They were carrying axes.

It was a shock to see them. And a greater shock to realize why the boys carried them as they followed the red-and-white herd. But surely she must have realized what the cows were being raised for—she must have known that they couldn't all be kept through the winter, that the oldest of them would never survive the long cold months. And most of all she remembered the quiet on the hilltop before they had left this morning, and how Aed had rested his hand between the horns of the oldest cow.

''I must go with them, Shannon. Come! Kiss me quickly, and then I will go—and we will be together once again, soon, soon—''

He pulled her close, and kissed her, and then to Shannon's complete astonishment, he turned his back and walked away, as casually as if he were simply going off for the afternoon and would be home for supper that evening.

Then, from behind her, came striding footsteps and a deep voice. ''Lasairian.''

He stopped. Shannon turned around and there, walking

up the hill, came Irial, the king, and Fergus, Lasairian's father.

They all stood in silence, studying each other, and Shannon could scarcely breathe. Finally Fergus spoke. "You are all looking well," he said, in his low, gruff voice. "No injuries? No illness? Good. Very good. Then come home now. Your family is waiting for you."

Shannon's eyes flicked to Lasairian. Family? She frowned, puzzled. She'd thought Lasairian had told her that he had only his father, that his mother was dead and he had no siblings. Well, no doubt he had cousins and such at Abhainn Aille, or maybe Fergus was just referring to the whole place as Lasairian's family. That must have been what he meant.

"Ah . . . ah, father, I thank you, but I am needed out with the herds, at least for a time." He paused, and straightened, and looked his father in the eye, but Shannon could see that he was nervous about something—nervous, uncomfortable, and very plainly wishing mightily that he was anywhere but here.

"They need me," he went on, after clearing his throat, "and I will not leave them now. I am well used to caring for them, and I—"

The king cut him off. "Your days with the herd are done. Come home. Now." He glanced at Shannon, and then back at Lasairian. "Your wife has need of you there."

A great relief washed over Shannon at his words, and a feeling of happiness. The king had acknowledged her at last, recognized her as Lasairian's wife. It would go a long way toward easing her acceptance into the community at Abhainn Aille.

"But—"

"Now, Lasairian."

Lasairian glanced at Shannon, and then back at the king. He gave a quick nod, and Shannon did not know which astonished her more—Lasairian's seeming reluctance to return to Abhainn Aille, or his complete silence on the matter. It was quite a rare thing to see him at a loss for words.

The three men turned and started down the hill, back to the place where two of the small boats waited. Shannon hurried after them, strangely disconcerted; it occurred to her that now she understood the meaning of the phrase, *not knowing what to think.*

She was happy to be accepted by the king, happy to know that she might truly have a home at Abhainn Aille with Lasairian; but she simply could not understand why he was behaving so strangely.

Why did he seem so anxious to leave her here alone? How could he let her go to Abhainn Aille by herself, alone among strangers who had little reason to welcome her, who saw her only as a curiosity at best?

Her initial relief was giving way to confusion, and with each step she took, the feeling grew, until it became anger.

By the time she stepped into the boat that would take them to the island, she was fairly boiling. She wanted nothing more than to ask Lasairian just what, exactly, was going on here. But now was not the time; not here, not now, with the king and the man who was now her father-in-law sitting right in front of them.

But just you wait, Lasairian, oh, just you wait until I get you home!

Chapter Twenty-two

They walked through the little cluster of houses toward the home Shannon knew to be Lasairian's. A number of people had come out to stare at her, but then quickly moved out of the way and ducked behind buildings and trees before peering out at her again. One or two actually hurried inside their houses and shut the doors and windows tight.

Shannon had expected the stares and long looks, but not the hiding. It was terribly confusing, but there was no time to puzzle it out now. She turned to Lasairian, hoping to find some reassurance from him as they walked; but as she did, she noticed that even Fergus and the king had paused beside one of the trees. It was clear that they were going no farther. She and Lasairian were left alone to make their way to his house, which now seemed disturbingly isolated beneath the single large overhanging pine tree.

Shannon felt increasingly frightened and confused at

everyone's strange behavior, but kept on heading toward the house. If nothing else, she wanted to get safely inside and away from all of these prying, staring eyes!

She reached for Lasairian's hand, only to find that he too was holding back, apparently unwilling to approach his own house. She could still see the people peering out from behind the houses and trees, could still feel their eyes upon her.

"What is going on here?" she asked, turning to him, both confused and angry now. "Why is everyone staring at me like this? Why are they hiding? And what—*what* is wrong with your house?"

He could only stand and look at her—and then his glance flicked to something behind her, something in the direction of the house. His eyes widened for a moment, and he looked as if he were about to speak; but though she could see the genuine pain in his expression, he only turned and walked away, back to where his father stood with the king.

Shannon turned away from him. It was either that or shout him down. And when she turned, she nearly forgot her anger, for in the door of Lasairian's home there now stood a woman.

A woman she had seen before.

Slowly the memory came back to her. This was the same cold, silent woman who had been in Lasairian's house on the day Shannon had come to Abhainn Aille—she had been in the house along with another, older woman, the talkative older woman who Shannon at first had thought was Lasairian's mother. Later she had taken them both for servants.

Now she could only stand and stare at the tall and silent woman, who held a very young baby to her shoulder, a woman who stood so calmly and naturally in the doorway of Lasairian's house that one would think she—

"I am offering you a welcome here." The voice was low, the words cordial, but the tone was formal and remote. "I am willing to share this house, this hearth, this man with you. Do you accept?"

The words echoed through Shannon's mind, and she felt as if the world was moving in slow motion. The woman in the doorway had sounded as though she were reciting, not merely speaking. It was a ritual of some sort, and as she continued to stand in the doorway with her baby, it seemed that she was awaiting Shannon's answer.

Over and over the words echoed:

I will share
this house
this hearth
this man
with you.

She closed her eyes. *This man . . . This man . . .*

Shannon felt dizzy. She thought she might actually fall. But when she looked again, she saw the older woman— the other one's mother—quickly take the baby from the younger woman's arms and hurry out of the house toward the trees.

Now Shannon understood why everyone was so tense— why they were hiding, waiting—not frightened, just curious and eager. They expected a confrontation, a catfight.

"You're his wife," Shannon whispered.

The woman frowned, giving Shannon a hard look, and then started once more into her litany. "I will share this house, this hearth, this—"

"Wife!" Shannon felt cold shock descending over her. "You're his wife—his wife—his—"

She could not stay in this place, in this dreadful situation, for one moment longer. Shannon turned and ran away, as quickly as her cold and trembling legs would carry her, past the people who stared from their hiding places, past the king, past Fergus, and most of all, far past Lasairian, as far from him as she could possibly get.

But in only a moment she had gone beyond the houses, and stood at the water's edge. One could not run far on Abhainn Aille.

She had gone to the head of the island, where the rushing waters joined together once more after dividing to race around the island. She could go no farther—but neither could she go back. She could only stand and watch as the waters raced away, feeling as though all the life and love and magic she thought she had found in this place were racing away with them, leaving her alone and deserted on this tiny point of land.

"Shannon."

She would not look at him. She continued to stand and stare at the rushing waters.

"Ah, Shannon . . . there is so much you do not know."

Her fists clenched. The cold shock that had descended over her settled within and closed over her heart. "What more do you have to tell me? What else is there that I do not know? What else have you kept from me, lied to me about? Is your name really Lasairian? Are you really a bard? Does the rain fall down or up, is the river wet or dry?"

She almost laughed. "You are right. I know nothing anymore. Everything I believed has turned out to be a lie. I believed in you, I trusted you, I loved you with all my heart—but you were nothing but a fantasy I pinned my hopes and wildest dreams on."

Shannon turned to look at him, at his white face, his

haunted eyes. "How laughable this must be to you! What a great, wonderful joke you've managed to play on a stranger! How many nights will you spend at the fire regaling your listeners with the tale of the foolish, deluded little woman who believed herself to be your wife? Who believed that you loved her beyond all others! Oh, I do congratulate you—the bard who has created his own real-life comedy to entertain his listeners for years to come!"

She was too angry to cry, too filled with pain to do anything more than stare him down and wait, with something like cold curiosity, to see what would happen next. Would he offer the usual apology? *Oh, darling, you have it all wrong! I can explain why I already have a wife. I'm sure you'll understand.*

He shook his head, and his voice was a whisper. "I have done nothing of the kind."

"Oh! I see. Then I must have been mistaken about that woman—that woman with the baby—who stood in the doorway of your home and politely offered to share you with me. Are you going to tell me she's the Avon lady? And that the baby is not yours?"

"The baby is not mine." He took another step toward her. "Whatever else you believe, you can know this: The baby is not mine."

She shrugged. "Not that it really matters now, anyway." She turned her coldest glare on him. "I only have one question for you, Lasairian: Why did you not tell me you were married?"

He tried to meet her gaze, tried to speak, but faltered, and looked away. "You did not want me to tell you. And I would not cause you pain if I—if I could avoid it."

She stared at him, incredulous. "Cause me . . . pain? Pain? What do you think you're causing me now? And how

271

can you stand there and tell me that I did not want to know?"

He continued to look down, watching the whitecapped waters rush away. "You were so happy. You were content to be my wife of the Beltane fires. I felt that—I believed that there would be time enough for you to find your place in my family when we returned to Abhainn Aille, whatever place you wished, however you—"

"Wait," she said. "You said—*wife of the fires*? Of the Beltane fires?" She turned to him, and her voice began to rise. "What does that mean? What does that *really* mean? What are you saying?"

Now he met her gaze, with a look of genuine puzzlement. "Wife of the fires," he repeated. "The marriage made at Beltane . . . the temporary marriage, the marriage for but one year."

As she stared at him in shock, he blinked, and then rushed on. "Surely—surely you knew this! Even you, the lady of the lost past, the lady of the Otherworld, would have to know what a marriage of the fires is!"

He was sincere. She could hear it in his simple, steady voice, see it in the straightforward expression on his face. She shook her head, just a little, and tried to breathe, tried to remember how to breathe.

"I did not know of this custom," she whispered, as time seemed to slow and stand still. "Please—do—explain it to me."

"Shannon—please—"

"Tell me!"

He swallowed. "The marriages at Beltane are but temporary contracts. They end at dusk on the night before the next Beltane. The man and woman are then free to go their separate ways . . . if they wish."

Thoughts from a long, long time ago leaped into her mind. She fairly reeled as sudden understanding struck her like a physical blow.

It is unlucky to marry in May . . .

It is unlucky for a bride to wear green . . .

Lasairian took a step toward her, then another. "How could you not know this? Every tribe in Eire follows the same ritual at Beltane. Are you saying you did not know our marriage was not a permanent one? Did they not have this custom in the—in the place where you are from?"

"No such custom," she answered, and closed her eyes. "No such luck." Shannon listened to the rushing waters for a moment. "But that doesn't matter so much. Whether for a day, or a year, or a lifetime, or more, we were married—weren't we?"

"We were," he said fervently. "We are."

"It is possible that I could misunderstand such a custom. I will give you that. It's not your fault that I had never heard of it. But—how could I know that you were already married! That you already had a wife! How could I possibly know such a thing? Tell me—is your other wife also a 'wife of the fires'?"

"She is not." Lasairian glanced down again, but then met her eyes. "Clodagh is my permanent wife."

Shannon closed her eyes as his words washed over her, leaving her cold, leaving her with yet another shock. "Permanent wife. Permanent . . ." She struggled to draw breath. "While I am only your short-term diversion—your little summer fling—your girlfriend behind your wife's back. Your temporary—*temporary*—"

"*You* are my wife," he said urgently, stepping up at last to catch hold of her hand.

She pulled away with all her strength. "How can you

273

say that? How *dare* you say that! You have a wife, a permanent wife, and you have lied to her as well as to me! No wonder everyone in Abhainn Aille cowered behind the trees as I walked up to your house! They thought they were going to see an all-out battle! Tell me, Lasairian, how does *she* feel about what you've done?''

''She already knows. She had no objection to your presence. She tried to welcome you.''

''Oh. She already knows. I see.'' Shannon's mouth tightened, as anger warred with pain. ''It seems that everyone knew about this but me.''

She struggled for control, but the battle was lost, and she knew it. Her eyes burned with tears, her voice shook. ''Why did you try to leave me here, alone, to find out that you already had a wife? Because you didn't want to be here when I found out? Because you didn't have the courage to tell me yourself?''

He looked down. ''It seemed the only way, Shannon. It was something which only you and Clodagh could work out together. I thought it best to leave you to it.''

''Your father didn't think so! The king didn't think so! I see that now. When we got here today, they thought I already knew! *Your wife needs you at home, Lasairian.* That's what the king said. And I thought he meant me! Oh, I thought he meant me!''

She covered her face with one hand, sobbing, trembling, yet too angry to run away, too much in pain to reach out for comfort.

''Tell me what I should have done, Shannon! I cannot send Clodagh away. It is—it is complicated. But I tell you, as I stand here, as I draw breath, as the tears wait behind my eyes—I do not love her, and I have never touched her.''

''Never—'' Slowly she looked up, not caring that he saw

her tear-streaked face and swollen eyes. "Never. I cannot believe that, Lasairian. If you were in my place, could you believe it?"

He looked at her for a long moment. "Perhaps not," he answered. "But I know someone who you will believe." With that he caught hold of her wrist and walked off toward the houses, keeping such a firm hold that she had little choice but to go along with him.

Lasairian walked straight to his own house with Shannon's wrist held firmly in his grasp, forcing her to hurry to keep up with his long, determined stride. She was too angry to struggle and too embarrassed to shout, certainly not out here where everyone was still staring wide-eyed at them.

As soon as they got somewhere private she would force him to release her. And then—then—

She nearly tripped over him. He'd stopped at the door of his house. Right in front of him was Clodagh.

"Come in," Clodagh said, in her remote, quiet voice, and moved back to allow them entry.

Still holding on to Shannon, Lasairian stepped inside. Shannon had to press close beside him to get through the narrow door. At last they stood in the cool shelter of Lasairian's own house, ankle-deep in soft, smooth rushes. Clodagh stood as calmly within the neatly kept home as though she'd just invited them in for tea.

More gently now, Lasairian led Shannon to the low bench beside the stone firepit at the center of the house. As Shannon sat down on the smooth, hard surface, she felt almost beyond emotion, so cold, so empty had the shock of this discovery left her. Now there was only a kind of cold curiosity, a detached wondering at what might happen next. What would they do, what could they say, that could possibly take away the pain of this moment, this endless hour, when she was certain she would never feel anything again?

"Clodagh," Lasairian began, "I need your help."

The woman said nothing, but merely stood and waited, hands folded.

"Shannon does not understand—our situation. She does not believe that ours is a marriage of formality only, that we do not—that we have agreed that nothing more shall pass between us than a courteous greeting and the occasional sharing of a meal. I ask you to explain this to her yourself, for I am certain that she will believe you, even if she does not believe me."

Clodagh glanced at Shannon. Nothing moved but her eyes. Her gaze flicked back to Lasairian. "Why should it matter to her what passes between us? I have offered her peace. I am willing to share this house."

"I understand. And I am grateful for your courtesy." Lasairian's voice was gentle. "Yet I find that Shannon is the one not willing to share. She is—accustomed to different ways. It is of the greatest importance, to the peace of our household, that she understand how it is with you and I. And so I would have her hear it from you, the lady of this house, who has no reason to tell her anything but the truth."

Clodagh regarded him for a long moment, and then raised her chin. "Then you have found happiness together."

"We have."

Now her gaze locked on to Shannon. "Very well," she whispered.

Clodagh took a step forward into the rushes, her arms crossed closely to her body, seeming to collect her thoughts. She drew a deep breath and began to speak.

"I am from the Liath tribe," she began, and Shannon felt another small shock. Of course, she did not yet know what had happened to Dowan! But though her breath caught in her throat, Shannon could not bring herself to speak. There would be no interrupting Clodagh.

"I was married, and I was content. Then, last year, at a few nights past mid-spring, Dowan decided to lead the men of Liath on a glorious raid to steal the cattle of Abhainn Aille."

Her voice dripped with bitterness. "Oh, it was not meant to be a danger. It was only to be a show of courage for Dowan, who fancied himself a prince and a leader and wanted a chance to prove it. None seemed to be forthcoming, so he made one for himself. No one was supposed to die."

"Die . . ." Shannon could not help whispering the word. "Who died, Clodagh?"

There was a silence. In the distance, the waters rushed past the island, on and on. "My husband died. My husband. My . . ."

"I am sorry," Shannon said quietly. "You loved him."

"I loved him," Clodagh answered. "I loved him more than my life. And if I had not already been carrying his child, I may well have joined him in the next life . . . in the Otherworld."

"Oh—surely you would not—"

Clodagh turned a fierce look on her. "He died for nothing. I begged him not to go. I told him he would only be feeding Dowan's monstrous vanity, that Dowan cared nothing for the men who fought for him, that he only wanted glory for himself. The lives of his men meant nothing to him.

"I would have killed Dowan myself if I could have, but it was not in my power. Neither could I go on living at Liath. Rage consumed me, rage and despair; I remained alive only for my child's sake, and to bide my time until I could take revenge on Dowan. And never would I touch another man. Not in this life or the next.

"And while I waited, we knew that the men of Abhainn Aille also waited, waited to take their own revenge in a never-ending cycle of blood and death.

"And so, the king of Liath sought out the king of Abhainn Aille, in an effort to preserve what peace there was. Neither of them had any wish to start a war. My king knew that I found life at Liath, indeed life anywhere, increasingly unbearable. He believed that he had found a solution: send me to live at Abhainn Aille, as a hostage, or a peace offering, as you will, to show that they wanted no more fighting between our two kingdoms. And, of course, the king was able to rid himself of an unwanted woman at the same time.

"That is how I came to live at Abhainn Aille, along with my mother, who also lost her husband many years ago. My son was born at midsummer. We have made a life for ourselves here, and for that I am grateful to Lasairian."

"But I thought—I thought you said you did not want another man."

"I did not. I still do not."

"Then why—"

"Why would I marry again?" There was the smallest trace of a smile. "I could appreciate the disruption my presence caused here. I had no wish to cause difficulty for anyone, so long as my own wishes were respected.

"After a time, Lasairian agreed to accept me as his wife, and care for my mother and my child. He assured me that the marriage would be in name only. In return I would care for his house, and see to his clothes and food and the like. It seemed a fair solution. It provided my family with a home, and gave me what I wanted most—a chance to live in peace and solitude, away from memories too painful to bear.''

She looked directly at Shannon. ''That is the truth of it. If you and Lasairian have found happiness in each other, then I am pleased, for I am one who can understand such happiness and know it for the rare thing that it is.''

That very evening, Clodagh and her mother gathered their things, took the baby, and left for a room in the King's Hall. ''But this is your home,'' Shannon said, as they stepped out the door. ''*Your* home. You have every right to be here. I have none. I cannot let you leave!''

But Clodagh only smiled to herself, and lifted her sleepy infant to her shoulder. ''I will come in the daylight, and work as I have before, and we will help each other; but this is Lasairian's house, and now it has become yours. If there is to be love in this house, then I am content.''

Then she was gone, into the evening. Shannon was left alone with Lasairian, alone in her own fine house with the man who was her husband.

Chapter Twenty-three

The night passed over them in quiet formality and polite conversation, followed by restless sleep. Shannon wanted nothing more than to talk to Lasairian about what had happened, what they would do now, and what would happen next; but she was still too stunned, too much in shock, to confront him now.

What words were there to cover such a situation? What more was there but raw emotion, feelings that words could never describe? Perhaps in time she would be able to speak about all of this, but for now she could only think, and wonder, and somehow try to heal.

And Lasairian seemed more than relieved to let her do just that.

A day passed. And another. Another one went by, and then another, and another. Again the days settled into a routine, but this time Shannon did not enter into it so joyfully. She kept herself relentlessly occupied so that the hours would pass, and the days, and the long, long nights. She could only hope that perhaps, if enough time passed, she might somehow make sense of what had happened and decide what she should do next.

Though just what she might do about her present situation was nearly impossible to imagine.

One morning she looked up to realize that winter had descended, confining everyone close to home during the long cold nights and short gray days. On returning to Abhainn Aille, Shannon had thought she would miss her outdoor life; but now she welcomed the long hours spent indoors doing simple, repetitive tasks. They gave her time to think, time to reflect, time to digest the things she had learned in one single, devastating afternoon hour on the day they had returned from the high pastures.

Lasairian, too, threw himself into work, putting as much energy into his intellectual pursuits as he once had into caring for the cattle. He would sit beneath the trees at the island's edge, his heavy wool mantle wrapped close against the chilling wet winds, chanting poems and songs. Some were of his own composing, some were recited to him by the other students of poetry.

Yet Shannon was not always alone. As she had promised, Clodagh came often to help with preparing food and making clothes. She taught Shannon to spin thread from wool and weave it into long narrow strips of cloth. She was always quiet and distant, never intrusive, and Shannon had to admit that she was both glad for the company and grateful for the things Clodagh could teach her.

But never could Shannon forget, not for one instant, that this other woman was Lasairian's wife, his true, legal wife. She herself was nothing more than a temporary wife, a wife of the fires, a spur-of-the-moment joining during the lusty madness that was Beltane. Not a wife at all . . . nothing more than a concubine.

She knew that things were different here. There was nothing shameful about being a second wife, even with the first one still very much married to the husband and spending most of her time in the same house.

But no matter what, Shannon would never be first here—not in Lasairian's eyes or anyone else's. As long as she stayed in Abhainn Aille, she would never be more than second best.

In the evening, Shannon and Lasairian retired within their small warm house, nearly always in the company of other young men and women of Abhainn Aille. They played board games with gold-trimmed wooden pegs, and told stories, and listened as Lasairian played so beautifully on his harp. Their hours were busy and full from dawn until long after sunset, when at last they would lie down together on the wide ledge and let sleep occupy what was left of their time.

Often they sought each other out in the warmth of the furs, in the comforting embrace that was as old as time; but even then, the distance remained between them no matter how closely they held each other. And no matter how eloquently Lasairian spoke while reciting his poetry or telling his stories, there were still no words for what lay between them.

"I will divorce him, if you wish."

Shannon looked up from where she knelt at the shore of the lake, rinsing out a linen gown in the cold, rushing waters. The dampness of the ground had begun to soak through her dark green woolen skirts, but she hardly noticed; she had been lost in thought, gazing out at the late-afternoon sun as it began to slide down through the gray layers of cloud.

Clodagh must have guessed what was on her mind . . . as if she ever thought of anything else. Then Shannon realized what the other woman had said. "Divorce?"

"He would be free to make you his permanent wife. The contracts could be renegotiated. It would be as if I had never been here."

Shannon stood up and threw her green-and-yellow plaid cloak back over one shoulder. Water ran unnoticed from the soaked linen gown. "You would be willing to divorce him?"

"It would make things much simpler."

Shannon's heart raced. "Clodagh—I would never ask you—"

"You did not ask. I am offering."

"But what would happen to you?"

Clodagh shrugged. "Little would change for me. I would remain in the Hall with my mother and child. And I would no longer be married. It was never my wish to be remarried."

Shannon hardly dared to breathe. "You're sure about this."

"I have thought of little else."

Of course. This situation was surely no easier for Clodagh than it was for Shannon. "All right, then. We'll go and find him together."

"I cannot do this. I will not. You do not understand, Shannon. I cannot do this."

Lasairian stood beneath a willow tree near the edge of Abhainn Aille, quickly wrapping his harp in its protective leather cover against the rising wind and needle-fine rain. He stood up, holding the bundled harp tightly against his chest as he faced the two women.

Shannon stood side by side with Clodagh. The heavy gray clouds seemed to be descending straight down over her, the sky darkening and lowering until Shannon thought it might just envelop her and close out this world forever.

At that moment, she could only hope that such a thing would actually happen.

Clodagh did not react at all. Shannon found it impossible to judge her response. But Clodagh had little to lose. Either way, her life would go on much as it had before.

For Shannon, though, it seemed as if her whole world had been turned upside down once again. She pulled her woolen cloak tight against the cold wind and tried to breathe, tried to find the breath to summon words. "I am not the one asking for this. Clodagh told me that she wished to be divorced. I would never have asked her to do this—or you."

She could hardly bear to look at him. "Please, Clodagh," she said, closing her eyes, "please tell him that I did not ask you to do this." She looked away, fighting for breath once more, brushing away the tears which stung her eyes.

"Shannon." There was a rustling as Lasairian set down the precious harp, and in a moment she felt his gentle touch on her shoulders.

There was nothing she wanted more than to lay her head on his chest, and pull him close, and give herself over to sobbing out the grief she had kept so tightly locked for so long. But once again she managed to keep her rigid control, and held herself away from him.

"Clodagh was sent to Abhainn Aille for the best of reasons," Lasairian began, in his gentlest voice, "but she was very much an outsider in many ways. She found it very difficult to find a place here, but neither could she return to the people of Liath—not without great risk to Liath and Abhainn Aille both.

"But now, as a woman married to a nobleman of Abhainn Aille, she has a place, she is protected, she has a certain status recognized by all." He paused, and his hands fell away from Shannon's shoulders. "I cannot ask her to give that up."

Shannon nodded, just once. "Would she be forced to return to Liath if you divorced her?"

"She would not. But you must remember, she was sent here not only to start a new life for herself, but to prevent retaliation for the death of her husband. If I divorce her—even of her own will—it would be seen as a cruel rejection of her and a terrible insult to her family. It could well start the fighting all over again."

"It would not start again. Dowan is dead. The threat is ended." She could feel Clodagh look at her, but kept her eyes down.

How cold her words sounded! Shannon was the one who had killed the man, however accidental his death had been. Clodagh had done nothing wrong. None of this was her fault. How could Shannon still feel so intensely antagonistic toward her?

Then Lasairian touched her shoulder again, and Shannon knew that she would do, or say, almost anything to preserve her ties with the man she loved.

But even so, she had no wish to hurt Clodagh or make her life any more difficult than it already was. Even in her own torment, Shannon still had the presence of mind to know that she did not want to gain her own happiness by trampling on someone else.

"Shannon—do you see, now, why I cannot divorce her? Why I cannot send her away?"

She let out a long breath. "I do. I do understand." And she did. In this time, in this place, this situation was normal and accepted. There would be dire consequences if the three of them tried to break up what alliances and necessity had put together.

And even if she could successfully wrest Lasairian away from his family and have him all to herself, she would only have made life harder for Clodagh—for Clodagh and her mother and her innocent child.

How much respect would she have for Lasairian if he would be willing to abandon three other people to such a hard and uncertain fate?

Lasairian turned her around to face him, and brushed a strand of hair back from her eyes. "It is so strange, Shannon . . . before you came here, I cared little about what might happen to someone else, so long as I was content. The worries of others were simply not my concern. But now—"

He leaned his head down to touch his forehead to hers. "Now, dear Shannon, the time spent with you has made of me a very different man. I am not the selfish youth I was at the start of the summer. I believe I have become a man, perhaps one who will someday be worthy of you."

He stood back and smiled down at her. "My love for you has brought us all to this. I am sorry for the pain that it has caused you; but I do not regret that at last, with you, I have learned to be a man."

*   *   *

The gray winter days went on and on, one very much like another; but then one day there was a softening in the breeze, a touch of warmth in the air. The pale sun found its way through the clouds and shone for brief periods on Abhainn Aille.

Spring was returning.

The people began to emerge from their close, stuffy houses, opening the doors and wooden window shutters for a little while each afternoon, glad for their first bit of freedom after so many weeks spent largely indoors.

There was a slight but definite relaxing among the people. They had made it through the winter and the cycle of life would continue. Even Clodagh began to unbend just a little. More than a few times Shannon saw her speaking calmly with Lasairian as they stood together beneath the trees; it looked as though they were finally becoming friends. Shannon, too, began to look once more to the future, holding on to the hope that somehow her future and Lasairian's would work out.

Early one afternoon she dressed in a freshly washed, cream-colored linen shift, and put the last stitches in a new gown of lightweight wool. Clodagh had helped her dye and weave the wool for it, and Shannon was quite pleased with the way it had turned out. The gown was a plaid of blue and cream with a small amount of yellow-gold, and felt wonderfully light and warm as she fastened her brown leather belt around it and pulled on her soft boots of folded leather.

Shannon picked up her basket and walked into the lovely daylight, the lake breeze cool as always, but warmed by the touch of spring sunshine. She started down the path which led to the nearest shoreline, looking for Lasairian.

In the basket was a carefully wrapped meal for the two

of them. He had taken his harp and gone out early, and now, though she looked in all of his usual places where he sat to practice, there was no one out beneath the trees. She stopped and listened for several moments, but heard no sound of his playing the harp.

She retraced her steps. He had to be here, somewhere, on the island. She walked farther beneath the trees and bushes, which were so thick on this side of Abhainn Aille, this time looking more carefully, pushing deeper into the small thickets here and there—

There! She caught a glimpse of his familiar blue mantle in one of the deepest parts of the brush. She'd walked right past him the first time. Perhaps he was asleep.

"Lasairian! Are you there?"

There was a rustling in the bushes. After a moment, he leaned back to look at her, and gave her his most welcoming smile. "Shannon! How good of you to come. I am so glad to see you."

Still holding the basket of food, she climbed awkwardly over the last of the bushes, trying to keep the thorns from snagging her new woolen skirt. "I've been looking for you," she said, stepping into the clearing at last. "I've brought you—"

She stopped, quite unable to move.

Sitting at Lasairian's feet were two lovely young women. She'd seen them often enough around Abhainn Aille, though they were younger than she was and Shannon had never spent any appreciable time with them.

But it seemed that they were spending some very fine time with Lasairian.

When she only stood and stared, Lasairian got to his feet and gave her a quick kiss on the cheek. "Of course, you have met Keelin and Keavy," he said. "Look here, they

were kind enough to bring me a midday meal! And now
you have joined me as well, and the sun has come out, and
the day has just become perfect."

He reached up and tried to take her hand, but Shannon
kept hold of her basket. It was all perfectly innocent; just
three people sitting together for a little picnic on a cold day
in early spring. All she could see were the lazy smiles of
the two girls still sitting on the grass, so confident in their
youth and beauty, practically daring her to say anything to
them, to make any claim at all on Lasairian.

. . . wife of the fires . . .

. . . temporary wife . . .

Shannon turned away, and stepped back over the brush,
and left the three of them alone together.

Now it all began to hit her hard. Shannon could no longer
deny the cold hard facts of the situation she found herself
caught in.

Oh, why had she not seen it before? How could she have
been so blinded by hope, so dazzled by wishes, that she
had not seen what was going on right before her eyes?

There was Lasairian, handsome, desirable Lasairian,
back now from his stint as a cattle herder and once again
the noble prince of Abhainn Aille. He had only grown in
respect among all of the people as he began to truly learn
to be a bard. And he was certainly more attractive than
ever to the women, who could not have failed to notice the
hardened muscles and sun-touched skin with which he had
returned from the fields.

Clodagh had said she did not want a man ever again.
But the fact remained that she was legally, permanently
married to a very handsome man who treated her very well.

Sometimes the desires of the body took over even when the heart would have preferred to wait.

Shannon certainly ought to have realized that.

And how could she have thought that the young unmarried women of Abhainn Aille would so quickly give up Lasairian? Or that he would give them up? Oh, he would tell her that they meant nothing to him, that they were just idle companions listening to his music and sharing a light lunch. But why should he give them up? His permanent wife had publicly stated that she wanted no intimacy with him. Everyone knew it. And as for a temporary wife—well, what would her opinion matter in such a situation?

It would matter not at all . . . not at all.

It was the final blow. Lasairian had all he could ever wish for in this place, and it would be up to Shannon to bend, to give, to force herself to accept things as they were. Even if it meant sharing him with every other woman on Abhainn Aille. Even if it meant watching as his first wife slowly came to desire him. As Shannon stumbled back into her house and barred the door, she knew that there was only one decision left to her.

Somehow, the weeks passed. Somehow Shannon managed to hold on as the days moved on like the river surrounding Abhainn Aille. Like the smooth and unchanging waters, time, too, could flow for quite a distance before one became aware of just how far it had traveled.

Lasairian was especially careful to be attentive and kind, spending as much time with her as he could. She found it impossible not to respond to his gentle touch, to his voice, to his fingers which played her senses as beautifully as they had ever played the harp.

Yet each day only confirmed the fear and suspicion that

had been brought home to her so forcefully on that afternoon in the thicket on the far side of Abhainn Aille. Not one day went by without her seeing the sly smiles of Keelin or Keavy or Monat or Morrin. Not one morning could pass without her hearing the distant liquid notes of Lasairian's harp, and knowing that at least one flirtatious young woman sat at his feet, smiling up at him. And everywhere, it seemed, was Clodagh, her presence becoming ever more close and constant.

Or was it just her imagination? Lasairian took such great pains to reassure her that all was innocent, that she had no need to doubt that he loved her beyond all others; but no matter what he said or did, the other women were always there, just out of sight, but ever-present just the same.

There was nothing left for her to say to Lasairian. He knew how she felt and tried as best he could to put her at ease; but he had the best sort of life a man of his time could imagine, and one that was quite acceptable for the time he lived in. She could never fully accept his way, and he would never really understand hers.

So, it had come to this. The cultural distance between them was simply too great. Shannon knew that she would never be able to resign herself to living such a life, could not go back to merely existing every day, ignoring her pain and pretending it did not exist.

At last, one evening, when the spring bloomed everywhere about them, she took one of the boats and set out alone for the mainland. She climbed to the top of the hill where the lone hawthorn stood, its perfume so sweet, so intoxicating. She reached up and broke off one of the slender outer branches, heavy with sweet white flowers, and returned to Abhainn Aille before anyone noticed she was gone.

The next morning, which was Beltane Eve, as Lasairian left their house and bent to kiss her, she found that she could not return his kiss. "I will meet you here at twilight, dear Shannon, and we will celebrate Beltane as we did last year. Once again you will swear to be my wife, and our love will be made real before the Goddess, beneath the shelter of the forest and the shining face of the moon."

But all she could do was reach up and lay her hand gently on his cheek, and look into his beautiful dark eyes one last time.

It was strange to prepare for such a long journey and yet have nothing to pack.

For a long time Shannon walked through the small neat house which had become so familiar, touching the smooth wooden plates, the heavy iron tools, the weaving loom in the corner, the fine woolen cloth she and Clodagh had made. Yet she saw nothing of her own, nothing that she wanted to take with her.

She would leave this place with even less than what she came with—only a gown of lime-green bedsheets and a pair of plastic sandals. The gold-and-emerald ring meant nothing to her any longer.

All the other people of Abhainn Aille were happily busy in preparing for the celebration of Beltane to come that night. No one paid any attention to Shannon as she walked at a steady pace to the front of the island, her gaze fixed directly on the ground just in front of her, listening only to the rushing of the waters and the chattering of the people, so that there was no chance of catching the sound of even a single note of the harp. No one paid any attention to her as she pushed one of the small leather boats into the water, climbed into it, and began to paddle it quickly toward the shore of the mainland.

Chapter Twenty-four

As Shannon moved the boat smoothly and easily through the water, her thoughts—which she refused to allow to turn to the past and which found the present far too painful—began to turn, by necessity, to the future. Assuming she could actually return to her own time, her own world, what would she do once she got there?

A distant memory faded into being, a memory of the man she had known in her own time as Ian Galloway—a man who in her own mind was one and the same with Lasairian.

Of course that could not possibly be the case. It was just that each of them had had the same powerful effect on her, and so her mind must have blended the two together until it seemed that—

But Shannon knew that she had no more chance of building any sort of future with Ian Galloway than she had of building one with Lasairian. The last time she had seen Ian, he had embraced his gray-cloaked lady at the Renaissance Faire and disappeared with her into the crowd.

As the little boat approached the shore, Shannon fixed her gaze on the distant hawthorn tree far at the top of the hill and banished all thoughts of Ian or Lasairian or anything else. It was not difficult to clear her mind; she felt nothing but a stillness, an emptiness, a resignation at what was yet to come.

At the climax of this year spent in ancient Eire, she knew that she had done all she could have to create the life she wanted. It was something she had tried to do in both this world and her own, and both times she had failed.

She could no longer find her way alone. Every path that she had chosen on her own had led to a dead end. Now, just as she had the first time, when she had circled the ghostly hawthorn tree in her father's backyard and invited the magic to do what it would, it seemed her only choice was to throw her fate to the universe once more and let the river that was time take her wherever it wished.

Not long now before the shadows lengthened into dusk. Shannon sat alone on a rock at the top of the hill, half-hidden by the forest—the same rock where, a year ago, she had sat combing her hair to calm herself. Now she sat very still with her hands folded in her lap, gazing out over Abhainn Aille, watching as the sun approached the waters.

The rest of the people, all those who would take part in the Beltane celebration, had gone into the woods to gather flowers and greenery and wood. She could hear the occasional shout echoing through the forest, or a ripple of laughter floating across the plain. She could only assume that Lasairian was out there too. She felt certain that Clodagh had remained on the island with her young baby, but next year . . . next year could be quite different.

And even if Clodagh was not at the Beltane fires, Keelin and Keavy and Morrin and Monat and all the rest of them would be there waiting for him, waiting to claim him at the Beltane fires, where freedom was the rule and all restrictions were lifted.

Shannon closed her eyes. It was nearly over now. The lowering sun eased closer and closer to the horizon. She had to gather her thoughts, think of the ritual, concentrate on it in her mind, prepare herself fully to call upon the magic once more to take her home.

Soft gray dusk hung over the land. Points of firelight began appearing in the forest, moving in and out of sight as the revelers lit their torches and carried them through the woods in their final forays to gather what they needed.

Shannon slid down from the rock. It was time.

She ran her fingers through her hair to push it back from her eyes and breathed deep of the soft evening wind, heavy and wet with the scent of the lake. She walked through the grass toward the hawthorn tree, to the place where it grew all alone, hanging out over the steep hillside which swept down to the shore of the lake.

The sight of Abhainn Aille, peaceful in the quiet sunset, yet surrounded by the mounting energies of Beltane gathering in the forest around it, was almost enough to turn her from her task—but there would be no going back now.

Eyes half-shut, she gathered her thoughts. In her mind she heard the notes of the harp, Lasairian's harp, and the familiar melody which the two of them had written together. In a moment her voice picked up the song, softly at first, just under her breath.

Then, as she grew more confident and allowed herself to

sink more deeply into the ritual, the song gave her courage. It caught her voice and lifted it sure and steady, and Shannon sang the melody as sweetly as she ever had—though never had it carried such sadness.

She began to walk around the tree, slowly, carefully, a step at a time, letting the song carry her forward. The world grew distant and surreal, lost in rising gray fog, becoming soft and indistinct beneath her feet, almost as if she walked on rainclouds, almost as if—

A hand closed over her wrist.

The song died in her throat. Looking up, blinking, she saw Lasairian standing before her. His breath was quick, as though he had been running, but his face was pale with hardly a trace of color. His dark and curling hair hung damp against the short blue cloak pinned over his shoulder. And the great dark eyes were haunted, stricken, flicking over her as though he were not sure she was still real.

She took a short breath. And another. But she could not speak; the magic she had started still held her in its grip as firmly as Lasairian held her wrist. Shannon could only look at him and wonder what she could possibly say when once again she found her voice.

"Shannon," he whispered, still holding her tightly, as if he feared she would vanish before his eyes. "Shannon, what are you doing?"

At the sound of his voice, the world began to return to normal once more. She again grew conscious of the grassy, rocky hill beneath her feet, the lake far below at the foot of the plain, the sunset fading into the waters. She pulled her wrist away. "I'm going home."

Before she could turn away from him, he caught her arm again. "Home! But this is your home! How can you think of leaving your home?" His voice actually trembled. "You know that if you are successful, we will never see each other again?''

She closed her eyes. "I know that."

His hand shifted, gripping her even tighter. "Once you said that you could never think of leaving me. What has happened to so change the way you feel? You said nothing to me about trying to return! About trying to invoke such a powerful magic! Shannon, do you know what you are doing?''

No longer did she hear the soft persuasive voice of the bard, telling her whatever she wanted to hear, whatever would persuade her to do things his way and keep things easy and comfortable for him. Now she heard real fear in that voice, real concern that he might lose her forever.

"I know what I am doing," she answered. "I am calling on the ritual once more, just as I did one year ago. I believe that if I try again, it will take me back home, in the same way that it brought me here."

His voice rose. "You *think* you can do this! You say that you will *try*! Shannon, you do not know the forces that you trifle with! I can tell you, magic is power! Magic is strength! There can be delicacy in magic, but never weakness!"

She looked straight at him, puzzled now. "Are you saying I'm not strong enough to get back? I got here once before, as you recall. I did it once. I'll do it again."

Shannon started to turn away, but he stopped her and forced her to face him again. His once-gentle fingers were like iron bands on both her wrists. "We were drawn together by a great power across the river that is time. That power came from our desire to know and love each other, no matter what the distance! Would you break down and destroy that love? Do you not see that if you destroy our love, you also destroy the power that brought you here?''

He shook his head, and his dark eyes glittered. ''If you attempt this thing in an effort to leave me, there will indeed be nothing left—no magic, no power, no more love left between us! Oh, the ritual may indeed take you, but you cannot know where! If you perform this ritual out of a desire to leave me forever, that is exactly what will happen! It will take you, but you could find yourself anywhere—or nowhere at all. Surely that is not what you want!''

His hold on her shifted, and now he held her hand gently, closely. ''Shannon, my life here is the finest, the most perfect, that any man could desire. I have my music, day and night; I have my friends, who gather to hear it, and laugh and talk with me; I have my father, who was a wiser presence than ever I could know, and who has not held against me the foolish actions of my youth; and I have the satisfaction of knowing that I have done a decent thing by providing Clodagh and her mother and infant with a safe and peaceful life.

''But most of all, I have you, my Shannon, my *one* love, to share my life with.'' He raised her chin with gentle fingers, and looked deep into her eyes. ''How can you ask me to leave all of this? How can you, yourself, leave it? How can you destroy all that we have built together?''

Her eyes narrowed as her anger rose. ''Destroy the love between us? What love would that be? You cannot, you will not, divorce your wife, even though she has offered to do so and has plainly stated that she does not love you and never wished to be remarried.

''But even worse, I do not believe you are willing to give up those very friendly and generous young women who are always around you—the ones who spend so much time sitting at your feet as you play for them, while I spend my days working! How kind they are, to bring you your midday meal in the very most secretive place on Abhainn Aille!''

He closed his eyes. The grip on her wrist relaxed. "Shannon . . . it is so hard, I know, for you to understand. Those young women are my friends, the companions of my childhood. And we have spoken so many times of why I should not—cannot—allow Clodagh to return to the Liath tribe. I thought you understood . . . I believed we had reached an accord about how we would live. . . .''

Even in her anger and pain, a small wave of guilt passed over her. "I do not want to ask you to leave your family, your friends. But there can be no real love, no lasting love, between any two people unless they place each other first above all others.

"You know in your heart that the women of Abhainn Aille would find other companions, even as they are doing tonight. Clodagh would be allowed to remain in the King's Hall until she can someday find another man to love. Your family would come to know that we had gone away together to make a life for ourselves. We can only trust that all those left behind will understand, and go on, even as I would understand and go on if someone I knew was lucky enough to find the person they truly loved.''

She shut her eyes, tighter now, in an effort to force back the tears. "I know that you have tried. And I have tried too, the best I know how. But we have reached a river that is far too wide, far too deep, for even the two of us to cross.''

His face was serious and still. For the first time, she felt the trembling of his fingers. "Magic is power," he repeated. "And the magic that brought you here was the magic of the two of us together.''

"But that magic has ended! It is no longer the two of us together! It is you and Clodagh, and all the other women, which provide you with your comfortable life here! I am only one part of that life, and I know that I cannot live with being only one part. I have tried, out of love for you; but I simply cannot live this way. And so I will go, and allow you the life you have chosen—the life which makes you happy."

As she had before, she reached up and laid her hand against his cheek, for her throat had closed and she could say no more, knew that the tears would overwhelm her if she tried.

"I cannot let you do this. I cannot let you leave me. I love you, Shannon Rose! The rest of my life, fine as it is, would mean nothing if you were not here with me."

The tears did come, but fear and anger gave her back her voice. "You say you love me, but only when it is convenient and comfortable for you! Oh, it was so easy out on the hills, thrown together as we were, working so hard each day just to survive. There was no time to worry about the future, and there were no other women to distract you as there had always been before.

"But now we are here, and I have learned since we came back—oh, how I have learned!—that I will never be the most important part of your life so long as we stay here.

"I made the sacrifice to find you. I left my own world and surrendered myself to the magic, hoping it would take me where I wanted most to go—and it did. It took me to you.

"And once I found you, nothing else mattered. I lived among cattle, I slept on a dirt floor, I faced dangers I never thought I'd have the courage to face. I found the strength in your love for me—and more than that, in the love I have for you.

"But now I find that you are not willing to do the same for me in return."

In the silence she searched out his eyes, his dark eyes filled with pain and fear. "Please, Lasairian—do not misunderstand me. This is your home! If you wish to remain here with your family, as I know you had always planned to do, you have every right to do that. I could never live with knowing that I had forced you to leave this place.

"But at this moment, the choice lies before you. You, now, must make a decision, just as I had to a year ago. You must choose a future with me—our future together— or you must choose a life here without me."

They stood staring at each other beneath the rising full moon, as the world descended into blue-black night and the shouts and cries of the gathered revelers began to reach them from the plain below.

Lasairian reached out to stroke her hair, as he had done so many times before. "Ah, Shannon . . . have you truly thought of what our life might be like in your world? I know nothing of the ways of it. Would I ever find a place there? Would I be . . . would I be the same to you, would I still be a man you could love? Or would I be only an outsider who could never learn your ways, an embarrassment to you, forever a stranger?"

She could only stare at him, and shake her head, as she listened to his last reasons—his last excuses, she thought bitterly—for not going with her. "I will not beg you to come with me."

Shannon turned away and placed her hand on the rough bark of the hawthorn tree. The sweet perfume of the white flowers lingered on the cool night air. "You said that magic was power. It seems to me that its power comes from a combination of things, never from just one single thing.

"I know that it was the magic of several things all coming together at the same time which allowed me to find my way here . . . the tree cut down on the wrong day, releasing its power uncontrolled; the song I sang, which I later learned that we created together; the full moon, shining down on the night that would have been Beltane.

"Even the penny I tossed so casually into the fountain was a part of it, I think; it was a gift to the Mistress of the Waters, to water itself, the source of all life. Surely nothing could carry more power than that.

"All of it served to bring the two of us together. Yet none of it was planned; it was not forced in any way. And in that same way, I will not try to make you go with me. The choice must be yours just as much as it is mine."

"But—would you go without this?" Lasairian reached beneath his cloak and withdrew a long cylindrical object, its copper surface shining softly in the twilight.

A shock ran through her. "Why did you bring that with you?"

He looked down at the gleaming cylinder, turning it carefully in the bright moonlight so that the leaves and birds and curving lines on its surface seemed to move. "When it was Beltane Eve, and I could not find you anywhere . . . I feared what you would try. I feared it."

"You're right," Shannon said, with a nod of her head and a deep breath. She never took her eyes from the cylinder. "You're right. Without this, without the calfskin piece finding its way to the future, how would I ever have come to you? I would never have learned the song, and so I would never have found my way here. . . ."

Shannon reached out to take the copper cylinder. But he

raised it up to his chest and held it close, looking steadily at her, his face solemn and still.

She drew back her hand. "I see," she said, her voice growing cold. "Did you think I would arm-wrestle you for it? Did you think I would beg you to give it to me?"

"I hoped you would not leave without it." His voice was so quiet she could scarcely hear the words.

"But I will leave! And if I do not take it, it will not be there for me to open, and I will never find my way to you. Your life will go on as it was intended to go, and I will never intrude upon it; and you will have only your peaceful, carefree life for all the years that you live.

"The only way that the song will come to my world is if you choose to bring it there yourself. I have made my own choice. I want to love you, I want us to love each other forever! But it's not enough for me alone to want it! You must want it as much as I do, and the only way I will ever know that—the only way that *you* will ever know that—is if you decide to make the journey with me."

She saw the finality of it in his eyes. Whatever he chose, there would be no going back. Here, at last, was a choice he could not avoid, a thing he could not put off until some other day.

He looked down at Abhainn Aille where it lay in the twilight, the sky behind it shining from the enormous rising yellow moon. Even from here they could hear the soft lapping of the waters at the shores of the island.

No lovelier home could possibly exist.

"I can offer you nothing in your world, Shannon. No gold, no home, no fine clothes . . . I would have nothing to give you except my love."

"That is all I had to give you, when first I came here. But I learned that it is all that really matters." She almost

303

smiled. "I have been offered gold and fine things before. And while I lived in the forest with you, I thought of them not at all."

He looked deep into her eyes, and she saw the fear and sadness in his own. He placed the copper cylinder back in his belt, reached out, and held her face gently in both hands. He said not a word, but kissed her with all the tenderness any man could possess; and as he stepped back from her and reached down for his harp, Shannon closed her eyes, and felt her heart breaking, and wondered, as if from a great distance, how she would have the strength to make the journey back if she had no heart.

Yet there was no choice now. She turned away, reaching out for the bark of the tree, the tears and the twilight leaving her in darkness.

Then, from out of that darkness, came the sweet notes of the harp. It was the familiar song, the song of their love together.

The melody drew closer. It was right behind her now. Then it faded, and she was conscious only of two strong arms around her, pulling her close, holding her with a power and certainty that could only come from the truest kind of love.

In a moment he eased his hold, and then came the notes of the harp once more. She took a step toward the tree and he moved to her side, continuing with her as she began the circle.

As Shannon walked, she added her voice to the beautiful notes of the harp, and as the world began to fade into a mist, she was conscious only of Lasairian's presence close beside her . . . so close that they could never be separated, not in any time, not in any place.

Chapter Twenty-five

Where are we going? Where, and when?

We are going to my world . . . we are going home!

How can you know this?

Because . . . because I choose to know it! No longer am I swept along like a leaf in a current. I am Mistress of the Waters now, and I choose where and when I go!

And where and when shall we go, Mistress?

To Ireland . . . one year before I left. We must not meet ourselves!

Ireland . . . one year . . .

Ireland . . . one year . . .

Ireland . . . one year . . .

"The sun is shining, Shannon. It was twilight when we left."

"It's morning! And we are still in Ireland! Look—there is Abhainn Aille!"

"Oh—Abhainn Aille—but there are only trees now, the houses are all gone."

"The houses are gone—but the people lived on, and became my ancestors! We are here, Lasairian! We are here!"

"But it does not look so very different. The forests remain, and the lake . . ."

"Look, there! Far out on the lake! Do you see it?"

"I do not believe what I am seeing. No boat could travel at such speed. And the size of it!"

"It's a motorboat, out for a pleasure cruise! Oh, we are here! Here, in the modern day! We've made it!"

"This is quite a fine path you've set us on. Solid as rock. Rain could fall for months, and it would never turn to mud."

"Paved roads are just the first of the many fine things I will show you in my time. And do you want to know one of the very finest things about paved roads?"

"Indeed I do want to know. And I have no doubt that you will tell me, if you can stop laughing long enough to find the breath for words!"

"Paved roads lead to cities! And towns! And civilization!"

"To—what?"

"Ah, Shannon—you did not have to sell your ring. Such a beautiful piece it was."

"But now I know why I kept it all that time. I had a need for it, and now it will serve that need. It will allow us to live here for the next year, until it is time for us to go back to my home in the United States."

"You wish to stay in Ireland for a year, before returning home?"

"We must not meet ourselves! We will go back just a few months before May Day—before Beltane—so that we can do the things that must be done to ensure I make the journey through time. You must arrange to have me work for the Renaissance Faire committee, and then—most of all—be your beautiful, charming self so that I cannot help but fall in love with you and search for you even in the Otherworld."

"Shannon, my head spins! But I will take your word that all of this will happen. After all, I know that you did come to my world, and now I have come to yours—and though I thought I knew what magic was, I never imagined it could be such as this."

"Magic. Oh, now I know what magic is. I always thought I had to escape to find magic. But magic is a life spent with you, risking all to bring you into my world. And I will show you magic such as you never imagined!"

"The size of this place! I almost cannot comprehend it. Five levels, stacked one atop the other! And a room which moves among them of its own accord!"

"Well, this hotel is one of the nicest in Ireland. And it's nice to be able to take the elevator when you're staying on the fifth floor."

"The view—we are looking down on the rooftops!"

"Oh, come here, and I will show you what is by far, hands down, the greatest miracle of the twentieth century. Start with this—doesn't it smell nice?"

"It does. And you call this—?"

"Lavender soap. And *this*—"

"Oh! There is—there is water spraying from the wall!"

"Soap and a hot shower. Never, I promise you, will you find anything more luxurious than this, anywhere or anywhen!"

"I do not know, Shannon. You tried to tell me that there was no greater luxury than a hot shower with perfumed soap—but I may have to disagree with you on this."

"There are many who would agree, and I am close to it myself. So, you have discovered that you like chocolate?"

"Like? There is no liking here. It is love, bested only by my love for you! I shall have to compose a poem for it, in all its many forms—hot chocolate, chocolate cake, chocolate chip biscuits—"

"Cookies."

"Of course, cookies. But no matter what they are called, I am not sure how I ever existed without them before! It is alone enough to make one wish to stay in this strange and magical place you call 'the twentieth century.'"

"I see! So, I have been supplanted by chocolate. Well, now that I know my place—"

"Come back here! I shall pull you so close, so close, just like this, that you will never walk away from me again."

"So, which do you love better—me, or chocolate?"

"Hmm. It is difficult, but I supposed I would choose you."

"Even over chocolate?"

"Even over chocolate."

"Flying is so lovely. Such power! Such sights!"

"I am glad you are not nervous. Many people are, even those who grew up knowing about airplanes from their earliest days."

"Do they not know magic when they see it?"

"There is magic everywhere in our world, Lasairian."

"You know—we may want to change your name."

"Change my name? Shannon, whatever do you mean?"

"Lasairian is a beautiful name, but it's very uncommon in this time and place; I don't believe I'd ever heard of it before I met you. So, do you mind if I change it to Ian? It's a familiar name to people here, really just a shortened form of your own name."

"If it pleases you, Shannon, you may call me whatever you wish."

"Oh, I knew you'd understand—"

"Of course, I shall begin to call you Non, since it is just the shortened form of your name—"

"You are incorrigible! If you call me Non even once, I will never bring you chocolate again!"

"I yield, Shannon Rose! I promise—I shall ever call you naught but Shannon Rose."

"Well, it is not so fine as the hotel in Ireland, but it will do."

"Bowling Green, Ohio, is a small place, but a fine one. No one will notice us in this apartment; we're just one more young couple among many. Besides, there is a place here that I am certain you will enjoy very much."

"Oh? And what place would that be?"

"A little place called Isabella's."

"Shannon, what are you doing? You must be careful, she will see you!"

"I never saw myself. Well, I did, but I had no idea of who I was actually looking at. And I also had no idea of just how silly I looked in lime-green bedsheets, decked out as Queen of the May!''

"Ah, but you are beautiful even up there by the mapyole so sad and serious even surrounded by the dancers of Beltane. And I could not help but fall in love with you, and bring out all the joy I knew you possessed even from the start.''

"It is so strange to see myself this way. How could I ever have believed that running away was the only way to find magic and beauty?''

"Come, come, pull this hood over your head and come away with me, before you see yourself!''

"Ah, kind sir, I will indeed come away with you—soon now, very soon—''

"Tonight is Beltane, even here, even now. I can feel it in the air, hear it in the water. No wonder I was so drawn to this day. The moon still makes my blood race. And look— there is the tree, I can see it, a ghost in my father's backyard. . . .''

"And there is the lost and lonely lady singing the song we wrote for her together.''

"And circling the tree . . .''

"And vanishing into the past, the faraway past, to find her true love.''

"Now it is our turn! Now we have come home together!'' Shannon turned with a joyful shout and ran toward her house. Daddy! Daddy! Come here, I have brought someone home to meet you!''